THE DAY OF EZEKIEL'S HOPE

DONNA VANLIERE

HARVEST HOUSE PUBLISHERS
EUGENE, OREGON

Unless otherwise indicated, all Scripture quotations are taken from the Holy Bible, New International Version®, NIV®. Copyright © 1973, 1978, 1984, 2011 by Biblica, Inc.® Used by permission. All rights reserved worldwide.

Verses marked ESV are taken from The ESV® Bible (The Holy Bible, English Standard Version®), copyright © 2001 by Crossway, a publishing ministry of Good News Publishers. Used by permission. All rights reserved.

Verses marked KJV are taken from the King James Version of the Bible.

Verses marked NKJV are taken from the New King James Version®. Copyright © 1982 by Thomas Nelson, Inc. Used by permission. All rights reserved.

Note: In the novel portion of this book, Zerah, Emma, and the two witnesses read from ESV Bibles, and Elliott reads from an NIV Bible.

Cover design by Faceout Studio

Cover photo © caesart, Marilyn Volan, Volodymyr Burdiak, Vadim Savdoski, FOTOGRIN, Meysam Azarneshin, Nick Brundle, aspen rock, brettphoto, pjcross, Victor Carretero Barbero / Shutterstock

Interior design by KUHN Design Group

For bulk, special sales, or ministry purchases, please call 1-800-547-8979.
Email: Customerservice@hhpbooks.com

The Day of Ezekiel's Hope
Copyright © 2021 by Donna VanLiere
Published by Harvest House Publishers
Eugene, Oregon 97408
www.harvesthousepublishers.com

ISBN 978-0-7369-7881-1 (pbk)
ISBN 978-0-7369-7882-8 (eBook)

Library of Congress Cataloging-in-Publication Data

Names: VanLiere, Donna, - author.
Title: The day of Ezekiel's hope / Donna VanLiere.
Description: Eugene, Oregon : Harvest House Publishers, [2021] | Summary: "In this gripping follow-up to The Time of Jacob's Trouble, bestselling author Donna VanLiere explores the end-times prophecies in the journeys of Emma, Zerah, and others who cling to hope even as danger closes in and civilization crumbles on an unprecedented scale"-- Provided by publisher.
Identifiers: LCCN 2020042698 (print) | LCCN 2020042699 (ebook) | ISBN 9780736978811 (trade paperback) | ISBN 9780736978828 (ebook)
Subjects: GSAFD: Christian fiction.
Classification: LCC PS3622.A66 D39 2021 (print) | LCC PS3622.A66 (ebook) | DDC 813/.6--dc23
LC record available at https://lccn.loc.gov/2020042698
LC ebook record available at https://lccn.loc.gov/2020042699

All rights reserved. No part of this publication may be reproduced, stored in a retrieval system, or transmitted in any form or by any means—electronic, mechanical, digital, photocopy, recording, or any other—except for brief quotations in printed reviews, without the prior permission of the publisher.

Printed in the United States of America

21 22 23 24 25 26 27 28 29 /BP-SK / 10 9 8 7 6 5 4 3 2 1

For Jme Medina, my longtime friend who is looking up
and my first encourager for this series of books!

"About the times of the End, a body of men will be raised up who will turn their attention to the prophecies, and insist upon their literal interpretation, in the midst of much clamor and opposition."

Sir Isaac Newton, 1642–1747

CHAPTER 1

Ashdod, Israel

Twenty-seven-year-old Zerah Adler watches from the front yard of a home in Ashdod as fighter planes over the Mediterranean Sea cast a long, threatening shadow as far as his eyes can see. "This is it!" he shouts, looking into the sky and shielding his eyes. Hundreds of thousands of Turkish, Russian, Iranian, Libyan, Asian, and other troops storm toward the northern Israeli border from Syria as the fighter planes soar overhead; other planes begin their ascent from aircraft carriers at sea and head toward land.

This is the time to wipe Israel off the map once and for all. The disappearance of millions of people from around the globe, combined with Iran's attacks on Washington, DC, and New York City, and Russia's nuclear attacks on US ships and major cities within the United States, has emboldened this military coalition as never before, and the clock is ticking. Iran, Turkey, Libya, and other allied countries have joined together with one common goal: destroy Israel and steal her treasures. With the exception of Russia, the countries share similar religious beliefs and are convinced the time has come for an Islamic caliphate to spread throughout the earth. Their determined military leaders are of like mind and share a sense of destiny: wipe out Israel and become the most powerful countries in the world.

Despite the two-state solution agreed upon by Israel and the

Palestinians under US president Thomas Banes's administration, which gave 80 percent of the West Bank and nearly half of Jerusalem to the Palestinians to establish their own country, the Palestinians, along with the terrorist groups Hamas and Hezbollah, had already spent several days screaming for the blood of the Jews, attacking Israel from within and at every border. Israel's weapons held back the terrorist armies, but also gave the Russian, Iranian, and Turkish coalition forces the time needed to move into action. Once Israel had diminished her armament, this murderous military front would move in for one massive final strike intended to annihilate the Jewish nation.

The Israel Defense Forces have been ready for this coalition attack for decades, equipping advanced fighting forces and amassing thermonuclear weapons in anticipation of her enemies pushing her to the verge of mass extermination. Every active and nonactive IDF soldier has been called into action. Israel's defense minister, deputy minister, the national security advisor, Mossad director and deputy director, and chiefs of staff from the Israel Defense Forces stare at the wall of computers and screens inside the Ministry of Defense headquarters in Tel Aviv as the coalition moves toward the border of Israel. The Defense Minister does not take his eyes from the screens as he issues the command to engage. "Go!"

As the words are spoken, a monstrous sandstorm arises and consumes each Israeli fighter jet on the tarmac—blinding the pilots, rendering them unable to find their aircraft through the thick silt. Tanks, artillery, nuclear weapons, and the Iron Dome are all disabled, seizing the entire IDF with fear. Their beloved country is moments from extinction.

From the war room in Syria, the presidents of Russia, Turkey, and Iran, along with Iran's ayatollah, who have come to watch Israel's final destruction, curse and cheer when they see the Israel Defense Forces are defenseless. "Allah is great!" Iran's supreme leader, the Ayatollah Behnam Mahdavi, shouts amidst the clamor. "Today, my friends, the sea will run red with the blood of the Zionist pigs!" He looks into a news camera and encourages his followers: "I call upon you to join the soldiers of the caliphate, attacking Jews and slaughtering them, killing them wherever they can be found!"

Beneath his feet, Zerah feels a mild tremor and he lifts his hands over his head. "O Hashem, you are our Savior and Redeemer!"

At that moment, the ground shakes beneath the enemy armies, disrupting their plan of attack. The earth emits a powerful, ear-splitting moan as mountains are overthrown and cliffs topple, border walls collapse, and the Western Wall in Jerusalem crumbles. The armies cry out in terror as the quaking grows more violent and fissures split the ground open, swallowing thousands of troops into canyon-deep crevices. Smoke, dust, and ash rise as the trembling continues, blinding the remaining troops. They wail and scream in their many languages, throwing each other into greater confusion and panic. They turn their weapons against one another, masses perishing at the hand of their allies. Painful boils break out on the once-healthy skin of each soldier and their curses and violence intensify.

Zerah's heart beats against his ribs as he watches the heavens burst open over Israel's enemies and a torrential deluge of rain and hailstones pours forth, beating and drowning all the hostile forces. As the rain and hailstones fall, fire pours down as well on the enemy aircraft, surrounding each plane in brilliant balls of flame. The entire sky over Israel glows orange and red, the infernos falling and lapping up the enemy armies.

CHAPTER 2

Brooklyn, NY
Ten Days Later

Twenty-five-year-old Emma Grady runs through the streets of New York City as buildings collapse around her. The explosions make the ground beneath her buckle, and she falls. She screams, but no sound comes from her mouth. She rises again to search through the rubble for her boyfriend Matt, her mom, her friends Brandon and Rick, and her sister, Sarah. A deafening sound envelops her, and she looks overhead as another building crumbles. She tries to scream again, which jolts her awake, her eyes opened wide in terror.

Covered in sweat, Emma bolts upright in bed; she feels as though her heart is exploding inside her chest. By the dim half-light in the room she realizes it must be just before sunrise. Her body aches; she feels two decades older. She swings her legs over the side of the bed, careful not to wake nine-year-old Lia, who has been sharing the bed with her. Signe, Ines, and three other older girls are sleeping on the floor. The house is shrouded in quiet. The power grid had been destroyed in the initial attack, and all of New York City has since been blanketed in eerie silence. Power grids in other cities across the country had also been hit, obliterating electricity to much of the world's most powerful nation. A country once buzzing with information and technology is now chillingly silent and wrapped in fear.

Emma glances toward the window and can make out an enormous blood-red moon through the curtain; it's appeared red both night and day for the last five days in a row. She hears bells ringing in the distance and knows the death wagon is coming down the street. Since the attack on the city and the violence that has erupted in the aftermath, there have been countless bodies that need to be carried away each day. Many ambulances were destroyed in the attack and simple box trucks are used to drive up and down streets at all hours picking up anyone who has died overnight from the virus that's spreading, from murder, suicide, overdose, or any other reason. Rather than use a horn that would confuse it with a regular truck, the death wagons are distinguished from other box trucks in that bells jangle from each side, alerting everyone to bring out the dead.

As fingers of light stretch across the room, Emma can see the photo of Mr. and Mrs. Ramos and their family sitting on the chest of drawers. It still feels so strange to be inside the Ramos's home. Less than three weeks ago, she and Mrs. Ramos were talking and laughing during Mrs. Ramos's physical therapy on her torn meniscus. Emma closes her eyes, attempting to shut out the memories. Her mind flashes back to putting her hands on Mrs. Ramos's shoulders and then stumbling through the air onto the therapy table. Mrs. Ramos, like millions of others within the city and around the world, had disappeared.

Before the vanishings, she always reached for her phone first thing in the morning to scroll through her social media accounts, check texts, and read her e-mail. It sits on the nightstand now, dead and useless without electricity and cell service. Emma turns to pick up the Bible on the nightstand; she found it in Mrs. Ramos's bag and has been reading it since. "I would always be happy to talk with you about God," Mrs. Ramos had said. "I love to talk about what Jesus has done for me." Emma looks down at the Bible. If only she had paid more attention to what Mrs. Ramos and her mom had told her. She flips open the cover of the Bible and pulls out the picture of her mom in between Emma and her sister, Sarah. Her throat catches as she looks at her mom, remembering again the horror of Sarah's voice screaming through the phone that their mom was gone. Emma's heart aches as she wonders whether her sister is safe in Indiana and if her streets are filled with bloody violence and chaos too.

As she slips the picture back into the Bible, she feels Lia's hand on her back. "Is it morning time already?"

Emma turns and pulls the blankets up to Lia's chin. She had found Lia in an alleyway just days after the vanishings, hiding next to a dumpster with heaps of garbage around her. Her mom dropped her off there following the disappearances, saying she would come back to get her. It was a lie; she never returned. "It's not time to get up. Go back to sleep," Emma whispers.

"Are you going out again today?" the young girl asks, squinting. "Are you still looking for stuff?"

Emma runs her index finger back and forth over Lia's forehead. "I don't know."

Lia reaches for Emma's arm, grabbing it. "I don't want you to go."

"One of us will be here with you. I promise," Emma says. "We are not going to leave any of you alone." She tucks the blankets around Lia again and leans over, kissing her forehead. "You need to get some more sleep. It's way too early to get up."

When Lia closes her eyes, Emma heads to the bathroom to get ready for the day. The small window above the toilet provides just enough light to see by as day breaks. Has the city been without power for three weeks now? It feels like a decade. When Emma ran from the rehabilitation room immediately after the vanishings, she grabbed Mrs. Ramos's bag to return it to her family and tell them that she was gone—only to discover that Mrs. Ramos's entire family had been snatched away.

Emma has now made peace with coming to Mr. and Mrs. Ramos's home and tracking down the homes of their children to round up food, extra mattresses, clothes, supplies, medication, and money. Very few food and supply trucks have made their way into the city since the pandemonium created by the vanishings and the attack, which had left the great metropolis staggering. All the major government and business buildings—including the United Nations—had been hit, obliterating the city. What the enemy hasn't devastated, residents have; looters have emptied and destroyed nearly every grocery and retail store, homes are threatened at every turn, and the streets are bloody from vicious attacks by roving street gangs. It has been frightening to see how quickly fear has created a mob mentality in cities all across the globe. Fright and anger have turned every city against itself, filling the streets with anxiety, grief, and helplessness.

An exact number has never been given, but it is believed that some 50 million Americans disappeared when Jesus snatched away his followers, rupturing the workforce and sending the economy into a wild downward spiral, causing the dollar to collapse. The fall of the US stock market caused loan institutions to crumble, and America's losses triggered a ripple effect around the world. This, in turn, crippled nations that were already struggling to keep their countries afloat, toppling their financial markets, creating rampant inflation, and throwing the world into a great depression.

As the United States fell, so did all other nations. With a national debt exceeding 52 trillion dollars and the labor force struck by the disappearances and the devastation caused by the attacks, it is impossible for the country to recover economically and maintain its position as the world's financial leader. With the US military hanging by a thread because so many members of the armed forces had disappeared, coupled with the missile strikes on US military bases in many parts of the world, the US leadership in NATO is finished as well. The country's role as superpower of the world is over.

Without electricity, Emma and her friends Brandon and Kennisha have relied on the shortwave radio they found in the Ramos's garage to bring them updates from around the globe. Keeping up with the news has been mind-numbing. The world is in upheaval, with little hope of improving. Before so many people had vanished, an election or a medical situation like the COVID-19 pandemic of 2020 would cause mayhem, emptying grocery store shelves, spurring fighting and looting in the streets, and inciting people to scream at each other on TV or social media, but boundaries were still in place. Law enforcement had kept the disorder from turning into all-out anarchy—but not this time. Lawlessness didn't merely creep in after the disappearances; it flooded in, deluging the world with chaos and rebellion.

Just days after the vanishings, President Banes, speaking from a safe house, declared the country, "Under a state of emergency." His words rang throughout the world. "To keep our citizens safe, with the help of the United States military, I am imposing martial law. Every individual must be in their home or sheltering in place an hour after sunset until sunrise. Those working must have all necessary paperwork to permit your presence in the streets. Additionally, in order to maintain peace, all firearms will be confiscated."

Emma was surprised at how many civilians were willing to give up their right to bear arms; they felt it was a small price to pay to feel safe with the military patrolling the streets. But Emma doesn't feel safe. Not for a moment. In the face of fear, the atmosphere in the city has not been one of unity and of safeguarding a neighbor. She has discovered that fear makes people angry, belligerent, hostile, selfish, hateful, and murderous. In New York and throughout the country, streets have turned into war zones as factions who were already against one another use the chaos of the disappearances to fight and kill their enemies.

Countries were rising up against each other as well. Though World War III did not unfold in the Middle East as pundits predicted prior to the invasion against Israel, wars had broken out all over the globe, resulting in deaths numbering into the millions. Earthquakes and famine conditions have followed, bringing further devastation. Transportation, businesses, hospitals, and governments around the globe are reeling. A new and unnamed virus is making its way around the world, which is attacking people's respiratory systems, making it hard for the infected to breathe. As patients gasp for breath, so does the world. There are times when Emma has to turn off the shortwave radio, unable to take in anymore.

She makes her way downstairs and finds her longtime friend Brandon in the kitchen, poring over the Bible opened in front of him. The countertops, cabinets, floor, and space against the wall are covered with supplies and canned foods. Packaged foods like rice, noodles, crackers, and cereal are kept in garbage cans with lids to keep rats out in case they somehow enter the house. After their arrival at the Ramos home, Emma and Brandon had written out the names and addresses of people in Mrs. Ramos's phone before it died. They reasoned that if Mrs. Ramos was snatched away by Jesus, then surely some of the people in her cell directory were believers as well.

Sure enough, they had found several empty homes and apartments, and secured as many goods as possible for their expanding family before looters had a chance to enter those places. Among their finds were children's clothes, propane for the gas grill, bottled water, pantries full of food, a portable camping grill, medical supplies, money, cans of gasoline, a solar phone charger, and bedding of all sorts. Emma despises the thought that they are like any other thieves out on the streets, but this is their means of survival. At least for now. With so few grocery stores open, and with goods at exorbitant prices, they have determined that they will get by on one meal a day until food trucks are making their way into the city again on a regular basis. That's what Emma prays will happen.

"Morning," she says, looking at Brandon. His eyes are tired like hers, and a dark stubble spreads over his usually smooth-like-milk-chocolate face. She realizes that until the last few weeks, she had always seen him clean-shaven. In the days following the snatching away, Emma had left the apartment she shared with her boyfriend, Matt, and Brandon left Rick, his partner. They ended up befriending Kennisha, a young, almond-skinned woman whose sister and niece had vanished. The children who were upstairs—Lia, Micah, Signe, Ines, and the others—were all discovered in the aftermath of the disappearances, and Emma, Brandon, and Kennisha had continued to scour the streets for other children who had been abandoned or were in danger of kidnappers who wanted them for trafficking.

Each time they found a child, they put word out through the members of their home church and other home churches in Brooklyn. So far, they had found homes for more than 60 children, and hoped to find more for the children who were asleep upstairs. While Emma, Brandon, Kennisha, and all the children were still new to one another, Emma felt as though they had known each other for a lifetime.

"What are you reading today?" Emma asks.

"I'm reading Revelation and Daniel again," Brandon says. They've read the books many times together, to the children and with their home church friends and visitors, who meet each morning at five.

"Has anything changed?" she says, trying to muster a smile.

"No. But we still win in the end." Sometimes the thought of what the ensuing years will bring is more than Emma can bear. Brandon notices her face. "Remember, we *do* win in the end."

She forces a nod. "Come on. Let's get to the streets." Brandon is wary. She looks as exhausted as he is. "Brandon," she says, sensing his hesitation. "We have to go now."

CHAPTER 3

Modiin, Israel

Zerah drives through the sea of people who are waving Israeli flags and dancing in the streets of his hometown of Modiin. For two weeks now, throughout Israel, Jews have been celebrating Adonai's victory over their enemies. The world has not stopped reeling and Israel has not stopped rejoicing and praising Hashem for decimating the enemies that had descended on their small country.

Videos and images of their enemies' swift and utter destruction have generated amazement and disbelief throughout the world. Today, the revelry continues as news of an enlarged peace covenant with Israel is coming soon out of Rome, where members of the European 10, or E10 for short—a coalition of nations that came together after the mass vanishings to lead and govern the world—have been working alongside Israel's prime minister Ari to achieve peace in the Middle East. Zerah opens the door of his parents' home and the sound of singing greets him. Inside, neighbors and family members are feasting and partying together.

"Get out!" his father Chaim shouts above the noise when he sees Zerah. Less than three weeks ago, when Zerah said he had been sealed as one of Yeshua's 144,000 servants, Chaim had banished him from their home. The old man storms up to him, his hands shaking from essential tremors. "Get out of my house!"

Zerah's mother Ada and his sister Rada rush to him. "Chaim, please," Ada says. "Please! We are rejoicing for what Adonai has done. Please don't do this."

Chaim's tremors worsen as he shakes a finger in Zerah's face. "He is dead to me!"

"Papa," Rada says, taking her father's hands in hers, her dark eyes pleading with him. "Hashem is mighty to save. Look what he has done for us, Papa! Please don't send Zerah away when we are celebrating Hashem's goodness to us." Chaim pulls his hands from hers and waves one toward her and Zerah as if dismissing both of them, turning his back on his family. Rada and her two children and husband, Amir, put their arms around Zerah. "Zerah," Rada says, "have you heard? The E10 will be announcing a stronger peace covenant."

"That's why I've come," Zerah says, running his fingers through his short black hair, thick like his father's. "I wanted to watch the announcement with you."

In the days following the destruction of her enemies, when the hearts of all Israelis have turned toward heaven, Zerah has been traveling throughout the country, sharing the message of how Adonai saved them, just as he said he would in the pages of Ezekiel. Countless lives have turned to Yeshua as their Messiah and the sound of the shofar can still be heard throughout the land.

"It's good, right?" Rada says, searching her brother's eyes. "A peace covenant with the E10?"

"It won't be with the E10," Zerah says, pulling her into the quiet of the kitchen. "It will be with the lawless one."

"Who's that?"

"We don't know yet, but we will."

Brooklyn, NY

Kennisha and several of the children are inside the kitchen waiting for Emma and Brandon to return home. Her hair is pulled up on top of her head with an elastic band. She's in her twenties, like Emma and Brandon, and had worked at the front desk of a hotel in Manhattan, but that feels like a lifetime ago. Kennisha lived with her sister and niece and spent many nights out partying with friends, more interested in a quick hookup than a long-term relationship, but all that changed when her sister and niece disappeared. When a Jew named Elliott from her apartment building showed up at her door looking for a Bible in the hours after the attack on New York City, she let him inside and hasn't been the same since.

As the door from the garage opens into the kitchen, Kennisha turns to see Emma, her face bloody and swollen. "What happened to you?" she asks, running to Emma. Micah, Lia, and Signe rush to her side.

"A man's fist happened," Brandon says, following Emma inside, opening a cabinet and setting, on the top shelf, the gun he and Emma had wrestled away from an attacker three weeks ago. "I hate apartments. We couldn't get inside. Instead, we got ambushed."

"By how many?" Kennisha asks, her eyes wide as she reaches for a small towel, running it beneath the water faucet and then wringing it out.

"Just one. He saw Emma, but he didn't see me."

Kennisha leads Emma to the kitchen table and looks closer at her face. One eye is beginning to swell. She uses the towel to clean up the blood. Without electricity there's nothing frozen or cold to help reduce the swelling, so she reaches for a large serving spoon, hoping the coolness of the metal will help.

"What would have happened if Brandon wasn't there?" she asks Emma.

Emma looks at the children and doesn't answer.

"You can't go do that anymore," nine-year-old Micah says, gazing at her. Emma had found him standing outside his apartment building in the days following the vanishings and brought him to the apartment she shared with Matt. She had tried to get Micah's drug-addicted father to take him back, but he never could and had asked her to take care of him.

Kennisha nods, glancing up at Brandon. "That's right, Micah. We have to stop doing this now. It's getting too dangerous."

"How are we supposed to get food when food trucks aren't coming into the city?" Emma asks, her voice quivering.

Brandon sits down in a chair facing her. "We'll go into Jersey or Connecticut or wherever we have to go until food starts coming in again."

Emma stares at him for a moment but doesn't want to argue in front of the kids. "What's new today?" she asks, indicating the shortwave radio and attempting to change the subject.

Kennisha pours each of them a cup of water; they can't waste propane on heating water for coffee. They keep the gas grill inside so it doesn't get stolen and move it outside only when they want to heat a can of vegetables or soup or boil some noodles. "I'm not moving to the news so fast," she says, handing the water to Emma and looking at her eye. "Seriously," she says, "this is beyond a food problem. We have to get out of here. The city's too dangerous."

Emma feels their eyes on her and nods. "I know. We have to leave."

"How?" 12-year-old Signe asks in her broken Polish accent. Both Signe and Ines were rescued by Brandon, their friend Elliott, and some others before they were about to be kidnapped by men who were trafficking children. Twelve-year-old Ines looks at Emma with her large, Haitian eyes filled with concern.

"We have to figure out how," Emma says, touching the cheek of each girl.

"We have to pray about how," Kennisha says, sitting down.

Emma nods, reaching for another spoon to put on her eye. Micah grabs one and hands it to her.

"What *is* the news?" Brandon asks, taking a long drink from his cup.

"More grisly descriptions of the charred troops in Israel," Kennisha says. "They have to fight off the birds from corpses so they can bury them. They're still burning the planes, tanks, and weapons and turning them into fuel." She turns up the radio.

"The new Iranian government has been formed on the heels of the massive overthrow of the remaining members of the Islamic Republic of Iran following the failed Israeli invasion," the announcer says in what sounds like a European accent. "This cataclysmic geopolitical earthquake destroyed the entire Iranian Revolutionary Guard by fire, plague, and floodwaters. Iran's Supreme Leader, the Ayatollah Behnam Mahdavi, along with President Fahim Manesh, and an unreported number of military and intelligence officials all died during the failed attack. Their deaths paved the way for Iranians to oust remaining government members, and Persians are said to be celebrating in the streets. We do not have a statement from the leaders of the E10 on this most recent event or on the hostile takeover of both the Russian and Turkish governments following the disastrous Israeli invasion, which has resulted in the deaths of thousands from among the countries involved. Concerning the invasion, the E10 will be announcing a peace covenant later."

"A peace covenant with Israel?" Emma asks. She leans back against the chair. "Just like Elliott said."

"So then it all begins, right?" Brandon asks.

"It all begins," Emma says. Her voice is heavy with a finality that both Brandon and Kennisha understand.

To discover more about the biblical facts behind the story, read Where in the Word? *on page 215, or continue reading the novel.*

CHAPTER 4

Rome, Italy

For the third day straight, loud, booming thunder can be heard and electrifying flashes of lightning surge across the skies above Rome, filling residents with fear. The sights and sounds have never been seen or heard like this before. President Banes of the United States steps to the podium atop the stairs inside the lobby of the Palace of Justice, where the E10 has set up offices. He has been in Rome, working alongside the other members of the E10 to restore peace and safety to the world.

After the attacks on the United States, President Banes knew the only way the US would survive was to join hands with other countries who would all work together to lead the world out of this madness. He is looking drawn and haggard as are most of the members of the E10, who stand behind or beside him as journalists from around the world press forward on the stairs or on the lobby floor, inching frontward to record statements, take pictures and video, and shout out questions.

President Banes lost his wife and two young children in the disappearances, while his ex-wife and two college-age children were all discovered safe. He has aged considerably. In less than three weeks, the late-50-something president's hair has become grayer, his eyes are now dark pockets, and his face is pale and lined with deep creases.

"On behalf of the E10, we want the great citizens of the world to be assured that we have been diligently putting zones into place in your region that will assist in feeding you and meeting your needs. The crash of the global markets has created opportunities for us to work hard on your behalf, and it is our great honor to serve all our global citizens." President Banes raises his voice to be heard over the deafening thunder. "To safeguard against further political or socioeconomic collapse, we urge your cooperation as we put these zones into place and create a new order for our world based on peace and safety."

In the years before the vanishings, Germany, the United Kingdom, Italy, China, Turkey, Iran, Mexico, Argentina, Brazil, and other countries had suffered from shrinking economies due to lackluster manufacturing productivity, skyrocketing debt, high unemployment, pandemics, and political turmoil. Trade wars, currency wars, civil wars, and cold wars were mere symptoms of a deeply troubled planet. The chaos of the disappearances has thrust that unstable world into a global depression.

President Banes continues, "We know that farming and food production have floundered since the global vanishings, and that food and gas prices are soaring, but we are creating a way for all of us to live and thrive together. We are no longer bound by borders but defined by our humanity, and in the days ahead, we encourage cooperation rather than confrontation so we can enable our new world to succeed and flourish. We each must extend our hand of unity and aid to our neighbor. Our open borders are the only way to bring peace, safety, and stability to our world."

Banes shuffles the papers in front of him, thinking of the millions who have poured over US borders since the disappearances and continue to do so at an extraordinary rate, putting pressure on the country's gasping-for-last-breath economy. "The E10 has labored tirelessly toward peace and security with all the earth's inhabitants. We have collaborated night and day with Prime Minister Ari of Israel to assure peace and safety in the Middle East. The peace covenant that my administration established between Israel and the Palestinians stands and the E10 binds both states to it. Since Israel's great victory, the governments of Russia, Turkey, Iran, Libya, Sudan, and other countries have been in turmoil. Their losses have been incalculable; their soldiers are still being buried; the destruction of their weapons is coloring the Israeli skies black with smoke. This war was unprecedented in the history of the world. We must never allow hatred and fear to drive us to war against one another. We must end the conflicts that are raging all around the globe before they destroy our great planet. We must have peace. We *can* have peace as one new and vibrant world."

President Banes bristles at his own words. Countless conflicts have broken out all over the globe and the death toll continues to rise. How many millions have died already? Prior to this, if a country got out of line and abused its power, other nations would come together and put that country back in line. But what will happen now? With the establishment of this new world order there won't be a system of checks and balances. Where can a country or people turn if every nation on earth falls under this one global government? What if the E10 is corrupt? Where can people go for help?

Individuals and countries can no longer look to the United States for aid. The disappearances, followed by the attacks on many major cities, have nearly brought the country to ruin, and in desperation, President Banes did away with the US Constitution so that his country could join the E10's governing body. He had been elected president partly due to his staunch belief in world globalization and multiculturalism, but when he thinks about how he abolished the US Constitution, he still gets sick to his stomach.

Reporters begin to shout questions over the noise of the thunder, but President Banes looks over his shoulder, nodding at the E10's Counsel Secretary Victor Quade, who steps to the podium. Victor was formerly the president of the failing European Council. Following the vanishings, he moved into action, along with England's Prime Minister Sophia Clattenberg and German Chancellor George Albrecht, to mobilize countries from around the world to work together as part of the E10. In his early forties, Victor looks youthful compared to President Banes; he is striking and charismatic, his smile illuminates every screen.

"These are days of wonder for our world," he says, his chest filling with strength at every word, making him a commanding presence. He does not raise his voice to be heard over the thunder as President Banes did, but talks in a way that makes the reporters want to lean in and catch every word. "A new world order has begun, a new dawning for our planet. We are the chosen ones. The universe has chosen us to clean up what the others have done to our eternal earth. We have been chosen to rid the globe of hate, bigotry, racism, violence, and false religion. The others were destroying us and our precious planet with their hostility, prejudice, intolerance, hatred, discrimination, and their twisted fervor against the good.

"Our beautiful world had been patient and longsuffering, but when it was time, it naturally cleansed itself of the destructive forces that were killing it. And now, we the chosen ones will restore our new interdependent planet to perfect peace, balance, and unity. We are already victorious because we have been chosen, and we take global pride in being the universe's chosen ones." Members of the E10 and many reporters applaud and cheer as Victor smiles warmly, waiting. "Prime Minister Ari and I shared a meal and tears together last night as I put this peace covenant together."

President Banes and other members of the E10 swap confused glances. Victor didn't put the peace covenant together; it was the collective work of the E10. Victor continues, "Prime Minister Ari, who has always been a fierce proponent of globalization, celebrates our new world order and is eager for world harmony, as all of us are. As President Banes mentioned, the E10 does recognize the peace covenant his administration put into place between the Israelis and the Palestinians. I am not only confirming that covenant but strengthening it, exceeding what was in place in order to ensure peace and safety and prosperity for Israel, the Middle East, and the entire world."

The members of the E10 make every effort to keep their faces straight as they become outraged by his words.

"Our planet needs Israel," Victor says. "Israel sits at the center of our world; she is our hub. Russia, Iran, Turkey, and the others thought that they would kill every Jew in Israel. Their greed and avarice poisoned their thoughts, and they believed they could steal the natural gas and oil that runs beneath the land and take over Israel's lucrative business and technology sectors. Their hatred convinced them that Israel's treasures belonged to them. But Israel is our treasure. We are each other's treasure. This will never happen again. Nations will not come against Israel." Victor pauses again, readying himself to speak more emphatically.

"I have put together a seven-year covenant with Israel. Because of this despicable war and the atrocious acts against Israel, I have made a provision within the covenant that permits the Jews to rebuild their beloved temple in Jerusalem. They have waited a long time for this; their previous temple was destroyed two thousand years ago. The temple will allow them to live in accordance with their faith. They will enjoy security and peace. The world has witnessed what will happen if any nation comes against Israel. If anyone as much as speaks a word of war against Israel, this body will unleash an unprecedented torrent of fire and fury against them." He lifts a piece of paper high into the air. "I have signed this covenant on behalf of the entire world. Israel will never again worry about annihilation, and we will all live in peace." President Banes and members of the E10 swap angry glances, some of them cursing beneath their breath.

The reporters immediately begin to bombard Victor with questions. "How can you sign the covenant on behalf of the entire world? Shouldn't each nation's leaders look at..."

Victor raises his hand and talks over the reporters: "The leaders of Russia, Turkey, Iran, Libya, Sudan, and all the nations who came against Israel—those leaders are gone. Those nations are now weak as a result of their foolishness. Fire and brimstone destroyed their armies. Their governments are in turmoil. They are desperate for peace. They have seen the power that will come against them. They have witnessed the devastation. And if pushed, we will do it again, but as I said, these countries—and the whole world—are now desperate for peace. I spoke with the remaining leaders of the countries involved in this contemptible war. They all want this."

A reporter from Africa yells above the crowd. "Are you forcing countries into this peace covenant?"

Victor smiles. "The E10 is the governing body of the world. We will *enforce* the covenant in order to keep the world safe. Citizens can no longer act individually, but as one. There can be no world order, no peace, if there are renegade nations waging war against other nations. We can no longer be against one another. We must be *for* one another. Our borders are open as we work with one another. This recent war against Israel has made the way for peace for all of us. We have much to learn from this war. The Arab and Muslim leaders recognize this and want peace."

Reporters shout above each other as Victor smiles and charms his way through each answer. When he waves to the sea of journalists to indicate he is finished, President Banes, Prime Minister Clattenberg, and Chancellor Albrecht confront him. "What was that all about?" President Banes asks. "That's not the peace agreement the E10 drew up. There was no talk of the temple or your signing on..."

Victor smiles as he talks with them, making sure he is facing the cameras as he does. "Your agreement was flawed. It needed to be strengthened. It needed longer, more powerful legs."

"You mean *our* agreement," Prime Minister Clattenberg says, her eyes challenging him. In her early fifties, the prime minister keeps her golden hair colored and professionally done. Her nails are always manicured and painted, and her suit dresses are fashionable and sleek, making her look younger than her years. "The E10's agreement."

"You can't change things in the twelfth hour. Not without discussion," Chancellor Albrecht says. In his late sixties, the chancellor is the oldest member of the E10 with gray hair and a paunchy belly from too much rich German drink and food and hours spent behind a desk. "You are the counsel secretary. *We* are the governing members of this council! With the exception of the United States, virtually every nation on earth has been against Israel's occupation of the land. The Jews are some of the most hated people on the planet, and you appease them without our approval!"

Victor is unfazed. "It's not appeasement. We will all find that this covenant keeps Israel, the Middle East, and the world safe."

"How does letting the Jews build a temple keep the world safe?"

Banes whispers hotly. “The covenant was strong as it was. Our greatest issues are wars and the worldwide depression, Quade. Stopping the killing and feeding people are our greatest problems. Not the Jews’ temple! Muslims will not allow a Jewish temple to be built on the Temple Mount. I don’t care if there’s a peace treaty in place or not. That means war!”

Victor’s mouth turns up a little. “War with who? You saw what happened. What Muslim will come against Israel after that? There isn’t an army on earth that would dare step foot in Israel right now.”

President Banes’s face begins to soften. Victor puts his hand on the president’s shoulder. “There isn’t one Muslim left on the Temple Mount now. Not one Muslim has ventured close to the Israeli border. They will allow the temple’s construction. Or deal with fire from the sky once again.”

Prime Minister Clattenberg shakes her head in disbelief. “You didn’t send the fire, Quade.”

He glares at her. “How do you know that I didn’t? Let’s focus on our work here! The peace covenant is the E10’s, of course. I only finessed it a little. Peace is in our hands, my friends.”

The four leaders then turn to the reporters to wave and smile at them in solidarity, but it was not the photo taken at that moment that made its way onto every Internet news site, magazine cover, or TV news program. Instead, it was a closeup of Victor Quade alone, smiling and waving from the podium with a headline that read “Architect of Peace!”

CHAPTER 5

Modiin, Israel

Zerah is at his parents' house when Victor's announcement is made, and the air is still noisy with celebration as he raises his arms to get everyone's attention. "Listen to me! Listen to me!" he says, trying to quiet the voices of longtime neighbors and friends. "You must understand what's happening!"

"We do!" old man Jacobs cries. He lifts his hands and tilts his face upward. "We are building the temple! All praise to Hashem!" The crowd cheers and begins dancing and celebrating again.

"No!" Zerah shouts. "You must listen to me!"

"Zerah, not now," his mother Ada says. "We have waited since 70 AD to rebuild our temple. Let us celebrate."

He puts his hands on his mother's shoulders. "No, Mom. This is a false celebration." Zerah turns to the many familiar faces from his childhood, the people who watched him grow up and become a doctor. They don't know the change Hashem has brought into his life, and he knows that when he tells them, their celebration will turn to anger.

"The prophet Ezekiel foretold of the great war against us. We were told thousands of years ago that Russia, Turkey, Iran, and the others would come against us and that Hashem would save us by fire and brimstone and rain and hail and plagues. We were also told thousands of years ago about this covenant of peace that Quade has signed with

Israel. Quade is the one the prophet Daniel called 'the prince who is to come and the one who makes desolate.'" A couple of people begin to interject, but Zerah lifts his hand to quiet them. "He is here in Daniel chapter 9." Zerah opens his Bible and the atmosphere changes instantly. Why is he holding a Bible? There is fury and anger in the voices raised against him, his father's voice among the loudest.

"Listen to him," Ada says, trying to restore peace. "I didn't believe him at first. I didn't believe my own son. But I was wrong. Zerah has been sealed by Hashem. He is telling you the truth."

"What do you mean *sealed*?" a neighbor asks.

"For his work," Zerah says. "I am one of his 144,000 servants who has been sent out to proclaim the life, death, resurrection, and coming again of our Yeshua Hamashiach."

The home erupts in shrieks at the name of Yeshua and many curse, shaking their fists. Chaim raises his hand to strike Zerah and stumbles forward as he tries to hit his son. Others throw punches that beat about the air, never making contact with Zerah. Confused and frightened, some run for the door.

"Please stay!" he yells after them. "Everything that has happened in the world is right here within Hashem's Word."

Ada clings to Chaim, begging him to stay, and Rada and her family watch in fear as he speaks to those who are still present. "We know through Moses that the seed of the woman will triumph over Satan. Moses also told us that that seed came from Abraham, Isaac, and Jacob. Adonai's covenant with David promised a kingdom and throne forever. The prophets of old predicted the coming of our Messiah."

He lifts the Bible upward and continues: "This is Hashem's Word, and it tells us that Yeshua is the descendent of Abraham, Isaac, Jacob, and David. Yeshua said to Jews just like us, 'You search the Scriptures because you think that in them you have eternal life; and it is they that bear witness about me.' At another time Yeshua said to them, 'O foolish ones, and slow of heart to believe all that the prophets have spoken! Was it not necessary that the Christ should suffer these things and enter into his glory? And beginning with Moses and all the Prophets, he interpreted to them in all the Scriptures the things concerning himself.'" More people storm out of the house and those who remain are still angry, but they are listening.

"The prophet Isaiah told us that Yeshua would be born of a virgin. Hosea told us that he would end up in Egypt. Micah told us he would be born in Bethlehem Ephrathah, of the clan of Judah, and he would be ruler in Israel. That day of Yeshua's ruling over Israel is very soon! The very pages of our Scriptures point to Yeshua. He is the king of the Jews."

Enraged, a few of the men in the crowd, including Zerah's brother-in-law, Amir, tear their shirts, charging at him as one mob. Though their fists flail at him they are unable to strike him and instead, they hit one another, which fills them with fright. Zerah raises his voice. "Please listen! Yeshua walked the earth, proclaiming that the kingdom of heaven is at hand, but our people rejected him, and the Gentiles were grafted into the vine for salvation, postponing the kingdom promise until the future. That future is upon us. Moses told us that Enoch walked with Hashem and then was no more because Hashem took him. A chariot of fire with horses of fire was sent from Hashem to the prophet Elijah, and he went up by a whirlwind to heaven. Enoch and Elijah were translated from earth to heaven just like that," he says, snapping his fingers.

Zerah then turns the pages of his Bible to 1 Thessalonians chapter 4. "A first-century Jew named Paul wrote this: 'We believe that Jesus died and rose again, even so, through Jesus, God will bring with him those who have fallen asleep. For this we declare to you by a word from the Lord, that we who are alive, who are left until the coming of the Lord, will not precede those who have fallen asleep. For the Lord himself will descend from heaven with a cry of command, with the voice of an archangel, and with the sound of the trumpet of God. And the dead in Christ will rise first. Then we who are alive, who are left, will be caught up together with them in the clouds to meet the Lord in the air, and so we will always be with the Lord. Therefore encourage one another with these words.'"

"What does this nonsense mean?" old man Jacobs says, his hands shaking atop his walking stick.

"You've seen the pictures of gaping holes in cemeteries around the world, where graves have been emptied. The dead in Yeshua were the first to rise," Zerah says to the hushed crowd. "You've seen the images from security cameras where people disappeared—in stores, banks, prisons, schools, wherever they were. Hashem told us long ago this would happen. He told us Yeshua would come for his own. And he did just as he said. He told us about the lawless one, the man of sin, the willful king—all names for the Antichrist."

Zerah then reads from Daniel chapter 9, and when he gets to the end, he pauses, reading slowly: "He shall make a strong covenant with many for one week, and for half of the week he shall put an end to sacrifice and offering. And on the wing of abominations shall come one who makes desolate, until the decreed end is poured out on the desolator." Zerah looks up, and tears are in the eyes of some of his listeners.

"Victor Quade is that man?" his mother asks, her voice trembling. "He's going to break the covenant that he just made?"

Zerah nods. "He will rise to power over the next three-and-a-half years, then will break the covenant. Then he will set out to kill every Jew on earth and destroy Israel."

"But he won't!" his sister says. "You just read that Hashem will destroy him."

Zerah smiles at her. "At the end of seven years he will be destroyed, but his goal will be to kill each and every one of you."

Some begin to scoff. "Why would he make a peace covenant with us? Why would he threaten to destroy our enemies again if he wants to kill us? Why not just kill us today, if that's his goal?" Javan says. He and Zerah used to play basketball together at a nearby park. Javan's wife stands next to him, holding their baby boy.

"If Quade killed you and destroyed Israel today, how could he gain the world's trust?" Zerah asks. "Don't put your trust in this man, Javan. Today is the day of salvation. Repent and put your trust in Yeshua because he is coming again."

To the dismay of most of the guests, some believe Zerah and claim Yeshua as their Savior. "It is blasphemy!" Chaim yells, shaking his fist in the air. "You are dead to me, Zerah!" he says to his only son, spitting at his feet. Several others begin to follow Chaim out, including Amir, Zerah's brother-in-law.

"Come with me," Amir barks at Rada.

She pulls on his arm to stay, crying. "No, Amir! I believe! I believe Zerah. Yeshua is our Messiah!"

Amir slaps her across the face and tries to wrench their two children from her grasp. Eight-year-old Taavi and his sister Batya scream in fright. "Blasphemy!" Amir shouts to his wife. "You are dead to me! The children belong to me!"

Rada and Ada wail in fright, trying to keep Amir from taking the children. "No, Papa, no!" Taavi cries. "Please stop it! I believe Uncle Zerah. I believe in Yeshua."

Amir's face is red with rage, but he doesn't strike his son. He looks at Batya, who is sobbing into her mother's neck. He then storms out of the house, cursing at them as he leaves. Rada crumples to the floor, weeping and clinging to her children. "What will we do, Zerah?" she cries, looking at him.

He bends down next to her and hugs her. "Pray that Papa, Amir, and the others will come to Yeshua." His mother's hand is on his shoulder and Zerah stands, looking at her; her face is wet with tears.

"Don't go, Zerah," she says, her voice breaking.

He smiles, kissing her cheek. "I have to go. I will see you again, Mom."

She grabs hold of his arm. "When?" He doesn't answer; he's not sure if he will see her again on earth, but he knows he will see her again when Yeshua returns with all the saints. "There are many things I still don't understand, Zerah, and I'm frightened of what will come," she says. "But I'm trusting Hashem with your life and ours."

Zerah kisses his mother and prays over this new fellowship of followers. Though several had left with his father, others who had grown up with him or watched Zerah grow into manhood, including Javan and his wife, are still present, comforting Rada and her children and believing together.

To discover more about the biblical facts behind the story, read Where in the Word? *on page 221, or continue reading the novel.*

CHAPTER 6

Jerusalem, Israel

Many parades and parties in Jerusalem have been interrupted by two crazy old men wearing mourning clothes of mohair sackcloth in a show of penitence as they make their way through the streets. Their clothes and words stand in harsh contrast to the carnival-like atmosphere throughout Israel, and their relentless cries for repentance are both baffling and maddening. At first people gave pause when they saw the pair, but after a couple weeks of this, people are becoming infuriated. Despite some of the best intelligence in the world, no one within the Israeli government or military has been able to identify the men.

Slate-gray hair falls just past the First Witness's shoulders, while his long and scruffy beard touches above the middle of his chest. The Second Witness is bald, with fine wisps of hair sitting in tufts at his temple. His full, silver-gray beard reaches below his neck. They walk through the crowded city jostling and bumping against people, crying out as they go, many times stopping and calling out a person's sin, whether it be hidden or public. At times this leaves the individual in tears of regret over their reckless life against Hashem, but most often it enrages the man or woman, leaving them incensed and seething at the old men's brash boldness.

"We are Adonai's witnesses!" the First Witness shouts on a crowded street in the Old City. The clouds above them dart swiftly as if recorded on a time-lapse video, making people crane their necks to look up to watch the strange sight. "Thus says Hashem: Disaster after disaster! Behold, it comes; the end has come; it has awakened against you. Your doom has come to you. The time has come; the day is near, a day of tumult. I will soon pour out my wrath upon you, and spend my anger against you, and judge you according to your ways, and I will punish you for all your abominations." People brush by, ignoring his ramblings. "Listen to us! For a long time, Israel has been without the one true Hashem. You have been without Hashem's truth, living by your own truth, not our holy Adonai's truth. In these times there has been no peace to him who goes out or to him who comes in, for many disturbances afflict the inhabitants of all the lands. Nation is being crushed by nation, and city by city, for Adonai troubles them with every kind of distress."

Most people rush past the witnesses, cursing them or ignoring them completely, but one stops to argue. "You are fools!" says a young man in his thirties. "Adonai has sent the earthquakes, the tornados, and pandemic? Did he send those clouds?" He points to the sky that is moving unnervingly swift. "Why?" His dark eyes are fierce and his bearded jaw is clenched in anger.

"In your distress turn to Adonai, Benjamin," the First Witness says. "If you seek him, he will let you find him."

The young man is unmoved by the fact the witness knows his name. "Let me *find* him!" Benjamin, says, laughing. "Am I lost, old man? Or has Hashem hidden himself or rejected us?" he asks, opening his arms wide to indicate the passing crowd.

A wry smile appears on the First Witness's face. "Hashem did not reject his people, whom he foreknew. But you are hardened, Benjamin. As it is written: 'Adonai gave them a spirit of stupor, eyes that would not see and ears that would not hear, down to this very day.'" Benjamin narrows his eyes, his body stiff and set against the old man's words as others in the crowd begin to shout at the witness.

The Second Witness raises his voice above the din and proclaims, "The wrath of Hashem has come, but he can still be found in your distress. Hear us, Israel! You are loved on account of the patriarchs, for Adonai's gifts and his call are irrevocable. Adonai wants a relationship with you. It is not about sacrifice. It is not about tradition. It is about Adonai's great love for you. You can be in relationship with him."

At this, rabbis within the crowd become enraged, racing toward the witnesses. "Blasphemy!" they scream, their faces red and twisted with anger. "Jews cannot know Hashem with such intimacy. We can only follow his commandments."

"This is what Adonai says," the First Witness declares, lifting his hand to quiet the crowd. "Son of man, I send you to the people of Israel, to nations of rebels, who have rebelled against me. They and their fathers have transgressed against me to this very day. The descendants also are impudent and stubborn: Be not afraid of their words, nor be dismayed at their looks, for they are a rebellious house."

The crowd that has gathered to watch is perturbed and some are growing hostile, but the two witnesses are undaunted. The Second Witness spots a bench on the sidewalk and steps up on it. "This is what Adonai says: 'Son of man, I have made you a watchman for the house of Israel. Whenever you hear a word from my mouth, you shall give them warning from me. If I say to the wicked, "You shall surely die," and you give him no warning, nor speak to warn the wicked from his wicked way, in order to save his life, that wicked person shall die for his sin, but his blood I will require at your hand. But if you warn the wicked, and he does not turn from his wickedness, or from his wicked way, he shall die for his sin; but you will have delivered your soul.'"

"Who has sinned?" an angry man in the crowd yells out, swearing at the witness. "Who is wicked here?" Others shout and curse along with him, but there is a softening among some who are listening, those who have ears to hear.

"Hashem will not be mocked any longer. His wrath and vengeance on a sinful, rebellious world is being poured out," the Second Witness says. "We must obey Hashem rather than you! Hashem raised Yeshua from the dead—whom your ancestors killed by hanging him on a cross. Hashem exalted him to his own right hand as Prince and Savior that he might bring Israel to repentance and forgive their sins. We are witnesses of these things. Over and over again you have rejected him, disobeying his Word, creating your own gods!" the Second Witness says. "And now is the time Hashem will judge this world of sin. Repent, O Israel, of your abominations! Choose life and live! Turn your back on Satan. Repent of your sins and follow Yeshua Hamashiach!"

When they hear this, many in the crowd become furious. The old men's cries of repentance have been a simple burr against their skin compared to this cry to follow Yeshua. Only Christians follow Yeshua, and the Jews have been persecuted by them throughout the ages. As several people rush forward to assault the two men, flames of fire burst forth from each witness's mouth, causing everyone to shrink back in amazement and fright.

"You make a covenant with Satan but grow angry at the name of Yeshua," the First Witness says, walking through them. "Wake up from your sleep! Yeshua seized all of those who were in relationship with him, who followed him, and he is coming again. Every eye will see him when he and all his saints and angels descend from heaven. He will return to the Mount of Olives, and on that day, you will have no more opportunities to follow him. Thus, says Adonai, today is your day of salvation!"

"We will not follow Christian doctrine, but our own," someone in the raucous crowd shouts. "Christians worship many gods."

"Hear, O Israel: Adonai is the One and Only," the Second Witness says. "Then Adonai said, 'Let us make man in our image, after our likeness.' According to Genesis 1:1, Elohim created the heavens and the earth. Adonai first manifested himself to us as Elohim…plural. He did not use a singular name but a plural one so that you would know he is many in one."

Some in the crowd pause at what the witness has said, wondering if it's true. But the majority of them have never studied the Torah, let alone the names of Hashem, and they shout at the witnesses, demanding that they leave Jerusalem.

Videos of that encounter and others are caught on cell phones and news about the old men spreads like wildfire throughout the world.

CHAPTER 7

Brooklyn, NY

Twenty-four-year-old Elliott Hirsch rides his bicycle through the war-torn streets of New York, fighting ferocious winds that began to blow yesterday, and shouting through a megaphone at anyone who will listen. "What will happen in the days ahead? Go to Marine Park in Brooklyn at noon for answers." He pedals from Queens to Brooklyn, making his way through neighborhoods and alerting as many passersby as possible.

On the day of the vanishings, Elliott was standing inside a cemetery when many of the graves burst open. After a frantic journey back to Queens, he locked himself inside his apartment and followed all the chaos around the world playing out on the news. In the days afterward, he became sleep-deprived and his nerves were stripped bare as he tried to make sense of it all. Then it happened—he was knocked to the floor by an intense, burning light and presence inside his apartment. It was there in that light, and in the powerful wind swirling about him, that Jesus spoke with Elliott, sealing him as one of his 144,000 Jewish witnesses who would take the gospel to every corner of the earth. Neither Elliott nor anyone in his Jewish family had ever spoken the name of Jesus, but all that changed for Elliott on that day, his own Damascus Road experience.

Elliott has since preached to thousands—in the streets, inside bars, at apartment houses, churches, rescue missions, warehouses, parks, strip clubs, and wherever people are gathered. This formerly shy and quiet man who had worked at a brokerage firm has caused great outbreaks of anger and violence as he shares the gospel of Jesus throughout New York City. He has been shot at numerous times, had multiple stabbing attempts made against him, had acid thrown on him, had gasoline poured over him along with a lit torch in an attempt to set him on fire, had makeshift bombs detonate near him while he preached, and many people have tried to run him over. But all weapons are powerless against the seal God has placed on Elliott's life. Shortly before 5:00 a.m., he rides his bicycle up the front sidewalk of Mrs. Ramos's house and knocks on the door.

"Elliott!" Emma exclaims as she opens the door, holding tight to it before the wind rips it from her hands. "We didn't expect you."

He pushes his glasses up on his nose as he enters, then hugs her, Brandon, and Kennisha. "What happened?" he asks, holding Emma's chin to get a better look at her eye.

"Just out for an early morning stroll," she says.

"What did you stroll into? And what does the other guy look like?"

Emma smiles. "Thanks to Brandon, he's probably still out cold in the street!"

Elliott puts his hand on her shoulder. "Throughout the city, people are being beaten when they're found pillaging." Emma opens her mouth to interrupt, but Elliott continues. "It's too dangerous to keep this up." He squeezes her shoulder. "I see it, Emma. I'm out there all the time. I've seen things that I do not want to see happen to any of you. You can't keep taking these risks."

She tries to smile, nodding, and Elliott walks to the children, kissing Ines and Signe on the top of their heads. He had helped save them from traffickers, and the girls hug him tightly. Elliott then looks around the room. "Did you hear the news?"

"Yeah," Brandon says. "We were praying about it when we heard you on the porch." Just a few weeks earlier, the thought of prayer had been far removed from all their lives, but since they have come to know Christ following the world's upheaval, prayer has been as natural as breathing for this little band of believers.

"It's him, isn't it?" Emma asks. "Quade is the Antichrist."

"He made it clear that the peace covenant has been strengthened by him and he's signing it," Elliott says.

"He also said that he would cause fire to fall from heaven again," Kennisha says, sitting on the sofa. "Who would believe he caused that and not God?"

Elliott sits next to her. "So many will believe." Turning to Emma and Brandon, he says, "I'll be at Marine Park at noon. We have to tell people about this. Can you help spread the word?"

"Of course," Emma says. "We'll tell the church. They'll be here at five. What will you say?"

"The truth," Elliott says. "People see Quade as an angel of light, a savior for the world. They need to know everything that's going to happen over the next few years. They need to know who he is and how he'll rise to power." Emma, Brandon, and Kennisha are silent as they consider the significance of Quade's identity. Elliott continues, "I need to get back to the streets, but I had to come see you."

Kennisha holds her hand up in the air, rushing to the kitchen. She returns with a small sack filled with a couple of granola bars, nuts, peanut butter between crackers, and bottled water. "Something to eat," she says, handing the sack to Elliott.

"Save it for the kids," he says.

Signe takes the bag from Kennisha and pushes it into Elliott's hand. "Take the food. You need to eat." Elliott smiles down at her and pulls her in for another hug.

Brandon puts his hand on Elliott's shoulder. "We'll pray before you go." He doesn't wait for Elliott to respond. "Father, we praise you that you have revealed Jesus to all of us. Help us get people to Marine Park so that they can hear your Word. Give us strong backs for this time. Show us how to live, and show us what to do today. In Jesus's name, amen."

Elliott hugs Brandon, slapping him on the back. "I'll see you soon," he says to all of them.

CHAPTER 8

Brooklyn, NY

Emma and Brandon ride their bicycles through the windy streets of Brooklyn, hanging on tight to the handlebars to help stabilize themselves through the powerful gusts. They are alerting anyone who will listen and telling them to show up at Marine Park. The streets have not been the same since the day Jesus snatched up his followers. The city, like many others around the country that were attacked, is the color of death: gray and ashen. The buildings that once formed the skyline are gone, reduced to heaps of rubble, a giant graveyard that sucks the breath from your lungs. The sounds of a city bustling with energy have been strangled and replaced with faint pants for breath.

The country had been on edge for decades. Before the disappearances, racial tension was at an all-time high. Anyone who believed the sovereign Word of God was considered a bigot, homophobe, or hatemonger. Political parties were no longer comprised of Americans in pursuit of the country's greater good but acted more like sworn enemies determined to destroy each other. Hatred and rebellion against law enforcement was spreading daily. Truth was hard to find and even harder to believe as pulpits were getting quieter and quieter about God's truth. Pundits battled it out on TV, radio, and Internet news, and tempers flared as people screamed at one another on social media. After the vanishing of millions from all across the country, there was no way that people would return to being civil and playing by the rules. Those who were once peace-loving citizens are fighting and killing over basic necessities, and the military and law enforcement officers are commonly seen as enemies. The bombings and earthquakes throughout the country have unearthed burrows of rats, badgers, and bears and destroyed living spaces for coyotes, foxes, mountain lions, and bobcats, displacing them and forcing them to forage for food in what's left of the city and suburbs. As a result of all this, the streets are now grim and bristling with fear to an extent that is far beyond what any science fiction movie has ever depicted.

Emma is thrilled to find Linda, a former coworker from Thrive Rehabilitation, at home. Linda and her husband have two grown children and are expecting their first grandchild any day now. She had been in the therapy room that day when Mrs. Ramos and others had disappeared. When Emma last saw Linda at Thrive, the place had been looted, and because there was no electricity, Linda couldn't access any of the patients' electronic files. During that encounter, Emma had told Linda about Elliott.

"Remember the man I told you about a few days ago at Thrive?" Emma says. "He told me how my mom disappeared, and why so many people are gone." Linda is feeling despondent and weary, but she looks at Emma with a glimmer of hope. Emma grabs her hand. "Please come to Marine Park at noon. He'll be there. Please, Linda."

Linda is uncertain. "How do you know what he says is true?"

"Because my mom told me the same thing while she was still here, and my mom never lied to me."

Linda pauses, then says, "Our neighbor was..." her voice catches as she tries to keep speaking, "...beaten inside her home by a mother and her two children. They robbed her. Took food right off her pantry shelves." She looks at Emma. "She's an old lady, Emma. A mom and her kids! How...?"

"People are afraid and hungry," Emma says. "They're desperate for food. And truth. We all are." Emma hugs Linda and whispers in her ear. "Please, Linda. Please come." Linda nods, wiping away a tear. Then she nods again, looking at Emma.

Emma and Brandon pedal away, shouting at people as they go. A block away from Linda's home is a plain-looking brick church that catches Emma's eye. The windows are broken, and the front door is hanging loose, another innocent victim of looters. "I think that was Mrs. Ramos's church," she says, stopping her bicycle.

Brandon squeezes the brakes on his bicycle. "How do you know?"

"I remember seeing the name of the church in her cell phone. I'm pretty sure that's it." She looks over her shoulder at him. "Let's go inside. There could be kids hiding."

They don't want to leave their bicycles out front, so they push them to the back of the building, where they see a door that has been broken down and haphazardly put back up. Brandon shoves it and a blast of wind blows it aside. He pushes his bike through the open door when he is struck over the head. Emma screams at the suddenness of the attack and bolts through the door to help Brandon. She glances up to see a folding chair held in the air and shouts, "No! Put it down!"

A young teenage girl holds tightly to the chair as two other girls who look to be 12 or 13 hold weapons of their own—a broken lamp base and a small pot.

"Stop!" Brandon says, holding up one hand and rubbing the back of his head with the other. "We're not going to hurt you."

"There's nothing here to steal," the teenage girl holding the chair says, her voice ragged and trembling.

"We're not here to steal anything," Brandon says.

"I knew a woman who came to this church," Emma says. "We want to help."

Brandon looks at the three girls and realizes they might be living here. "Who are you here with?"

All three begin shouting. "Get out! Leave us alone!"

Brandon holds up his hands as a peaceful gesture and the three girls react in fear, prompting Emma to step closer. "We just want to know that you're okay," she says. Emma glances around the room, noticing blood on the floor. "Is anyone hurt?" she asks, noticing a red trail that goes through the doorway and stretches into the hall. "Is someone else here?" she asks as Brandon takes a step toward the door.

"Get out of here!" one girl shouts.

Emma steps closer. "Please. We just want to make sure that you're safe."

Brandon walks into the hallway, following the path of blood. He stops when he sees a man's body in an office. The man's head lies in a dark pool and Brandon recognizes immediately that he's dead. He runs back to Emma and the girls, shaking his head when Emma looks at him. The girls begin to cry.

"He didn't know that I was here," the oldest of the girls says, an Asian with long black hair, dark eyes, and cream-colored skin. "I heard Taylor screaming and I ran back here and saw him hurting Bella. Taylor jumped on his back, but he smashed her up against the wall. I ran back into the church and found that," she says, pointing to a tall, broken marble candlestick. "I didn't mean to kill him." Tears flow down her cheeks, and Emma puts her arm around her.

"You saved their lives," Emma says. "You've told us Bella and Taylor's names, but not yours."

"Jordan."

"You're very brave, Jordan," Emma says. "All of you are."

"We didn't know what to do with him, so we dragged him into that office," Jordan says.

"You can't stay here," Brandon says. "It's too dangerous to be on the streets right now. Do you have any family?"

"My mom disappeared," Jordan says. "My dad is still here, but he left us a few months ago to live with his girlfriend. I tried to go there, but they didn't have room for me along with all of her kids, so I found this place."

"I lost my mom too," Emma says. "How about you, Bella?"

Bella's curly blonde hair looks as if it hasn't been washed since the disappearances; it sits lifeless on her shoulders. "Taylor and I lived with foster parents," the petite girl says as she looks at Taylor, a beautiful girl with chocolate brown curly hair, dark skin, and soft features. "After they disappeared we tried to stay in the apartment, but people broke in. We started running and ended up here. The doors were open because people had already stolen everything. The only reason that candlestick was left was because it was already broken."

"When is the last time you've eaten?" Brandon asks.

The girls look at each other and shrug. "Three or four days," Taylor says. "The only thing left here was some crackers. Those ran out a few days ago."

"Okay," Emma says. "You need to eat, and we have some food. We'll also find you a home to live in with adults. It's not safe for you to stay here alone."

"We can take care of ourselves," Jordan says.

"We know that," Brandon says. "But now is the time for people to stick together and help each other. We need your help just as much as you need ours. There's no electricity here, and that makes for dark, scary nights inside this church with people like him on the street," he says as he points to the office, indicating the dead man, "along with dogs and other animals looking for food and these weird winds. It's better for all of us to be together."

Jordan is quiet, looking at Emma and Brandon. "You said you knew a woman who came to this church. Who was it?"

"Mariana Ramos," Emma says.

Jordan responds with a sad smile. "I knew her. She and her husband owned the 316 Deli."

"We're living in their house," Emma says. "Mrs. Ramos would love for you to come and eat a meal there and get a good night's sleep without worrying about how to survive alone."

To discover more about the biblical facts behind the story, read Where in the Word? *on page 227, or continue reading the novel.*

CHAPTER 9

Brooklyn, NY

When Elliott arrives at Marine Park a few minutes before noon, despite the gales, the lawn is teeming with people anxious for answers amidst the escalating chaos and confusion. Emma and Brandon are tired and hungry as they push their bicycles into the area and are followed by Jordan, Taylor, and Bella. The winds catch Emma's hair as she looks up at a brilliant purple sky flashing with beams of light and gasps at the sight. Each day a new marvel appears in the skies to keep people looking up, and she wonders how many see God's hand trying to lift their faces upward. She looks over the size of the crowd and her eyes widen. "Look at all these people, Brandon!"

"It's enormous!" Brandon says. "I didn't think people would come, but here they are!"

Emma tries to see to the back of the crowd, but it's impossible. "I hope Matt and Rick will be in one of these crowds someday." When she left Matt and Brandon left Rick, there was little hope that either of them would become believers too. Emma calls to Elliott when she sees him, and he smiles, beckoning for her and Brandon to come to him.

As they approach him with the girls in tow, Elliott lifts his Bible and says, "Can each of you help me read from this today?" They both manage a nod, but Elliott doesn't give them time to say anything else. He raises the megaphone to his mouth to address the mass of onlookers, and Emma and Brandon make sure to stand with Jordan, Taylor, and Bella between them so the girls feel safe.

"My name is Elliott. I am a New Yorker, and I am a Jew," he says into the megaphone. "What I am about to say to you are not my thoughts. They are God's words from the Bible. He is not some god we have created. He alone is the one true God. I know that you are frightened, but I'm here to tell you that God loves you so much that he sent his Son Jesus to die in your place for your sins so that you can live with him someday." Elliott is unable to see everyone in the crowd; their numbers push well beyond the trees bordering the park and bending at the power of the prevailing wind. His words are already stirring up murmurs, and he continues.

"Nearly three weeks ago I stood in a cemetery when many graves burst open. The coffins inside were empty. Many urns were empty. That's because Jesus stepped into the air above us and commanded his dead followers to come to him. And because they were his sheep and his sheep hear his voice, they were snatched away, just before those who were alive in Christ were taken up as well. All of them were called to him because they knew him, the one true God and Savior. Many of you were with someone who was snatched away that day, and you are still wondering why they disappeared." Elliott can see people in the crowd wiping their eyes. The reminder of their sudden and unexpected loss is still a grief too hard to bear. "The danger of this new world became apparent immediately, and you're wondering what will happen next. I wondered too, but now I know. What I am about to say is not science fiction. It is not a horror story from a madman's mind. As I said, it is the truth of God from his Word, the Bible."

Elliott holds his Bible high into the air, its pages flapping in the wind. "Listen to me: I am a man who never spoke the name Jesus until a few short days ago when Jesus sealed me for his work." He could tell by many faces in the crowd that people were wondering if he was in his right mind. "I have been chosen to tell you about God's love for you, about salvation in Jesus Christ, and about what will happen in the years ahead. Right from the very beginning, God knew the end of all things and he told us about them." Elliott then opens his Bible and reads. "I make known the end from the beginning, from ancient times, what is still to come...What I have said, that I will bring about; what I have planned, that I will do." Elliott lowers the megaphone so he can turn a couple pages, then continues, "I am the LORD; that is my name!...See, the former things have taken place, and new things I declare; before they spring into being I announce them to you."

Elliott closes the Bible and looks at the people before him. "Throughout the Bible God told us what would happen. He told us that he would give us his son as our bridge to heaven, but none of us here believed, and that's why we're still here. God told us that he would send his son to rescue his bride—that is, all those who put their faith in Christ and walked with him. Jesus told his followers that he was going to prepare a place for them, and that he would come back to take them to live with him. He did exactly as he said! He came back and took his people to be with him."

Elliott then reads from 1 Thessalonians 4 about the dead in Christ rising first, just like the dead inside the cemetery that day. Many weep as Elliott is speaking, realizing that he is proclaiming truth. "Today is the day of salvation! Today is the day to turn from sin and place your life in Christ. Jesus said, 'I am the way and the truth and the life. No one comes to the Father except through me.' Jesus is our way. He is our truth. He is our life. He is our only way to God the Father." Tears fill Emma's eyes as she listens to Elliott and prays this entire crowd will believe as she does. Elliott clears his throat and continues. "The Bible says, 'The arm of the Lord is not too short to save, nor his ear too dull to hear. But your iniquities have separated you from your God; your sins have hidden his face from you, so that he will not hear.' Our sins separated us from God. That's why we're all still here. If you want to know Jesus, you must admit that your sins separate you from him and confess with your mouth that he is Lord. You must believe in your heart that God raised him from the dead. You must turn from practicing the sin in your life and follow him."

The crowd becomes noisy as people rally against what Elliott is saying, while others speak aloud the name of Jesus. Elliott looks at Emma and Brandon, smiling at the sound of people coming to Christ. He raises the Bible and speaks into the megaphone again. "God also told us that Jesus will return to earth with all the people he snatched away, including those you loved. One day he will burst through the clouds in the sky, and every eye will see him."

"When?" voices from the crowd shout above the shrieking of the wind.

"When God the Father tells him to," Elliott says. "Like I said, God told us from the very beginning about the end. I've asked two friends to help me read the Bible's book of Revelation to you. This will help you understand what is happening and where we are headed. This is not a made-up story. It isn't allegory. It's prophecy from God, and it will take place."

For the next forty minutes Elliott, Emma, and Brandon take turns reading through Revelation. The hair and clothes of the crowd are waving and blowing as the winds seem to pick up but the people are silent, listening to the words, the weight of them capturing their attention. When Elliott reads the final words of Revelation 22, he does so almost as a prayer: "He who testifies to these things says, 'Yes, I am coming soon.' Amen. Come, Lord Jesus. The grace of the Lord Jesus be with God's people. Amen." Elliott closes the Bible, and Brandon and Emma step aside. The crowd is eerily quiet.

"How can we live through that?" an elderly woman near the front asks.

Elliott holds up the Bible. "We're told this calls for patient endurance on the part of the people of God—to keep his commands and remain faithful to Jesus. Get into a group and learn God's Word. Keep his commands. Remain faithful to Jesus. Tell everyone about him. Read Revelation again and again. Read about Jesus. In Matthew 24, Jesus said, 'Watch out that no one deceives you.' Many deceivers are in the world today. A great deceiver is on the rise internationally right now. The Bible tells us this deceiver will confirm a covenant with Israel, and he will break it three-and-a-half years later."

As people murmur, Elliott lifts his hand to silence them, talking louder into the megaphone. "The Bible says that now is the time for understanding. The hour of trial Jesus warned about has now come upon the whole world. During the next seven years, we will see God's judgments fall on this world. His purpose for these judgments is to make himself known so that we will come to him. Victor Quade is the Antichrist, that man of lawlessness who will rise to power."

Some in the crowd become agitated at this. Although the city has been without power and cell phone service for some time now, many have been able to receive the news through battery-powered and shortwave radios, as well as from people traveling into the city. Victor Quade and the other members of the E10 are being hailed as heroes. With their help, there is now a plan in place for peace not only in the Middle East, but the entire world.

One woman shouts, "He's trying to unite us. What you're saying will only cause division."

"The Word of God *is* divisive," Elliott says. "For some of you, the truth will sound divisive, but for others, the truth will be life eternal. God told us that the Antichrist would come, and now he's here."

"That's why the universe got rid of so many of you," a man yells, stirring others against Elliott. "People like you divide us and destroy our planet!"

"Do not be deceived!" Elliott says, his voice full of concern. "The Bible says that in the beginning, God created the heavens and the earth. He made this universe, which listens to him. The universe is not able to make people vanish. Only the one true God has the power to do that."

"But Quade said we're the chosen ones," another woman shouts. "The others were taken because they were filled with hate and were destroying everything."

"Don't believe the lie! Quade is a liar and follows the father of lies, Satan," Elliott shouts over the wind. He turns to 2 Thessalonians 2 and reads, "Don't let anyone deceive you in any way, for that day will not come until the rebellion occurs and the man of lawlessness is revealed, the man doomed to destruction...He will use all sorts of displays of power through signs and wonders that serve the lie, and all the ways that wickedness deceives those who are perishing...For this reason God sends them a powerful delusion so that they will believe the lie and so that all will be condemned who have not believed the truth but have delighted in wickedness."

"Victor Quade, the lawless one, is rising according to the work of Satan. He will be given power, signs, and lying wonders to deceive you. You will perish if you do not receive the truth that can save you." He holds the Bible over his head. "This is what God's Word says. Understand that if you refuse the truth of Jesus Christ, you will be given a strong delusion so that you believe the lie. And if you succumb to the lie, you will be condemned. Jesus is still calling people to him. If you don't know Jesus, now is the time of salvation." Elliott pauses, then says, "Stay in God's Word. Walk with him! Go and tell others about him because Jesus is coming soon! He is..."

At that moment, shots are fired by a small group of men and women who have run into the park. Emma screams, grabbing Jordan and Bella to run and flee. She looks over her shoulder for Brandon and Taylor, then calls for Elliott, who is still standing and shouting to the crowd, "Believe now! Call on the name of Jesus Christ!"

"Elliott!" she yells as two men fire at him.

"Go!" Brandon shouts at her. "He's okay." Brandon pushes Emma through the running crowd as shots continue to ring out. Emma and Bella stumble over those who have fallen in the stampede, and Emma struggles to lift Bella, crying out as bullets hit a woman next to her. Emma is shocked into silence as the woman's lifeless body falls in front of her. Jordan runs back to help and grabs Bella's hand as others are shot beside them, blood splattering onto their clothes as they scream. Emma struggles to help pull Bella up and the three of them dash to the street, running toward home, their lungs feeling as if they're about to burst, making it hard for them to breathe.

"We need to go back!" Emma gasps while running. "Elliott!"

"No!" Brandon says, leading them to an alley. "Elliott can survive bullets. We can't."

As they run, a man from behind cries out, "Emma! Emma!"

Emma turns and sees Lerenzo pushing his way through the crowd. She met Lerenzo, an immigrant from Guatemala, shortly after the vanishings. He had helped her move Micah's belongings to Kennisha's apartment when Micah's father could no longer care for him. Emma has thought of Lerenzo often; he reminds her so much of Mrs. Ramos's son: dark hair, dark eyes, and a broad smile. Lerenzo's grandmother in Guatemala had tried to tell him and his family about Jesus, but they weren't interested in listening. America was the land of promise. Who needed Jesus there? But on the day Jesus snatched away his followers, Lerenzo's work as a truck driver left him in a mess. Vehicles sat abandoned on the highway while people wandered helplessly, wondering what had happened to a passenger or a driver. In an instant, Lerenzo recalled his grandmother's warnings, and he had buckled to the ground in despair.

"Lerenzo!" Emma shouts over the gusts. "This is Lerenzo," she says, turning to Brandon. "The one from Micah's building."

"I was at the park," Lerenzo says. He's still catching his breath, rattled by the terror that had broken out. "People are dead." He looks at them and stammers, "Are you hurt?"

Emma shakes her head. "No. None of us are. We were next to people who..." She is unable to finish, and Bella wraps an arm around her.

"Every bullet missed Elliott," Lerenzo says, dumbstruck by it all. "Why were they trying to kill him?"

"Because he's a Jew preaching about Jesus," Brandon says, looking around. "Remember, the universe supposedly purged Christians, and Christians are to blame for the upheaval in the world. Come on! We need to get home." They continue to run through the streets toward Mrs. Ramos's house, where they close and lock the door behind them.

Three hours later, they are still shaken by what happened. As they talk, they realize that if they had been among those killed, their souls would be in heaven right now with Christ. As Lerenzo prepares to leave, he looks at Emma. "It was good to see you again," he says with a smile.

Emma smiles in return and wonders what life would be like if they had met years ago. Maybe they would have become believers together. If she had listened to her mom, she wouldn't be facing all the horrors of today. But before she dwells on the "if only" for too long, she catches herself and says to Lerenzo, "You should come to our home church."

CHAPTER 10

Rome, Italy
Four Months Later

Members of the E10, their aides, and three generals with the Global Union Forces sit around a massive table inside the Palace of Justice. A bank of screens covers the breadth of the front wall and they feature the many events taking place around the world: earthquakes and tsunamis in parts of Asia; rare, out-of-season typhoons and flooding in Japan and the Philippines; cyclones in parts of Africa; the strange sights in the sky and unpredictable weather changes; volcanoes erupting in Central and South America; more earthquakes in Greece, Italy, Romania, Turkey, and the United States; hospitals filled to capacity from disaster victims and the pandemic patients; towns that have been reduced to heaps of rubble from missile attacks. On some of the screens are dead bodies strewn along streets and wild animals consuming them for food. Prime Minister Sophia Clattenberg cringes and looks down at the table; the scenes of screeching monkeys fighting for food in flood-ridden Thailand, hyenas attacking humans in Africa, and tigers chasing down people in India send a chill down her spine.

Footage of the president of China meeting with Chinese military leaders takes up several of the screens, and video portraying military troops training by the thousands prompts Chancellor George Albrecht to ask, "What is happening in China?"

"China has countless troops engaged in the ongoing battle with Vietnam and the Philippines over control of the South China Seas," General Voss with the Global Union Forces says.

"We told them to stand down," President Banes says, scowling at the images.

"We're keeping a close watch, sir," General Voss replies.

Prior to the disappearances, the United States, along with the United Nations, kept China in check. Even so, China had continued to flex its considerable military muscle and cut off vital trade routes, engaging in conflicts with Vietnam, Japan, Taiwan, the Philippines, India, and other countries in the general region. Tensions were now at the point war had been declared on Vietnam and the Philippines.

General Bernard points to a screen. "Over the last several days, we've seen terrible losses in the Philippines."

"China has been strong-arming its neighbors for centuries," Victor says. "This is nothing new."

"But the Chinese government must be made aware—again—that they are not to be engaged in war or raising up another army at this time," says Bruno Neri, a 40-something member of the E10 from Italy. "Do we have intel from Echelon?" One of the most secret intelligence operations in the world, Project Echelon is situated on 560 acres in the bleak Yorkshire moors of England and is the world's largest electronic monitoring station. "Are we listening to what's happening there?"

"Yes, sir," General Bernard replies. "But the Chinese have been aware of Echelon and other monitoring stations for many years. They are always guarded in their conversations and movements."

Bruno curses and slams a manila file folder onto the table. "Are they part of the Global Union or not? This is a time for worldwide peace! Not war."

With the click of a button, the pictures turn next to vicious conflicts and bloody battles taking place around the world. Nations and people groups are rising up against each other, claiming lives and destroying property. "The world hasn't gotten your memo, Bruno," Sophia says, watching the screens. "How many millions have died already in these wars?"

"The world has gone mad," Maria Willems says. Maria is from the Czech Republic, is in her late thirties, and has long, dark hair that she keeps in a smooth ponytail on most days. Today she looks ashen and grave as she watches the killings, bombings, attacks, and natural disasters.

"The word *apocalypse* comes up in more and more news stories," President Banes says.

Victor scoffs. "This is not the apocalypse. We're not part of a Hollywood science fiction movie. The world isn't charred and desolate. We're not wearing rags. We're all still here and healthy and building a strong, unified, peaceful world, Thomas."

President Banes grimaces. He hates it when Victor calls him by his first name. He turns to look at him. "Look at what is happening on those screens, Victor. We're far from unified, and we're not all here. Many have vanished, and because of these wars and natural disasters and growing pandemic, many are now dead."

"These disasters," Victor says, his eyes scanning the screens in front of him, "these wars and the pandemic will further reduce the population of the earth. Only the strong will remain. It is as it should be."

"Why would you say that?" President Banes says gruffly. "Look! We are in a time of global depression, Victor! Only the wealthy can afford food and gas right now. We have accomplished nothing," he says, indicating the members of the E10. "The world is escalating out of control, and we sit inside this building without any clear direction or help for the nations."

"Many are at war," Bruno says. "We have always had wars. They will play themselves out."

President Banes watches as the video footage changes from food lines to people removing debris from streets to those carrying their wounded or dead. On other screens people are repairing homes, standing in lines for jobs, waiting to get medical treatment, and fighting over piles of garbage or rubble in search of food. On one screen, a man dressed in a white robe is standing in front of multitudes in Rio de Janeiro. "Who is that?" President Banes asks, pointing to the screen.

"He claims to be a savior," an aide for the E10 replies. He clicks the remote in his hand and another image pops onto the screen, this time of a man in Chile with a throng of followers behind him. "This man also claims to be a savior."

On several other screens, the group sees individual men standing before large crowds and explaining the reason for the disappearances. "And who are those men?" Victor asks, pointing. "What are they doing? Are they also claiming to be saviors?"

"We don't know who they are, sir," an aide replies. "But they're preaching."

Victor turns to look at the aide. "Preaching what?" He looks closer at one of the screens. "Is he in Tehran?"

"Yes, sir. From what we understand, many of the Persian people are believing in the man Jesus." The aide points to other screens. "This man is preaching in Nigeria. This one is in Indonesia. This man is in Pakistan. This one is in India. This one is in Beijing. This man is in New York City, and this one is in Tel Aviv." The crowds listening to these men are enormous. "From what we've seen, all these men are telling people that on the day of the disappearances, Jesus Christ came for his people. That is why they disappeared."

"Insanity," Bruno says.

"Is that one at a pride parade in Tel Aviv?" E10 member Adrien Moreau asks. Adrien is from France, in his late forties, and has a shock of dark hair and a tall, powerful frame.

The aide nods. "Yes, sir. He stopped the pride parade so he could preach to everyone from the top of a float."

"Preached what?" George Albrecht asks, squinting to see the screen.

"Jesus," the aide says. "Again, it's what they are all preaching."

The members of the E10 are baffled. Sophia points to one of the screens. "That man stopped a pride parade in Tel Aviv, the gay capital of the Middle East, and talked about Jesus to a city full of Jews, and no one did anything?"

"They tried to get rid of him," the aide says. He rewinds the video and shows parade participants trying to forcibly remove the man from atop the float. "They couldn't. There's something about all of these men and the others like them that..."

"What do you mean, the others like them?" President Banes asks.

"So far we have estimated there are at least five thousand of them around the world. Possibly more," the aide replies.

"Five thousand! Who are these men?" Victor asks. "Have you done facial recognition surveillance on them?"

"Yes. They are Jews, sir," the aide says. "The man in Tel Aviv is Dr. Zerah Adler. This one in New York City is Elliott Hirsch. He worked at a brokerage firm before the disappearances. The one in Tehran is..."

Maria silences the aide and the E10 leaders are perplexed. "You're joking, right?" Maria says. "*Jews* are telling people about *Jesus* in Muslim countries?"

"Yes, ma'am."

"It's impossible," Adrien says. "That is an African man!" he says, pointing to the screen. "He is a black man!"

"He's a Jew, sir."

Adrien scoffs. "He would be killed talking about Jesus in Muslim countries."

The aide clicks the remote in his hand. "People have tried to kill them." Images pop up on some of the screens showing people trying to kill the men with guns, knives, machetes, grenades and other explosive devices, vehicles, and drones.

"Impossible!" Bruno says. "They need to be suppressed. That ideology has always been dangerous, and it's why the universe expelled those who follow it. That message is a serious, critical threat. Especially now."

"How is this possible?" George asks, watching a screen as the Jewish man in New York City survives what looks like gunfire and many in the crowd fall dead.

"Witchcraft," Victor answers matter-of-factly.

"Or God himself is protecting them," President Banes says.

"There is no God, Thomas!" Victor says, pounding the table with his fists. "Or are you as big a fool as all of those people listening to them?" He doesn't allow President Banes to answer but shifts his attention to the aide. "These men are nothing more than cockroaches. Are people ignorant enough to believe them?"

"Some, yes," the aide says.

Victor sneers, waving his hand as if to shoo away simpletons. "Fools! This is one of the many reasons why this body exists," he says, tapping the table with his index finger. "Christianity was a disease that was fatal for our world, and the universe purged itself of these lower forms of human organisms. This body must lead the world in its regeneration. You must save people from this ignorance. They've gone mad."

"The earth itself has gone mad," Sophia says as the screens once again show devastation from earthquakes, typhoons, wildfires, and volcanoes.

Victor turns to look at her. "Look at what we did in Israel."

President Banes begins to chuckle, then realizes Victor isn't laughing. "Are you serious? Sophia has said this before. You had nothing to do with Israel's victory. This body had nothing to do with it."

"We told Israel's enemies that we would deal with them if they attacked," Victor says, looking around the table at each member of the E10. "They were dealt with just as I said."

President Banes laughs. "We didn't deal with them. That was a supernatural act of God! These men on the screens are somehow being protected. By God."

Victor again pounds the table, hurling obscenities as his face turns crimson. "No one believes there is a God!"

Sophia raises her hands to quiet them both. "Perhaps there is no God, Victor, but I don't think any of us believe that we had anything to do with Israel's victory."

"Belief comes from speaking the word," Bruno says. "When we all speak the word as one, the world will believe."

Sophia shakes her head in disbelief. "Look at the world," she says, glancing at the screens. "It's coming unhinged. How can we be a global union if this council is not united?"

Bruno looks at her. "When we speak the word, *we* will believe. When we speak the word, the *world* will believe."

"Believe what?" President Banes shouts. "This lie?"

"It's not a lie if you believe it," Bruno says, his lips turning up into a slight smile.

CHAPTER 11

Rome, Italy

They don't believe it!" President Banes says, pointing to the screens showing the Jewish men preaching around the world. "And neither do they." He's looking at a large screen at the center of the wall. The E10 members focus their attention on the image of the two witnesses in Jerusalem, who are standing outside the Dung Gate. An aide turns up the volume so everyone can hear.

"Hashem has saved you, and yet you mock him," the Second Witness says to the crowds who are making their way to the temple site. Daily, thousands have come to observe the beginning of construction on their beloved temple. In doing so, they have encountered the two witnesses, and their disgust and loathing for the two men has been broadcast throughout the world as they curse and spit at them, try to strike them, run them over, and even fire on them. But the men continue to walk throughout Jerusalem calling for repentance and salvation in Yeshua.

"You do not repent or surrender to Hashem, the one true God. You do not listen to him but to the false gods in Rome. You have not turned to Hashem; instead, have made a covenant with evil."

"Ugly fools," Adrien hisses. "Who are they?" he asks, looking at General Lazenby. "Has facial recognition identified these maggots?"

General Lazenby shakes his head. "No, sir. There are no matches."

President Banes can't believe this. "That's impossible. Neither of these men are in any databases?" He doesn't wait for a reply. "What about DNA?"

"We can't get close enough for DNA samples," General Voss says.

"Then find a way!" Bruno barks.

The First Witness's voice becomes louder on the screen. "Adonai, the Father of Abraham, Isaac, and Jacob, is making himself known to you; he has glorified his servant Yeshua. Yeshua is a Jew like each of us. He was sent to the lost sheep of the house of Israel. Your prophets foretold of Adonai making a new covenant with you. He would place his law and Ruach ha-kodesh within us; his presence would move from the tabernacle or the temple and reside within us. Wake up, O Israel! Yeshua became your sacrificial Lamb. His shed blood established the new covenant with you."

"What is it with the Jews and sacrifice?" Bruno asks. "How can the people stand there and listen to this idiocy?" The other E10 members ignore him, fixated on the screen.

"Your ancestors handed Yeshua over to be killed, and you disowned him before Pilate, though he had decided to let him go," the Second Witness continues. "You disowned the Holy and Righteous One and asked that a murderer be released to you. Your ancestors killed the author of life, but Adonai raised him from the dead."

This arouses venom from the crowd, and again several attempt to attack the witnesses, only to be blanketed by an instant dust storm that arose after one of the old men scraped his foot on the ground. Members of the E10 gasp and curse at what they see on screen, but Victor watches in fascinated silence.

"Now, fellow Jews," the First Witness says, "you have acted in ignorance, as did your ancestors. Repent of your sins and turn to Hashem so that your sins may be wiped out, that times of refreshing may come from him, and that he may send the Messiah who has been appointed for you—Yeshua. Heaven has received him until the time comes for Hashem to restore everything, as he promised long ago through his holy prophets. Hashem declares anyone who does not listen to him will be completely cut off from their people."

"Sounds like a loving God," Maria says. "This is why the universe removed all the fanatics."

"Not all of them," Bruno says, cursing.

"You are heirs of the prophets and of the covenant Adonai made with your fathers," the First Witness continues. "Know this: Yeshua is the stone you have rejected, which has become the cornerstone. Salvation is found in no one else, for there is no other name under heaven given to mankind by which we must be saved."

Adrien points at the screens, flabbergasted. "Why are they listening to this?"

"They'll kill them," George says, watching the men. "No Jew is going to tolerate this. I can barely tolerate it."

"The man of destruction, the lawless one, is a foolish shepherd, and you are fools for following him," the Second Witness says.

"Who is the man of destruction? Is he talking about Prime Minister Ari?" Sophia asks.

"He will overcome and destroy you," the Second Witness says to the crowd. "The E10 are liars and follow the father of lies."

Members of the E10 sit up straighter, bristling at what the witness said. The crowd rails in anger, voices rising together in defense of the E10: "The E10 protects us," and "They help us." Several in the crowd lunge at the witnesses but lose their sight, falling to the ground and groping for someone to help them.

"What happened to them?" Sophia asks, leaning forward. "Can't they see?"

The First Witness raises his hand to silence the shocked throng. "That you may have eyes to see! You are looking to people and not to Hashem for your help. The all-powerful Adonai destroyed your enemies as they came to annihilate you, and your voices sang praises to him for a few days. But now you sing the praises of the false gods in Rome. You place your trust and hope in the man of sin, and Hashem will not put up with your disobedience much longer. This is the time of your trouble, O Jacob! It is time for you to repent, to surrender and listen to Hashem. Today is the day of salvation in Yeshua, who is your pure and spotless sacrificial Lamb. You have rejected him, and now you are witnessing the wrath of Adonai on your sin and disobedience."

Bruno curses as he listens to the Second Witness. "Why can't they be removed?"

"We're still trying, sir," General Voss says.

Some of the onlookers begin to weep at the words of the witnesses, crying to Hashem for forgiveness. Several soldiers move quickly, approaching the two witnesses in an attempt to reason with them. "Please, sirs, again, we need you to get out of Jerusalem," a soldier with a dark, age-lined face says. "We are trying to build our temple and..."

The Second Witness holds out his arm, stopping the soldier so he's unable to move. "This temple has become your idol. Wake up! Thus says Adonai: 'I am sick of your sacrifices. Don't bring me any more burnt offerings! Why would you parade through my courts with your worthless sacrifices? The incense you bring is a stench in my nostrils! I hate all your festivals and sacrifices; I cannot stand the sight of them!'"

These words are blasphemous to the crowd, causing many to bellow louder. As several soldiers rush toward the men, the First Witness lifts his hand and shouts, "Come!" A dark shadow against the pale sky bends and dips as a great swarm of predator birds swoop down with shocking swiftness to attack their prey, flapping about the soldiers and squawking. The soldiers cry out in alarm, waving their arms and running away to the astonishment of the multitude around them.

The Second Witness looks at the soldier who has told them to leave. "Hashem does not want your temple. He wants you! You are the temple of Hashem, and Yeshua Hamashiach is the cornerstone." Some onlookers begin calling on the name of Yeshua, and the Second Witness raises his palm to the skies. "This is what Adonai says: 'I will speak the word that I will speak, and it will be performed...in your days, O rebellious people, I will speak the word and perform it.'"

"Jews are so dramatic," Adrien says, watching the screen.

More soldiers arrive and move toward the witnesses. The Second Witness looks up to the sky. "Rain," he commands. A sideways deluge pounds the soldiers, blinding their vision and causing them to stumble as they attempt to run away. "Because of your disobedience and your unbelief, as Adonai lives, before whom I stand, this will be the last of the rain these years, except by my word."

"They are insane!" Bruno says. "Nobody can stop the rain!" He laughs, watching the spectacle on the screen unfold.

But the rain stops and the black skies are replaced with sunny brilliance. "My God," President Banes says. "Who are these men?"

Victor clicks a button and shuts off the screen. "They are nothing more than sorcerers and illusionists. All of them. The Jews telling fantasies around the world and these two parasites. Low-class street performers."

"Time will tell," President Banes says.

To discover more about the biblical facts behind the story, read Where in the Word? *on page 235, or continue reading the novel.*

CHAPTER 12

Brooklyn, NY

Brandon is the first one up, and he's careful not to wake the other boys as he steps out of the bedroom at 4:00 a.m. This is late for him; he normally wakes up at 3:00. The house is always strangely quiet. After weeks without electricity or cell service, he thought he would become used to the deafening silence, but it's still unnerving to him. His life prior to this was one of constant noise and busyness; he always wore earpods as he listened to music, a podcast, or watched something on YouTube, and he spent many hours a week on social media.

But now he doesn't even know where his cell phone is anymore. He uses this time in the mornings to study the Bible, pray, and listen to the shortwave radio, collecting news from around the world. Once he and the others know what's happening, they know how to pray. His work in the publicity department of a publishing house in Midtown ended when Iran dropped the nuke on the city and the building was destroyed. He has been plunged headlong into this upside-down world and hasn't had time to grieve the losses in his life. He and Emma have been so busy trying to find food and supplies for their ever-growing family that he hasn't had time to think about finding another job or where to move. The city has become increasingly unsafe and unable to meet the physical needs of its residents, and there is so much happening in the city and the world that he doesn't know how to wrap his mind around it all.

Brandon grew up with a single mom in Louisville. She was a good, honest woman who often worked two jobs to support him. He exchanged a short text with her once after the disappearances, and at the time he was thankful that she had been left behind. But now he prays for her every day, asking that she will come to believe in Jesus. Without cell service, he hasn't been able to talk with her or text with her, and he prays for her safety. He also prays for Rick, the man he spent the last few years of his life with, and for Matt, Emma's former fiancé. Several days ago, Brandon and Emma came across Luke 9:23 and they now pray these words daily: "If anyone would come after me, let him deny himself and take up his cross daily and follow me." Before the vanishings, Brandon, Emma, and their friends had lived their lives in pursuit of what and who they wanted, giving little thought to God and what he wanted.

"I want to be your disciple, Lord," Brandon says aloud in the kitchen as he gets a cup of water. "I deny myself and take up my cross today to follow you. Help me, please. Show each one of us in this house how to live for you and what to do today. Lead us to those who need help."

When Brandon walked away from Rick, he never thought he would give up such an important part of his identity, something that had been fundamental to his sense of self and to what he believed for so long. It wouldn't make sense to give up something or someone so valuable for something or someone less valuable. That would be insane. But everything changed when Brandon learned who Jesus really is. Jesus is more valuable than any relationship, thought, or belief Brandon has ever had. From the Bible, he understands that a believer should be willing to die for that relationship with Jesus because it's so precious. He now realizes that for years he was wrong: celibacy and singleness aren't synonymous with death. Not having sex or a romantic relationship doesn't mean being doomed to loneliness. From the Bible, he now understands that giving things up is part of the Christian life. Throughout history, Christians have given up comfort, money, sex, their homes, jobs, relationships, and countless other things—all out of love for Jesus.

They were captured by Christ's love and were willing to do what it took to be with him because Jesus gave them the love, purpose, grace, mercy, and a destination that they longed for.

Brandon looks out the window above the kitchen sink at the supermoon that has looked close enough to touch for the last four days. Prior to this, the skies were red during the day and in the evening, a phenomenon he has never seen before. "And I will show wonders in the heavens above," Brandon whispers, quoting a verse from the book of Acts. The moon illuminates the small deck adorned with a round patio table and four plastic chairs, and Brandon wonders about the life the Ramoses lived here. How he wishes he could go back to the times when someone would send a faith-based article to him or mention God at a family Christmas dinner! Back then, as far as he was concerned, God was a bigot, homophobe, and racist. He believed God existed; he even believed that Jesus was his son, but he had set his mind as to what God was like and wanted nothing to do with him. If only he could go back and have a conversation with someone, or read the articles and Bible verses that a well-meaning aunt or friend had sent his way! But when that happened, he discarded the articles or emails as trash, as nothing but hate coming from haters.

"Any news?" Emma asks, startling Brandon. She and Kennisha have come downstairs together.

Brandon shakes his head. "Haven't turned it on yet."

Emma clicks the shortwave radio on and begins tuning it, trying to find voices that will come in clearly. She finds a voice speaking English and settles here for a moment to listen. "An 8.5 magnitude earthquake struck Indonesia at seven-fifteen this morning. And a 9.0 magnitude quake struck Beijing. According to sources, much of the city is in rubble. In the United States, a 9.0 quake struck the middle of the country along the New Madrid fault line just moments ago. The new Madrid fault line is six times larger than the San Andreas fault line, and according to our sources, this earthquake was so massive it has actually split the country in two." Emma glances at Brandon and Kennisha and gasps, slumping into a chair at the kitchen table. The announcer continues, "Through the states of Illinois, Indiana, Missouri, Arkansas,

Kentucky, Tennessee, and down to Mississippi, the earth has split. Scientist warned for years that this could happen, and today it has. In Mexico, a..."

Emma turns down the radio, looking ashen. "My sister and your mom," she says, looking at Brandon and beginning to cry.

Kennisha sits at the table, squeezing Emma's hand. "We don't know that anything has happened to them. They could be all right."

"It split the country in two!" Emma exclaims.

Brandon kneels in front of her. "I have to have faith that my mom is okay, Emma. And even if she died, I've been praying that she and your sister and all our friends will come to know Jesus. We need to have faith that they've come to him. We can't give up."

Emma tries to smile through her tears. "Who knew that one day I would say you're the level-headed one?" Emma turns the radio back up and they listen as the announcer describes the two holy men in Jerusalem as being mentally disturbed and outrageous.

"This is from late yesterday in Israel," the announcer says before playing the audio of one of the witnesses.

"Because of your disobedience and your unbelief, as Adonai lives, before whom I stand, this will be the last of the rain these years, except by my word." Emma, Brandon, and Kennisha look at each other.

"Israel is working to remove the men from the temple site," the announcer says. "Soldiers approached them today, but one unit's skin inexplicably broke out in seeping, painful ulcers, incapacitating them. Another unit was blinded as they advanced on the old men, a third unit lost muscle control and was seen writhing on the ground, while a fourth unit was engulfed in blazing flames and a fifth unit was attacked by a large cloud of bees that appeared out of nowhere."

"Those are the two witnesses we read about in Revelation, right?" Kennisha asks. Brandon and Emma nod. "In Revelation, it says how long it won't rain. Do either of you remember how long that is?"

Brandon reaches for his Bible and opens it to the book of Revelation, flipping through the pages until he finds mention of the two witnesses in chapter 11. He taps his Bible as he reads: "They have the power to shut the sky, that no rain may fall during the days of their prophesying, and they have power over the waters to turn them into blood and to strike the earth with every kind of plague, as often as they desire."

"Turn the waters into blood and strike the earth with every kind of plague?" Kennisha asks. "What all could that mean?"

Emma's face looks grave. "How long do they prophesy?"

Brandon backs up to the beginning of the chapter. "I will grant authority to my two witnesses, and they will prophesy for 1,260 days, clothed in sackcloth." He looks up at them. "That's three-and-a-half years."

"No rain for three-and-a-half years," Emma says. "They'll turn the waters into blood! We need to tell all our friends. We need to collect as much fresh water as possible right now."

"When they get here this morning, we can talk about it," Brandon says, referring to the group that meets in their home each morning.

Emma looks at them and she is overwhelmed by the news of the day. "I noticed that whenever Elliott leaves, he says, 'I'll see you soon.' And I don't think that he means that he'll..."

Brandon and Kennisha exchange glances, knowing where she's headed. "Emma, don't," Kennisha says.

"No," Emma says. "We need to talk about it. If something happens to me, I want you to know that I *will* see you soon. If something happens to one of you, I know that I'll see you soon. That's an awesome truth for us!" Tears fill her eyes at the thought of it.

Rather than talk more about what a three-and-a-half-year drought or the severe earthquake means for food supply, transportation, health concerns, or any of the other thoughts scrambling through their minds, they join hands and pray for everyone affected and ask that they'll be given strong backs to endure what's ahead. They also pray for the peace of Jerusalem, for Elliott and the other 144,000 Jewish evangelists around the world, and for wisdom as they take care of the children they rescue.

When they finish, Emma goes to the garage and pulls three garbage cans into the house. They had salvaged these from the streets and sanitized them so they could store food in them. She and Kennisha clean them again and use the sprayer hose from the kitchen faucet to begin filling one with water. "The two witnesses will turn water to blood," Kennisha says. "Do you think collected water like this will turn as well?"

Emma watches the water pooling at the bottom of the can and shakes her head. "I don't know. I pray it doesn't."

CHAPTER 13

Brooklyn, NY

Emma and Kennisha are almost finished filling the final garbage can with water when a pounding at the back door makes them jump. Brandon cautiously reaches for the door and opens it. Standing there is Nick, a member of their church group. He is earlier than usual, and they notice the expression of alarm on his face.

"Nick," Brandon begins, but Nick immediately talks over him. He speaks so rapidly that Brandon, Emma, and Kennisha struggle to understand as he mixes Spanish with his English.

"Three children were taken from our apartment building," he says breathlessly as he moves past them into the kitchen. "One of them was Victoria." Kennisha gasps at the thought Nick's niece may have been kidnapped.

"When?" Brandon asks.

"Thirty minutes ago or so." Nick's dark eyes are filled with either sadness or rage; it's hard to tell which.

"Do you know who took them?" Emma asks, her heart beating wildly.

Nick shakes his head. "I don't know them, but I followed them. There were too many of them for me to do anything by myself. They took the children to the Coffee Shop."

Emma had read years ago of similar shops in the red-light district of

Amsterdam and on the streets of Thailand but never thought she would see such things within her own country, let alone a couple of blocks from where she lives. The windows of these shops are filled with men, women, and children who are sold for sexual purposes, and brothels had begun operating in what were once coffee and ice cream shops. They call the area the Coffee Shop District, or Coffee Shop for short, and have, along with some members of their home church, risked their lives several times to rescue children who had been abducted for prostitution or trafficking.

Brandon blurts out, "Let's go get them!" They know they have to act fast because children are sold daily in those shops.

"I can come too," Emma says. Brandon looks at her. "Women go in there for sex too, and you need a third. We always go in threes."

Kennisha reaches for a jar of money from a top cabinet, pulling out 60 dollars. "Isn't the rate twenty dollars for fifteen minutes with a child?" The words make her feel sick to her stomach.

Nick nods, and Brandon takes the money. Brandon then puts one hand on Nick's shoulder and his other hand on Emma's. "Direct us, Lord!" he prays. "Show us what to do and give us the words to say. Give us success in saving these children from this evil."

Brandon slips a gun beneath his jacket, leaving the other one with Kennisha. She hugs all three of them before closing the door behind them. Brandon, Emma, and Nick walk through alleyways and other discreet paths so they are not noticed by the military personnel who are guarding the main streets. With city shelters beyond occupancy since the bombing, addicts and the homeless have been left to fend for themselves and lie strewn in the alleys. With the power grid completely disabled from the attack, the streets are normally pitch black at this hour, but the brightness of the supermoon lights their way.

Emma, Brandon, and Nick talk quietly, formulating their plan, but Emma's heart is pounding so loud she can hear it in her ears. By the time they reach the Coffee Shop, sweat is rolling down her chest. "Help us," she prays.

"Are we ready?" Brandon asks. His voice is quiet and uncertain, and Emma knows he is as nervous as she is right now.

"Let's get them in Jesus's name," he says, walking across the street that used to be lined with a local supermarket, family-owned restaurants, an ice cream store, and the coffee shop. As the moon shines on the storefronts, their stomachs turn as they make out the scantily clad or naked men, women, and children in the windows. How has America so quickly come to this?

"Which store is it?" Brandon whispers.

"The second one," Nick says. "I saw my niece and the two boys taken into that building."

Emma's breath is coming in short, ragged gasps as she follows Brandon and Nick into the building. Except for a couple of gas lanterns, the building is dark, and if darkness can be felt, Emma feels it here as her hair stands up on the back of her neck from knowing what takes place here. A long hallway is lined with curtains on either side. Emma knows that behind those curtains, atrocities she can scarcely think about take place against innocent women and children. A man who looks like he was probably an accountant just a few weeks ago walks down the hallway toward them, waving a lantern in their faces to get a better look. He eyes Brandon up and down and gets right to business. "What are you looking for? Cowboy? Jock?"

"Hispanic," Brandon says.

"I don't have a man available right now. Only two Hispanic teen boys."

Brandon shakes his head. "A girl."

The man looks him over. "Not what I expected." He glances at Nick and Emma. "What about you two?"

"Two kids," Nick says.

"That's not what we talked about!" Emma snaps.

Nick follows her lead, turning on her in anger. "If they have them, we will try it!"

The man chuckles, his bulging belly jiggling above his belt. "Don't knock it till you try it, right?" The man is delighted with the business. "What age?"

"Let's take the Hispanic teens," Emma says, with something like the sound of the ocean rushing through her ears.

"No," Nick says. "I want two black boys. Around ten or eleven."

The man nods. "A man who has made up his mind. All right with you, sweetheart?"

Emma wants to bash the man in his fat face, but she nods as she feels nauseated, about to gag.

"How about you?" he asks, looking at Brandon. "Age?"

"Twelvish. I don't like short hair. Can we all be in the same room together?"

The man scratches his head, looking at them. "That'll cost you more."

Emma feels her heart racing faster and prays that 60 dollars will be enough.

"How much?" Brandon asks.

"Sixty," the man says. "But for only ten minutes."

Emma can't believe it. "Okay. But we get to pick."

The man shrugs. "I have only a few this morning. The others have already left."

Emma prays that the children from Nick's building aren't among those who have left already. Brandon leads the way as they follow the man to the end of the dark hallway, where he slides open a curtain, revealing at least 12 to 15 children who appear to range in age from about 8 to 16 and look frightened out of their minds. Emma's blood runs cold; she can't imagine what they have already seen or done within this house of horrors.

Brandon recognizes Victoria and points to her, urging her with his eyes not to reveal that she knows him. The man directs Brandon to a room across the hall, and as Victoria stands to her feet, she notices Nick. But his face is like flint as he pretends he doesn't know her. The man then steps across the hall and slides open another curtain. Looking at Nick and Emma, he holds his arm out and waves it toward the children, indicating for them to take their pick.

"Those two," Nick says, pointing to two black boys who are clinging to each other.

"You two," the man says. "Come here." The boys shake their heads, groaning as the man steps closer to them. They try to shrink into the corner, but the man reaches down, yanking at their shirts. The boys drop down to the floor, screaming and crying as they try to get away. The man swears and barks in their faces, turning back to Nick and Emma. "Pick two others. These two aren't ready yet!" He gets in the boys' faces, cursing at them. "You won't do this again. I promise you that!"

"Those are the ones we want," Nick says, stepping further into the room so the boys can see him. "They're young and wiry."

As Nick speaks, he's hoping that the boys will recognize him from their apartment building. "I told you I wanted two black boys, and these are the only ones around the age that we wanted." Nick looks directly at the boys, praying that they recognize him. The older boy appears to have figured this out; he takes his younger brother by the hand and stands. The younger brother cries, trying to pull away, but the older brother keeps his eyes on Nick, walking toward him.

"That's more like it," the man says, directing them across the hallway. Nick and the boys join Brandon and Victoria.

"I need to go to the bathroom," Emma says.

"You still have only ten minutes," the man says, pointing to the door next to them. "Clock's ticking."

Emma darts inside the room and quickly sees there is no window in the tar-black space. She peers out the door and can hear that the man has gone back to the room with the group of children. She quietly bolts for the next door, gently opening it. She can see an exit door with two men standing just outside it in the alley, the moon's light shining through the exit. Her heart is in her throat as she rushes to the room where Brandon and Nick are with the children. "An exit door is two rooms down, but there are two men standing by the door," she whispers.

Brandon and Nick look at one another. "If they're at the back door, we need to bolt for the front," Brandon says. "Did either of you see anybody else at the front?" Emma and Nick shake their heads. "We need to go now," Brandon says. He directs Nick, Emma, and the kids to go in front of him, then whispers to the children, "As soon as Nick opens this curtain, run as fast and quietly as you can out the front door." As he says this, he points in the direction they are to go.

Getting ready to run, Nick peeks out from behind the curtain to make sure no one is in the hall. The moon provides just enough light through the front door to indicate the hall is clear. Nick looks at the children, puts his finger to his lips, and opens the curtain so they can quietly slip by him and hurry down the hall toward the front of the store.

"Hey!" the man yells, rushing from the room holding the kids. Brandon lunges from out behind the curtain, striking the man's head with the gun. The man slumps to the floor, and Brandon flings open the curtain to see the group of children sitting wide-eyed with fright.

"Get out," he whispers. "Run to the front! Go! Go!"

The children bolt past him and Brandon opens more curtains along the hallway, looking for other possible captives. Five women are in one room together and seven more in another. "Run!" He whispers, looking behind him with the gun in hand. The women run past him, disappearing through the front door as Brandon opens the last curtain, revealing two men together. One of the men curses Brandon, who then quickly sprints to the front and out the door. He bolts across the street and to the alleyways where Nick and Emma are already running with the children to the house. Later they will try to return the children to their own homes or find guardians for them, but right now they just want to hide them someplace safe.

Brandon's breath comes in short bursts and his lungs feel as if they will explode. "Thank you, Lord!" he whispers, his heart flailing against his ribs. He knows this escape was made possible because of God's help. There is no other explanation.

CHAPTER 14

Jerusalem, Israel

The two witnesses walk past the hundreds of construction workers along the Western Wall and head toward the Temple Mount, where the Muslim holy sites—the Dome of the Rock and al-Aqsa mosque—once stood. Both structures fell during the earthquake as Israel was being invaded and have since been removed to make room for the new temple.

The architectural rendering and plans for the temple have been ready long before this day. Authentic sacred vessels, instruments, and furnishings were made in past decades from gold, copper, silver, and wood, according to the exact specifications given in the holy Scriptures. All the sacred clothing items have also been made ready for use in the temple services. There is no resistance against a Jewish presence on the Temple Mount; the Muslims who had long guarded the site died during that great and terrifying invasion of Israel. Thousands of Jews work unhindered 24 hours a day, and at the rate of their progress, they believe the temple will be completed in one more month.

Soldiers from the Israel Defense Forces surround the construction site, and several of them look in surprise at the spectacle of the two old men walking toward them. "No one except crew members and authorized personnel are allowed on site," one soldier says, tired of these buffoons.

"Adonai has sent us," the Second Witness says, walking past him.

The soldier grabs the Second Witness's arm. The bald man turns to look at the soldier, then puts his hand atop the soldier's. "Move aside, Aaron."

The soldier blinks as he looks at the old man, baffled at how he knows his name. The old men walk past him as another soldier approaches to help stop them. "For your safety, we have to keep you away from the site," Aaron says, squaring off in front of them.

"Hashem loves you, Aaron," the Second Witness says. "Repent of your sexual immorality that separates you from Hashem. Give your life to Yeshua and follow him." Aaron's body is stiff; he is shaken and baffled.

The witness then looks at the second soldier. "Make amends with your father, Levi. Humble yourself and seek forgiveness for stealing money from the company. The kingdom of Hashem is near. Today is the day of salvation." Levi is stunned at the old man's words and feels powerless to move.

The two men walk closer to the temple site, shouting above the noise. "We are witnesses of Hashem, the Lord of Israel," the First Witness says. The sounds of pounding tools, jackhammers, and heavy equipment drown out his words, so the witness raises his voice. "We are the two olive trees and the two lampstands that stand before Hashem of the earth," he booms, his words thundering over the racket like a sonic explosion. Hundreds cower in their tracks, and machinery and equipment are silenced as workers position themselves to see the two men.

"Hear us, O Israel! Hashem, the father of Abraham, Isaac, and Jacob loves you, the apple of his eye! But he will not be mocked any longer. His wrath on a sinful world has already begun. Open your eyes! Wake up, O Israel! You have made a covenant with Satan."

"Get them out of here," hisses Asher Bunim, the lead contractor. Asher is a strong, hard-muscled man in his late forties with a shock of thick, black hair and piercing dark eyes. To be chosen as lead contractor for this holiest of construction sites was the greatest honor of his life, and anger burns inside his chest with each word spoken by these ludicrous old men. "Remove them!" he shouts. Four soldiers move toward the witnesses to seize them, but the Second Witness holds up his hand, and a powerful whirlwind immediately swirls around the soldiers, throwing them to the ground.

"Prime Minister Ari is a wolf in sheep's clothing," the First Witness says. "He has made a pact with Satan that will destroy Israel, and you must repent." He names each and every member of the prime minister's cabinet, along with rabbis and prominent men and women in Israel, calling them liars and deceivers and naming their sins. More soldiers move toward the two men, pointing and directing for them to turn around and leave the construction site, but the First Witness opens his mouth and blocks their way with fire. "Hashem, the sovereign Lord of heaven and earth, knows your works," he says. "You have made a mockery of his Word and rejected his son, Yeshua Hamashiach!"

Asher runs toward the men. The Second Witness lowers his hand so Asher can get close; his face is flush with rage as he hurls profanities at the two witnesses. "Get out of here now!"

The Second Witness looks at him. "Asher, your sins will kill you. You must turn to Yeshua and give your life to him before he returns."

"Blasphemy! Get off this site before I kill you myself!"

"The darkness of pornography gripped your soul years ago and you stand defiled before Hashem," the First Witness says.

Asher works at controlling his face, careful not to grimace or blink. He opens his mouth to speak, but the Second Witness raises his hand, silencing him. Asher tries to say something but is mute and stumbles backward, away from the witnesses, terrified. The Second Witness looks out at the workers on the construction site and bystanders who are watching. The old man's voice pierces through the stillness like a trumpet: "Turn from your life of sin while there is still time. Rebel against Satan and cling to Yeshua Hamashiach! He does not want any of you to perish."

The voices of soldiers, construction workers, and bystanders rise together against the two witnesses, a unified mob shrieking at the sound of Yeshua's name. A new unit of soldiers rushes toward the witnesses, along with construction workers, but the Second Witness raises his hand and they fall to the ground, writhing in pain and screaming for the agony to stop. "Hashem the Almighty performs signs and wonders in the heavens and on the earth," the Second Witness says to the hundreds of people watching in disbelief. "Just as he rescued Daniel from the power of the lions, he will deliver us." The mouth of every construction worker, soldier, and bystander is shut tight, and a spine-chilling silence envelops them all.

The First Witness raises his arms and lifts his face toward the sky. "Thus says Hashem: 'By this you shall know that I am the LORD. Behold, I will strike your streams, your rivers, your ponds, and all your pools of water, that they may become blood. And the fish that are in the waters shall die, the waters shall stink, and the people will loathe to drink the water. No life will be in those blood waters, but only in the blood of Yeshua.'"

The two men then walk away from the site, leaving hundreds of people mystified, shaken, and silent.

To discover more about the biblical facts behind the story, read Where in the Word? *on page 243, or continue reading the novel.*

CHAPTER 15

Rome, Italy

Members of the E10, along with their aides and the three generals representing the Global Union Forces, look at the images on the screens in front of them. Conflicts rage throughout the world as people continue to kill one another, and thousands upon thousands die each day. Despite the E10's assurances of peace and security, ethnic unrest has reached unprecedented levels. A borderless world has not made a safer world, but rather, one rife with hatred. Before the disappearances, there wasn't a nation on earth that was untouched by ethnic unrest. Now it is a problem of even greater global proportions as ethnic groups, who were dormant powder kegs prior to Jesus's snatching up of his followers, are killing one another unhindered.

Thousands have been killed as China fights for what they call their "string of pearls"—ports that ring India, Bangladesh, Myanmar, and Sri Lanka—in an effort to control those ports. Genocide is taking place in numerous volatile regions around the globe. President Banes struggles to watch a screen filled with hostility and bloodshed coming out of his nation, and Prime Minister Sophia Clattenberg covers her mouth and shuts her eyes against the brutality in front of her.

Food and gas prices are at extortionate rates and the ongoing conflicts around the globe, coupled with the drought and the second day of water turned to blood, makes feeding the hungry nearly impossible.

Water-borne diseases are causing diarrhea, vomiting, and even a flesh-eating bacteria to spread across the map. Alligators in the United States and China and crocodiles in Asia, Africa, South America, and Australia have fled the waters, looking for unbloodied waters elsewhere, and countless people have been attacked or killed by them. Wars and natural disasters have made habitable areas much scarcer, with people and wild animals fighting for the same spaces and competing for the same foods. Fleas carried by rats are dispersing the bubonic plague in areas devastated by war and in crowded, filthy cities where garbage collection has been abandoned since the vanishings. In all this, the death tolls have been astronomical, with no signs of slowing. Through the ages, people have spoken of hell on earth, but nothing in the past compares to what is happening now. This is it. *This* is hell on earth.

"These conflicts are in direct opposition of our continued rhetoric of peace and safety," President Banes says with controlled sarcasm as new images of war appear on the screens.

"These conflicts, wars, and diseases will continue to purge the weakest from our world," Bruno responds.

"Who is strong enough to live without water, Bruno?" President Banes asks. "We are fortunate. We've had some juice and other canned drinks here. But what about those people around the world who are facing day two of bloody waters?" Bruno begins to speak, but President Banes shouts over him. "What about the farmers? Livestock? The people already in famine conditions? Where do they go for clean water?"

Banes points to the footage on the screens. Dead cattle, sheep, goats, and horses are strewn like rubbish across pasturelands everywhere. Most of the world's fish have died, their bloated bodies floating atop waters or littering beaches and shorelines, the putrid reek of death saturating the air. Livestock drank the plagued waters, killing many, and cholera, which previously had been a growing problem in the tropical regions of Asia, Africa, Latin America, India, and the Middle East, is now spreading throughout the world.

The E10 and their families have been vaccinated against every possible disease and have a team of doctors present within the building to care for them. "We can't lead if we're not healthy and strong," Bruno said on the day he proposed the E10 secure their own medical services. While many in the world stand in days-long lines waiting for vaccinations against deadly diseases, the E10 is safe within the confines of these walls.

"Those blood waters are killing everything," President Banes says, looking at the stomach-churning images.

"It is *not* blood waters," Bruno snaps. "We heard scientific proof this morning that the drought and the red water have been caused by the moon's gravitational pull, causing red algae to flourish and are merely temporary."

President Banes shakes his head, repeating more specifically what the scientists had told them earlier: "The disappearances have interrupted the moon's gravitational pull and turned the waters to blood."

"They did not say blood, Thomas!" Victor shouts. "We must not be given over to fantasies or paranoia."

"Those old men in Jerusalem are not superhuman!" Adrien says. "They cannot cause a drought or turn waters to blood."

"Maybe he turned the waters red," Maria says, pointing to a screen depicting a man in Lima, Peru, wearing white clothing and leading a hundred or so people through the city. The man waves his hands, and a powerful windstorm sweeps over the city. He waves his hands again and the wind comes to a total standstill, leaving onlookers spellbound. "Who is he?" she asks.

"He is one of the many who are claiming to be a savior," an aide replies.

"A god?" Victor inquires.

"I assume, yes," the aide says. "He has told people to follow him and to put their lives in his anointed hands."

"Anointed!" Victor says, leaning in. "Is that like…magical?" He looks at the members of the E10. "He is a god with magic hands. He can make the wind blow. Anything else?" They all watch the screen as the man claps his hands and a great flock of birds soars through the crowd, making the people shriek. He claps his hands again and the birds land atop buildings, light poles, and cars. "Impressive," Victor says. "But if he is a true god, he cannot be killed, correct?"

Bruno sees where Victor is going with this. "That is a correct." He looks at General Voss. "Do you have men or a drone in Lima? The sheep there must know if their shepherd is a true god."

General Voss nods, and an aide hands him a phone so he can communicate with his forces inside Lima. The E10 waits patiently for several minutes before a shot rings out on screen, causing Sophia to jump. The man in white lies sprawled on the street, blood saturating his shirt. "He is not a true god," Victor says, getting up and walking to the screen, touching it on the place where the man was shot. "A true god cannot be killed. Or if he is a god, he will rise from the dead." He cocks his head, staring at the dead man. "Will you rise, dead man?" He waits a moment. "No. I don't believe you are a god."

"Is this our plan for everyone who claims to be a savior?" President Banes asks. "We kill them?"

"They are deceiving the entire planet, and we must continue to be the voice of truth and reason," Adrien says. "Not these false gods."

"What about them?" Sophia asks, pointing to the screens that show the Jewish men preaching throughout the world, including the two old men in Jerusalem. "They don't claim to be saviors."

"They are termites," Victor says, still looking at the dead man.

"Termites can do a lot of damage," George says. "Turn it up," he says to an aide, pointing to a screen featuring images of a Jewish man in India. Victor returns to his seat to listen.

"Jesus says, 'The reason I was born and came into the world is to testify to the truth. Everyone on the side of truth listens to me,'" the Jewish man says as he stands on the field of the packed 120,000-seat Salt Lake Stadium in Kolkata, India. "There is no other truth but Jesus!"

"Go to another one," Maria instructs the aide, shaking her head in repulsion.

A stunning image of an overflowing Rungrado May Day Stadium in Pyongyang, North Korea, causes Sophia to gasp. "How many people are there?"

"The stadium holds 150,000," an aide says. "But as you can see, people are on the field and have overflowed into the parking lots."

Sophia is mesmerized by what she's seeing. "How do people even know to show up for these meetings?"

"Many of them have said they were prompted by a dream," an aide replies.

"A dream?" Sophia asks with great interest.

"Yes," the aide says. "A dream that told them specifically to go to these meetings and listen to these men."

"Impossible," George snorts.

Sophia asks the aide to turn up the volume as they read the caption at the bottom of the screen that translates what the Jewish speaker is saying. "Why is my language not clear to you?" the Jewish man asks the crowd. "Jesus asks you this today. 'Why is my language not clear? Because you are unable to hear what I say. You belong to your father, the devil, and you want to carry out your father's desires. He was a murderer from the beginning, not holding to the truth, for there is no truth in him. When he lies, he speaks his native language, for he is a liar and the father of lies.'" The speaker stops reading from his Bible and looks out at the vast crowd. "Are you listening to the lies out of Rome or to Jesus?" Many seated at the table in Rome bristle at his words, but Victor watches him with great curiosity.

"The E10 follows the father of lies!" The Jewish man looks down at his Bible again, reading the words of Jesus: "Yet because I tell the truth, you do not believe me!...If I am telling the truth, why don't you believe me? Whoever belongs to God hears what God says. The reason you do not hear is that you do not belong to God." He looks to the crowd again. "Are you hearing what God says today? Are you hearing the truth of Jesus, or are you hearing what is coming out of Rome? Are you hearing man's truth? Man tells us that the drought and the blood waters have been caused by the moon, yet the two witnesses of God have told us they are the wrath of God poured out on a disobedient world so that all may know him. Who will you believe? Now is the time, now is the moment for you to hear the truth of Jesus! Not the truth you have created. Those who disappeared from this world heard and believed the truth of Jesus. Today is your day of salvation!

Pray, 'Lord Jesus, have mercy on me, a sinner. I believe you are Lord, and there is no other.'"

"No more of him," Bruno says, slapping his hand on the table in anger. "Why weren't those people stopped so they could not get into the stadium?"

The aide clicks on the computer keyboard and pulls up video that fills each screen. "Many times, local police and soldiers try, sir, but most of these meetings are spontaneous. Here's footage from the stadium in Abuja, Nigeria, where the military tried to intervene." What looks to be hundreds of armed men attempting to hold off a massive crowd proves futile as the crowd stampedes them, rushing into the stadium. Gunfire erupts, but even as some fall wounded, the crowd continues pressing into the stadium, eager to hear the speaker who is there.

"Remarkable," Sophia says.

The aide switches over to the Gelora Bung Karno Stadium in Jakarta, Indonesia, which is also filled to overflowing. Thousands of people in the stands are weeping as they lift their hands to the sky. "What are they doing?" George asks.

"They're praying," President Banes says.

"To what?" George asks.

"To whom," President Banes says. "To God."

"There is no God, Thomas!" Victor bellows. "This body has to continue to inform you of that!"

CHAPTER 16

Rome, Italy

The Jewish man is already well into what Victor calls "his venom" when, in a heart-stopping moment, the stadium rocks with explosions and members of the E10 gasp, watching people run for their lives. Countless attackers, hell-bent on murder, pour into the stadium from every entrance, opening fire on the crowd, seeking to kill those that the explosions didn't. The E10 watches in horror as the screen fills with blood and the lifeless bodies of hundreds of Indonesians.

"And this is what prayers to their god accomplished," Victor says, sneering as he watches the violence unfold.

Sophia wants to turn away from the gore but is mesmerized by the man who continues to preach all through the explosions and gunfire. "Call on the name of Jesus, and you will be saved!" he shouts into the microphone. The E10 is spellbound, wondering how he has survived the explosions around him and the barrage of bullets. "Call on Jesus! Call on Jesus, and you will be saved!"

"How…?" Sophia stammers, watching him. "Is he a god?" she asks, directing her question at Victor, who is up on his feet again, fascinated by what's happening on the screen. "Listen to him," Sophia says. "He's instructing them as if it's one final thing to say before they head out the exits. He's not terror-stricken. Why?"

"There have been many deaths around the world at these sorts of events," General Bernard says.

"So you're saying they expect this?" Sophia asks. "That's why his voice isn't edged with terror? That doesn't make any sense."

"They are God's men," President Banes says. "He's protecting them."

Sophia turns to look at Banes, struggling to understand as the other members revile him, the room exploding in voices. "We are God!" Bruno shouts. "This body!"

"These men are not gods," Maria says, her voice shaking. "They are vile pretenders. That man is responsible for the murder of those people, and this governing body should hold him accountable."

"How do you hold a man accountable who doesn't die when a bullet passes through him?" President Banes asks, blanketing the room in silence. "If an explosion doesn't rip him to shreds, what can you do to him?"

The atmosphere has changed from shock to anger and then confusion as Victor, standing in front of the screens, raises his hand to speak. "Throughout time there have been counterfeits, sorcerers, and magicians who cast their spells over the innocent. The world must never fall for their poisonous lies again."

"Why can't these men be contained?" Bruno asks, watching screens showing the Jewish speakers in Singapore, New Delhi, Belfast, Amsterdam, Cambodia, Mexico City, and countless other places. "Have you tried body snatchers?"

General Lazenby nods at an aide to pull up a video. "Without success—yes, sir." Footage of a spider-looking drone with claw-like legs is shown targeting and trying to lift one of the Jewish evangelists from the ground. The preacher swats the drone away as if it's an annoying fly and continues speaking.

"It was a defective drone!" Bruno snaps. "You killed the man in Lima! Why can't these men or those lunatics in Jerusalem be shut up?"

"I assure you, we are trying, sir," General Lazenby replies. "Military forces throughout the world have tried to forcibly remove them. It is our understanding that the IDF has tried several times to remove the two men from Jerusalem without success, and we still have not been able to obtain facial recognition data or secure DNA."

George sighs, looking up at the ceiling. "This is getting tiresome,

General. This body has said this mythical message of Jesus is dangerous to our new world. We've now heard these men speak. It's a message of being set apart for this one man, Jesus. It's not a message of interconnectedness or interdependence with the world. It was these hatemongers and bigots that forced the universe to purge so many from among us. The purging must continue. Now you repeatedly say that you're trying to eliminate them."

"We are, sir…"

"Then try harder!" George barks. "Use greater force! How hard is it to get rid of one man in front of a unit of soldiers?" Most members of the E10 nod in agreement. "Or two old men walking around Jerusalem? These men have become thorns in our flesh. Remove them!"

"Perhaps we need to think this through from another angle," Victor says, walking to his seat. He looks at General Lazenby. "Over and over you have told us that these men can't be killed."

"Yes, sir."

"You said yourself that qualifies them to be gods," President Banes says to Victor. "But they've never claimed to be gods or a savior like the other cult leaders. If those men aren't gods," he says, pointing to the Jewish missionaries and two old men in Jerusalem, "then what are they?"

"They are vermin!" Victor snaps. "And they will be taken care of. But in the meantime, let's kill their message." Members of the E10 and the generals wait for more. "Get rid of everything that has the message of their fictional leader."

"The Bible?" President Banes asks. "We can't get rid of every Bible in the entire world."

"Of course we can," Victor responds.

Bruno is inspired by the idea. "We start by tearing down steeples and crosses, any symbols of this man on buildings or those ghastly crucifixes. Prevent people from using church buildings for places of worship. Tell them they can no longer assemble."

President Banes scoffs at the suggestion. "Prevent people from assembling together? That's not what this body is for!"

Victor speaks over him, his ideas pouring forth at rapid speed.

"You can eliminate everything from the Internet that spreads this ideology," he says. "Every site, blog, video, song—completely rid the Internet of anything relating to this man. Then destroy physical books about him or anything he taught. This includes all videos uploaded of those two old fools in Jerusalem and of the Jewish men spewing hate around the world. News of them must be suppressed. All videos and news must be blocked. The world doesn't need to hear them. The world needs hope! The only videos we'll allow are the ones we make with AI."

"We'll use artificial intelligence to make what sort of videos?" President Banes asks.

"Of them, of course," Bruno replies, pointing to the screens. "The technology has been in place for years. We'll make videos of them, using their voices, but their message won't be this."

Sophia knows exactly where this is headed and asks, "What will their message be?"

"Hate," Adrien says. "Thousands of videos will flood the Internet around the world."

"Fake videos," Sophia says.

"No one will know that except us," Maria says. "They'll be the ones with the fake message. Not us."

President Banes opens his mouth, but Victor talks over him. "We'll eradicate their holidays," he says. "Get them off the calendar. Then let's pay people to turn in their Bibles or anyone who has a Bible."

"You said pay them," Sophia says. "Pay them what?"

Victor shrugs. "Food. You've said yourselves that some people have food, while many others don't."

"What is the goal in getting rid of all this information?" she asks.

Adrien leans onto the table. "Because without information, people will just be taking the word of some Jew standing on the street. There will be nothing to back up what he's saying, especially after we flood the world with videos of their *true* message." Several members nod, mulling over these ideas.

"But what about free speech? Freedom of religion?" asks President Banes.

"That was *your* Constitution, Thomas," Victor replies. "This new world requires something that will move people forward, not backward."

"Because the messengers can't be killed," Bruno says, "we kill the message." President Banes and Sophia shake their heads, but the others are in agreement. "Only fools will listen to these men," Bruno says, smiling.

"What about other religious holidays? Will those also be struck from the calendar?" President Banes asks.

George looks upward, thinking. "I believe it's reasonable to strike all religious holidays from the calendar. If we leave them on there, people are given no room for unity."

"What about other faiths?" President Banes says. "What about Islam, Buddhism, Judaism, and all the others that are in the world? Will we abolish their religious materials? Their places of worship? The Jews are building a temple in Jerusalem. Or are you specifically targeting Christianity?"

"It is *this* ideology that is devastating our globe," Adrien says. "Look at those screens! No other faith is posing this kind of threat. There aren't thousands of men preaching jihad throughout the world. The Buddhists don't have a threatening message. We have to start *here*. We *must* confront this extremism head on. This ideology has been a problem long enough. The universe expelled what it could when it took so many in the disappearances. But now, we have to be faithful and do our part to help."

Sophia furrows her brow. "Faithful and do our part to help? What does that even mean? Are you suggesting extermination?"

Voices clamor on top of each other as Victor leans forward, his elbows resting on the table. "Of course no one means that, Sophia. I think what has been suggested here, which has been made very clear, is that the message needs to be exterminated. We'll remove the message and get rid of their books and buildings. If they persist in congregating or spreading lies, we will simply imprison them." He turns to look at the generals. "What about the militia throughout the world? They have been surrounding these events, correct?"

"Not surrounding them, but in the sense of being out in the streets, yes, sir," General Voss responds.

"They must *not* be surrounded," George says, following Victor's train of thought. "There must be no protection for these people."

"Which is extermination," Sophia says. "Because we know that these groups are targeted. We can't sit back and allow this to…"

"This is not on us, Sophia," Maria says. "These people will be taking their lives into their own hands if they choose to go hear these Jewish fools. We must have a peaceful world religion, not this extremism. If we aren't one, we are nothing."

Adrien nods in agreement, pointing at Maria. "There has been much interreligious dialogue over the last several years, but now it is time for something more than talk of coexistence. We must have a religion of peace and unity."

President Banes shakes his head. "So people aren't allowed to discover or find out answers to their own questions about faith? This governing body has all the answers?"

"We must be one," Bruno says. "The world is much too dangerous a place if we are not."

"*That* is the most dangerous ideology of all," President Banes says.

"We are supposed to lead people," Sophia says. "Not dictate what they think. *That* is extremism," she says, looking at Adrien.

"It is only with one faith that we will be unified," Maria says.

Sadness crosses President Banes's face. "Unified to what end?"

To discover more about the biblical facts behind the story, read Where in the Word? *on page 249, or continue reading the novel.*

CHAPTER 17

Jerusalem, Israel
One Month Later

The ministers of defense and internal security are pacing inside Prime Minister Ari's office, looking weary and aggravated. "Mr. Prime Minister," the minister of internal security says, "we strongly urge you not to do this. Do not give our state's secrets and treasures away to these people. We've worked too hard to…"

"These people?" Prime Minister Ari responds. "They are the ones who brokered our peace covenant, Gershom. If it wasn't for the members of the E10 and Victor Quade, we never would have built our temple. You saw how they marveled during their tour of the temple yesterday. Those were Victor Quade's actual words. 'This is a *marvel*! I've never seen anything quite so exquisite.' He just stood there with his eyes taking in the beauty and splendor of our temple."

"And we are grateful, Mr. Prime Minister, for their covenant of peace and for their presence here today for the dedication," the minister of defense says with a look of concern. "But I agree with Gershom. It is too dangerous to take these leaders deep into our state's business. We simply cannot reveal our brightest and boldest inventions in technology, medicine, and agriculture."

"And it is too dangerous to share our latest discoveries in oil and natural gas and in our water osmosis plants," the minister of internal security says. "These revelations will be too tempting for our rivals to ignore."

The prime minister considers their words, then responds, "They believe in us. The E10. They traveled all the way here. I am proud of our nation. I want to show them that they have reason to be proud as well. Israel could help solve the global drought. We can take great pride in this."

Prime Minister Ari and members of the E10 stand in one of Israel's first osmosis desalination plants, which opened in 2005. The prime minister is beaming as he tells them, "Nearly all of Israel's drinking water is from the sea, and we extract it from the air, making Israel immune to the droughts that frequently plague the Middle East—as well as this drought that has come upon the whole world. Now water facilities like these can benefit all humanity! We could not purify the red waters, but we are researching ways to do just that in case the waters turn red again. As you can see, we are back up and running at full speed ahead."

Members of the E10 can scarcely believe what they're seeing; Israel's system for collecting and cleaning water could resolve the crises that are crippling the globe. Prime Minister Ari swells with pride. For once, with these inventions, their technology, and their production of oil and natural gas, Israel will be considered a world leader. The E10 is amazed at what Israel has accomplished in the face of worldwide adversity. Because of this water system, the drought has not struck their wheat and corn as it has other farm produce around the globe, and Israel's farms are producing plenty of other foods for the entire state without worry. With Silicon Valley in California reeling from a recent earthquake, Tel Aviv is clearly the leader in high-tech industry now, with research and production taking place in fields like bioengineering, nanotechnology, medicine, and defense.

"We are providing solutions for the real-life problems of today's world," the prime minister says inside a lab where members of the E10 gaze at a human heart that has been cloned. "This is better than an actual human heart," the prime minister says, noting the admiration from the E10. "No disease."

"Magnificent," Prime Minister Sophia Clattenberg says, bending forward to examine the beating heart more closely.

It has long been known that Israel found the cure for cancer; their scientific findings have gone out around the world and their anti-cancer medicines yield the state billions of dollars each year in exports. The prime minister gives each of his guests the finest gifts from Israel's inventions, including artificial intelligence, a beautiful and expensive sample from their diamond-cutting industry, the newest in cell phone and computer technology, the latest technology in skin therapy that reverses signs of aging, and medicine that will extend life. He simply has to send them home with the best and brightest that Israel has to offer.

"Absolutely stunning," Victor says, taking it all in.

Millions converge on Jerusalem for the opening of the temple. Anticipating an enormous celebration, the Israeli government began building a rail system in 2001. The high-speed system, complete with an underground nuclear bunker, takes passengers from the Ben Gurion Airport all the way to Old Jerusalem at the Western Wall to the Donald J. Trump Station, named after the forty-fifth president of the United States and the first to recognize Jerusalem as the capital of Israel.

The government saw to it that several hotels in Jerusalem were built as well, creating rooms for an additional 100,000 visitors to the city. The governing authorities also created a map that divided the country into zones. The citizens who lived within each zone were assigned a day to come celebrate the opening of the temple, but from the looks of the bloated streets, it appears all of Israel has ignored the zones in order to celebrate on this remarkable opening day of dedication.

The temple reflects the dazzling splendor of the ancient structure built by King Solomon and is adorned with gold, bronze, quarried stone and marble, and choice woods from around the world that have been acquired over the last several years. In keeping with the earlier temples, this one faces east and is 45 feet in height, 90 feet long, and 30 feet wide. In keeping with the commands in the ancient Torah, all stone for the temple was dressed at quarries, and never within the temple site. And as was the case with the ancient structure, much of the temple has been overlaid with gold.

Shofars sound as priests who are descendants from the tribe of Levi wash in the laver. The Ark of the Covenant is carried on poles, just as in the days of ancient Israel, and a team of priests guide it via a procession through the crowded streets of Jerusalem. During King Solomon's reign, a vast system of labyrinths, mazes, chambers, and corridors were constructed underneath the Temple Mount complex and it was here, in the bowels of the earth, that a place was built to hide the Ark and the sacred vessels of the temple from enemies. This location was recorded by the Jews; and through the ages, there were a select few who knew where the chamber was located, but that knowledge was eventually lost.

Many years ago, an attempt was made by Israel to excavate in the area of the secret chamber, and the result was widespread Muslim rioting. The Muslims didn't want their own holy places on the Mount disturbed, but they also knew there was much to lose if the Ark was discovered because it would serve as solid proof that the past temples had in fact existed and the Jews did have a legitimate right and inheritance to the Temple Mount. The Muslims had no idea that ultimately, their protests had protected the Ark and the vessels. During the invasion of Israel the massive earthquake unearthed the precious Ark, and Israelis have been praising Hashem for the discovery.

As the team of priests carrying the Ark slowly makes its way through Jerusalem, the entire nation dances and shouts in victory. After 2,000 years, the holy temple has been rebuilt! Dignitaries from around the world and members of the E10, including President Banes, Prime Minister Sophia Clattenberg, Chancellor George Albrecht, Bruno Neri, and Victor Quade, sit alongside Prime Minister Ari and his wife. Victor and Prime Minister Ari share warm smiles for the cameras as they celebrate this pinnacle of peace together.

"We would not be celebrating this day were it not for the sacrifice and service of the entire E10," the prime minister exclaims to the enthralled crowd in front of the temple. "Israel is eternally grateful for your work toward peace and security, your belief in a world united together in harmony, and for your unwavering support of our great nation. Our temple would not be here today without the strengthened peace covenant by Counsel Secretary Victor Quade, and we celebrate this day with all of you." The members of the E10 stand, smiling and waving, and Prime Minister Ari lifts Victor Quade's hand high in the air as F-15 Eagle fighter jets do a flyover in the skies above them.

Prime Minister Ari has directed his minister of defense to use any means necessary to keep the two witnesses out of Jerusalem and away from the temple ceremony. Their presence is always disruptive, and they leave catastrophe in their wake. Four months have gone by since they announced that there would be no rain, and the earth has suffered—first by drought, and then for two days by the plague of blood waters. People had gone so far as to kill one another for clean water.

Prime Minister Ari, members of the E10, and others were quick to claim these disasters were merely coincidences, and that there was no way these two old fools carried such power. But the earth is still reeling from unseasonably warm temperatures and quickly drying lakes, rivers, and other bodies of water. Farms had suffered greatly—first from losing so many farmhands in the mass disappearances, and now from the inability to keep their crops and animals watered. The blood waters had further sickened livestock, causing even more farmers to stop business altogether. Food and meat processing plants were also grappling with the water shortage, and during the blood waters, they had no choice but to close their doors. Until the drought ends, many more processing plants have closed their doors.

Though world leaders and the media had declared the drought and blood waters were only coincidental, they hated the two witnesses nonetheless. And before today's dedication ceremony for the opening of the temple, Prime Minister Ari made it clear to the minister of defense that these two men were not to set foot in Jerusalem.

CHAPTER 18

Jerusalem, Israel

All through the day, whenever the two witnesses are spotted in the streets, soldiers from the Israel Defense Forces have been dispatched to stop them. But by the time the soldiers arrive, the witnesses disappear. A new call comes from the Via Dolorosa, which is believed to be the path that Yeshua walked to his crucifixion. There, the witnesses are preaching and calling people to repent of their sins. The crowd curses and screams, throwing rocks or food at them; no one wants them to ruin this historic day.

Zerah works his way through the crowd, eager to see the witnesses. Everywhere that he has preached throughout Israel, hatred for the witnesses in Jerusalem has been hurled at him; he has been violently threatened each and every day. Zerah begins to run as he sees soldiers from the IDF pushing their way through the crowd to confront the witnesses. "Hashem's Word is perfect!" Zerah yells, elbowing his way to the front of the onlookers. The witnesses nod when they see Zerah. The First Witness had met him when Hashem sealed him as one of the 144,000 Jewish servants to preach throughout the world, and he raises his hand to greet Zerah. "Hashem is just in all of his ways," Zerah says. "Listen to these prophets of Hashem!" Some in the crowd attempt to push Zerah away, but they are unable to get near him.

Lieutenant Colonel Eliezer Berenbaum squeezes through the crowd and steps before the witnesses. "Come with us," he says, holding up his hand to halt the five soldiers behind him. "Please."

"You know we will not do that, Eliezer," the First Witness says.

The fact that the old man addresses him has no effect on the lieutenant colonel. He is here to remove these men, not to be swayed by their mysterious ability to know people's names. "You will either come with us peacefully, or we will have to remove you by force."

The Second Witness moves toward him. "Eliezer, you have been searching the Scriptures since Yeshua called his bride home. You know who we are. You have read about us yourself."

Eliezer's heart races to his throat but he remains unmoved. "Your wife, Dahlia, has also been reading," says the Second Witness. "She has told you that she has come to hear us. We met her in the Shuk and she told you that she believes. Doesn't she, Eliezer?"

The lieutenant colonel can't hold the old man's gaze and looks to his men behind him. "Bring them in," he commands, keeping his composure.

Zerah cranes his neck to see what will happen. Soldiers rush forward, but the witnesses pass through them as if strolling to the market. They begin to preach as the soldiers pursue them, looking like Keystone Cops and embarrassing themselves. The lieutenant colonel barks orders at the soldiers, commanding them to seize the witnesses and to fire upon them if necessary. "Halt!" the lieutenant colonel shouts to the witnesses, but they continue to walk and preach, calling people by name and pointing out their sins. "Halt or we'll shoot!"

"Behold," the First Witness says to the crowd, "your sins have separated you from Hashem. You use your bodies as instruments of unrighteousness; you practice lawlessness. No one who is born of Hashem practices sin because Hashem's seed abides in him. Your sins have hidden his face from you so that he does not hear. For your hands are defiled with blood and your fingers with iniquity; your lips have spoken lies and your tongues mutter wickedness."

"Repent of your sins," the Second Witness says, walking through the crowd. "Call on the name of Hashem! Make yourselves clean; remove the evil of your deeds from before his eyes. Though your sins are like scarlet, they shall be white as snow. If you are willing and obedient, you will eat the good of the land. But if you refuse and rebel, you will be eaten by the sword; for the mouth of Adonai has spoken." Tears fill the eyes of many in the crowd as others push forward in fury.

At the sound of weapons being drawn, the two witnesses turn and extend their hands toward the soldiers. The weapons become live snakes that bite the soldiers' hands and make them scream as they try to fling off the slithering reptiles. A new unit of soldiers quickly lunges for the old men, but the First Witness stomps his foot, causing the ground beneath the soldiers to open and swallow them. The crowd gasps, and Zerah watches in astonishment.

The lieutenant colonel calls for yet another unit, requesting backup. Soldiers rush through the street to confront the witnesses from the other side, and the crowd is urged to keep its distance. Zerah somehow manages to make his way to the front again. Two soldiers carrying flame throwers aim the weapons at the old men and flames engulf the space between them and the witnesses. The witnesses walk through the fire and yank the weapons away from the soldiers' hands.

"That you may have ears to hear and eyes to see!" Zerah yells above the noise of the crowd.

The lieutenant colonel ignores Zerah and the voices shouting around him. "How are you doing this?" he asks the witnesses, his voice quivering.

"You know how we do this, Eliezer," the Second Witness says. "Do you believe what you have read in the Word of Hashem?"

Eliezer's eyes lose their iron gaze as he nods. The old man puts his hand on the back of the lieutenant colonel's head, patting him like a father would a son. "Go and tell others, Eliezer. Yeshua lives."

"He does," Eliezer says, tears welling in his eyes. "Yeshua lives!" He turns to the crowd. "Our Messiah lives!"

Zerah whoops and shouts, thrusting a fist into the air. Some of the soldiers turn against the lieutenant colonel, cursing and spitting at him. The crowd turns violent as well, attacking him. The two witnesses continue their journey down the Via Dolorosa and the crowd leaves the lieutenant colonel's beaten body in the street to rush after them.

As the two witnesses make their way toward the temple, IDF soldiers spread out and attempt to block their way. The old men open their arms in front of them and the soldiers fall backward, as if paralyzed, creating an open path to the temple. Furious with rage, Prime Minister Ari, along with his security detail, pushes his way through the throng of people to face the witnesses, who are now on the steps leading up to the temple. "You will not ruin this historic day for Israel!" the prime minister barks, his face wet with sweat.

"We listen to Adonai," the First Witness replies, walking past him.

"You will stop!"

The Second Witness turns to look at the prime minister; his eyes are full of love for him. "Ephraim, we will not stop until Adonai commands us to. In Israel, every Jew—every man, woman, and child—must repent and turn to our Messiah, Yeshua." The prime minister begins to speak, but the witness grasps his shoulder. "Repent of your whoring with Victor Quade and the E10."

The prime minister's face turns red as he opens his mouth and hurls obscenities at the Second Witness. The Second Witness continues, "Repent of your mistress, Ephraim. Stop your sexual sin with her. Confess to your son, Abraham. He's the only one who knows of her and he hates you for it. Redeem the time, Ephraim. It is short. The time is fulfilled, and the kingdom of God is at hand; repent and believe in the gospel. Turn to Yeshua."

The witnesses leave Prime Minister Ari gaping at them and walk up the temple stairs to face the members of the E10. President Banes's heart lunges at the sight of the small old men, who seem larger on TV, but their commanding presence takes his breath away. One of them catches his eye, and President Banes's mind is flooded with images of his wife and two children, who disappeared in the vanishings. "They are with me, Thomas." President Banes shakes his head, wondering whether those words came from his own thoughts or if he truly was "hearing" another voice. The witnesses stand in unsettling silence in front of the E10, making the members uncomfortable.

"Satan will have your souls," the First Witness says, and Bruno balks at the words. "He has come to steal, kill, and destroy."

Victor looks at the men with disdain, as if they were nothing more than doddering, amusing caricatures. As the witnesses turn to address the multitudes, IDF soldiers rush their way up the stairs. The two witnesses open their mouths, spewing fire and killing some of the soldiers. A colossal wall of blazing fire continues to rage before them, keeping soldiers and the crowd from reaching them. "Their magic is certainly impressive in real life," Victor says to Bruno.

"Unbelievable," Bruno says, leaning forward to get a better look.

The Second Witness declares, "Thus says Hashem, 'Be still and know that I am.'" Many among the throng of people begin to murmur and curse him, but the Second Witness raises both his arms in the air, holding their mouths closed. "That you may have ears to hear!" he shouts. Every street in Jerusalem is suddenly quiet. The shofars have been silenced; the singing, shouting, and laughter have all been quenched. Members of the E10 are baffled; they, too, are unable to form any words on their lips.

Zerah looks at the people around him, thoroughly amazed by the power of the witnesses. "Wow!" he whispers, trying to take it all in.

Another unit of soldiers moves toward the witnesses from atop the temple stairs, but the Second Witness opens his mouth with an outpouring of fire that blocks the soldiers' way. Now the stairs are surrounded by fire, with Prime Minister Ari and members of the E10 inside the wall of flames with the witnesses. "Hear the Word of Hashem, all you people of Israel who come through these gates to worship him!" the Second Witness proclaims.

The First Witness looks over the top of the flames to the people closest to him and to those who are packed in like cattle around the temple and in the streets. He speaks, and his voice rings out with the clarity of a bell: "This nation has not obeyed Hashem or responded to correction," he says. "Truth has perished; it has vanished from your lips. This is what Adonai says: Reform your ways and your actions. Repent of your sins. Turn to my son, Yeshua. Do not trust in deceptive words and say, 'This is the temple of Hashem, the temple of Hashem, the temple of Hashem!' This temple cannot hide your disobedience or your sin before me. You are trusting in deceptive words that are worthless."

Members of the E10 look to one another, wondering if he's speaking of them.

"Will you steal, murder, commit perjury, sexual perversion and adultery, and worship other gods, then come and stand before me in this house, which bears my name, and say, 'We are safe'—safe to do all these detestable things? But I have been watching! declares Hashem. Do you not see what I have done because of the wickedness of my people Israel? You disobey my Word, and the earth trembles." As he speaks, the witness's words are broadcast throughout the world, enflaming anger and outrage in some and arousing curiosity in others.

The Second Witness raises his hand. "This is what Adonai, Hashem of Israel, says: 'When I brought your ancestors out of Egypt and spoke to them, I gave them this command: Obey me, and I will be Hashem to you and you will be my people. Walk in obedience to all I command you, that it may go well with you. But they did not listen or pay attention; instead, they followed the stubborn inclinations of their evil hearts. They followed after other gods.' "

The Second Witness pauses, looking at the sea of faces in front of him. "Hashem says, 'I sent my son, Yeshua, and your ancestors rejected him. Your disobedience scattered you across the globe, but in 1948 you became a nation again in the land I promised you. I said I will do it, and I did it according to my Word. Yet you embrace the E10 and Victor Quade, who made a hollow covenant with you, turning your ears to them and placing your hope in their empty words.' " Victor burns with anger at the old man as he speaks. " 'It is the work of Satan that you would believe their lies and die. I sent my son that you would live!' "

The First Witness turns to look at the members of the E10. "The E10 is not your god." Victor and the member of the E10 sit up straighter, listening. "Their words are futile. The grass withers, the flowers fade, but the Word of Hashem stands forever." The First Witness turns his gaze to Victor Quade and says, "The Word of Hashem endures forever!" Unable to speak, Victor's jaw clenches and rage courses throughout his body. A chill runs down President Banes's spine, and he refrains from looking at the other members.

The First Witness turns again to the crowd: "Therefore, this is what our sovereign Hashem says: 'My anger and my wrath are being poured out—on man and beast, on the trees of the field and on the crops of your land—and it will burn and not be quenched.'" He lifts his arms upward. "'Throughout the earth, locusts will feast on your fields, consuming them so that you may eat of the Bread of Life and drink of the Living Water, who is Yeshua. While there is still time, repent and turn to me.'"

A great wind blows over the throng of people and, in the distance, what appears to be an inky rain cloud forming on the horizon speeds straight for the crowd. But as the cloud comes over them, everyone covers their heads and runs as they realize this dust storm is alive with a massive swarm of winged creatures. Some people cry out to Hashem while others swear, and everyone is swatting at the buzzing horde of locusts.

With that, the walls of fire die out and the two witnesses move down the stairs without a glance at Prime Minister Ari or the members of the E10. They each place a hand on Zerah's shoulders and look him in the eyes before departing through the city streets. They have ruined the opening-day festivities for the rebuilt temple, and the members of the E10—including Victor Quade—bat away the droning locusts as the two disappear from view.

To discover more about the biblical facts behind the story, read Where in the Word? *on page 255, or continue reading the novel*

CHAPTER 19

Brooklyn, NY

Emma, Brandon, Kennisha, and several others from their home church are canvassing the streets for abandoned children when the clouds above them darken. The roar of something like a waterfall descends upon the neighborhood and Emma turns her face upward, her eyes taking in the sight. There's no time to say anything as the buzzing throng dives from the sky, flapping their way through all the streets and through every open window or door. People scream and curse as they run for shelter from the pulsating menace, and Emma, Brandon, and Kennisha race toward home.

Jerusalem, Israel

Following a long day, Prime Minister Ari tries to prepare for his evening address to the state. But locusts have made their way into his office through open windows and under doors. He waves his arms, shouting at the aides inside the room to do more to get rid of them. His shouting stops when he sees the two witnesses appear on the TV screen. They are standing in front of the temple, and the prime minister uses blistering language at the sight of them, demanding that the IDF remove them at once. An aide clicks a number on his phone to convey the prime minister's directive.

"This is what our holy Hashem says to Israel," the First Witness proclaims from the temple steps. "'You became very beautiful and rose to be a queen. And your fame spread among the nations on account of your beauty, because the splendor I had given you made your beauty perfect. But you trusted in your beauty and used your fame to become a prostitute. You lavished your favors on the serpent who passed by, and your beauty became his.'"

Prime Minister Ari can feel his blood pressure rising. "What are they saying?" he shouts at the staff and television crew inside his office. "What do they mean?"

The First Witness continues, "Hashem says, 'Can a virgin forget her ornaments, or a bride her attire? Yet my people have forgotten me days without number. You went to him, and he possessed your beauty. You offered the riches of my land.'"

"What do they mean?" Prime Minister Ari screams, pounding his desk. His mind staggers back to the warnings his cabinet members gave him about showing Israel's treasures to the E10 and his heart thumps wildly in his ears.

"'Woe! Woe to you,' declares Hashem," the Second Witness says. "'You engaged in prostitution and aroused my anger with your increasing promiscuity. The greed of your enemies consumes them.'" The prime minister slumps in his chair, listening. "'You adulterous wife! You prefer strangers to your own husband! All prostitutes receive gifts, but you give gifts to all your lovers, bribing them to come to you from everywhere for your illicit favors.'"

Prime Minister Ari feels sick to his stomach and watches in dread as the two old men continue their ramblings. "What are they talking about, Mr. Prime Minister?" a staff member asks.

"Shh," says the prime minister, holding up his hand for silence.

"King Hezekiah received envoys and showed them all that was in his storehouses—there was nothing in his palace or in all his kingdom that Hezekiah did not show them." The prime minister's office is heavy with silence as dread shrouds the prime minister's heart. "Then Isaiah the prophet went to King Hezekiah and asked, 'What did those men say, and where did they come from?' Hezekiah replied, 'They came from Babylon.' The prophet asked, 'What did they see in your palace?' 'They saw everything in my palace,' King Hezekiah said. 'There is nothing among my treasures that I did not show them.' Then Isaiah said to Hezekiah, 'Hear the Word of Hashem: "The time will surely come when everything in your palace, and all that your predecessors have stored up until this day, will be carried off to Babylon. Nothing will be left," says Hashem. "And some of your descendants, your own flesh and blood who will be born to you, will be taken away."'"

"There is no Babylon, Mr. Prime Minister," the same staff member says. "This is absurd." The prime minister does not answer him.

"Therefore, you prostitute, hear the Word of Hashem!" the First Witness says. "'Because you poured out your lust and exposed your naked body in your promiscuity with your lovers, therefore I am going to gather all your lovers with whom you found pleasure. I will gather them against you. I will sentence you to the blood vengeance of my wrath and jealous anger. Then I will deliver you into the hands of your lovers, and they will make desolate your holy places. They will strip you of your clothes and take your fine jewelry and leave you stark naked. They will bring a mob against you, every nation against you. They will burn down your houses and inflict punishment on you. I will put a stop to your prostitution, and you will no longer pay your lovers.'"

The Second Witness adds, "'Ah, sinful nation,' declares Hashem. 'Return, faithless Israel. I will not look on you in anger, for I am merciful; I will not be angry forever. Only acknowledge your guilt, that you rebelled against Hashem and scattered your favors among foreigners and that you have not obeyed my voice. Return, O faithless children, for I am your Master.'"

Prime Minister Ari motions for someone—anyone—to turn off the sound and buries his face in his hands.

"Prime Minister?" Prime Minister Ari looks up with terrified eyes at one of the workers with the production crew. "One minute to air."

The prime minister pulls himself together and, as the jet with the E10 flies over Israel on its way to Rome, he addresses the nation, claiming the locusts are only a temporary problem and declaring that their new temple is a miracle and wonder.

As Victor Quade looks out his airplane window over Israel, he thinks the very same thing.

CHAPTER 20

Rome, Italy
Three Months Later

Victor Quade stands at the podium atop the stairs of the great lobby in the Palace of Justice and as he begins to speak, the clamor of the reporters dies down. "It has repeatedly come to the attention of the E10 that the rhetoric of the two men in Jerusalem and the men who are preaching throughout the world is dangerous, narrow-minded, bigoted, intolerant, and the greatest threat to the security of our global union. Their ideology continues to stir hatred and violence, and countless people have lost their lives in the places where these men have spoken. It is the belief not only of this governing body but of every citizen of our New World that we need a safer, peaceful, broad-minded perspective that keeps us unified.

"In our efforts to create a safe and reconciled world, we are asking for your help. It will take all of us working together to rid our world of bigotry, hatred, homophobia, racism, violence, xenophobia, and intolerance of every kind. From what we have seen, it is our belief that the message these men are presenting—about the mythical Jesus Christ—is sending our world into a downward spiral of confusion and hostility.

"We spoke of this concern in months prior, and I reiterate on behalf of the governing body of the E10 that it is of utmost importance that we all work together toward peace and unity. One way we can achieve these goals is by bringing to authorities any Bibles or religious literature or information dealing with this man Jesus. All traces of this ideology must be eradicated. Anyone attempting to promote this ideology through the printed or spoken word or the Internet will be punished and imprisoned. Steeples and crosses will be removed from buildings, and any so-called churches will be monitored for religious activity and will instead be used to further advance the causes of peace and unity in our world. It is our collective duty to report anyone who is not compliant with our new and peaceful standard of living. These are measures we must take in order to provide the peace and safety our world longs for and that are within our reach."

The reporters shout over one another, vying for Victor's attention. He nods toward a dark-skinned man in the front. "Are these measures only for those with the message of Christ? What about Muslims? Atheists? Sikhs? Buddhists? Hin..."

Victor cuts him off. "We are aware of the world's many religious bodies, but in fairness, it is this particular belief that is causing the most upheaval. We must begin here. Once this message is removed, we will be free to create a more unified world." Victor ignores the other reporters and turns from the podium, going back to work.

President Banes turns off the live feed at his office in Virginia. After Washington, DC, was attacked and the White House and all major government buildings were destroyed, the president's office was set up in Fairfax, although most of his time these days is spent in Rome, working with the E10. He pulls up a picture of his wife and two young children on his phone, knowing that if they were here, he or someone else would be obligated to turn them over to the authorities. The thought makes his eyes sting, and he turns off his phone.

CHAPTER 21

Brooklyn, NY

Emma holds a lit gas lantern near a pot of rice mixed with cream of chicken soup. Kennisha spoons a portion onto each of the plates in front of the 16 children they have in the home. The garage shelves still have food that Mrs. Ramos had in storage for the 316 Deli, and the kitchen counters are piled high with the canned goods and other non-perishable foods Emma and Brandon had found in homes.

But how long will these goods last? With so many mouths to feed—even though they eat only one or two small meals a day, they know the food will run out quickly. Emma moves the gas lantern closer to the pot of rice so Kennisha can see better. This is day number three of darkness in the world, and Emma feels like she's going mad. Temperatures have plunged around the globe, and constant nightfall has challenged the psychosis of man and animal alike. Three days earlier, one of the two witnesses in Jerusalem had stretched out his hand and said, "Darkness shall cover the land, a darkness that shall be felt by the old and young, the great and the small."

This plague follows seven days of the entire world being mute so that everyone would have "ears to hear and eyes to see." The witness had said, "Thus says Hashem, 'Who has made man's mouth? Who makes him mute, or deaf, or seeing, or blind? Is it not I, Adonai?'"

Remarkably, the 144,000 witnesses were not affected by this plague, nor any of the other plagues. They were able to continue proclaiming the gospel during this time when no one could speak.

Without the ability to communicate, countless jobs were unable to be carried out and struggling economies suffered even more. Emma and everyone else in Mrs. Ramos's house decided to pass this time of muteness by reading the Bible from cover to cover and praying and fasting as never before. The world around them took on a new sense of disturbing silence, but Emma and all those in the house heard from the Lord in ways they never thought possible. But then this plague of darkness came along, playing with Emma's mind and making her feel as though she's going crazy.

"I'll take this to Bella," she says when Kennisha hands her a plate of rice. Emma sets down the gas lantern so Kennisha and the children can see in the kitchen, grabs a cup of water, and picks up a flashlight to make her way up the stairs into Kennisha's bedroom, where Bella has been sick for two days. Many from their home church have been fighting a virus, the pandemic that has swept the globe, and Emma and Kennisha are doing what they can to keep Bella's fever down and fluids inside her. Medication isn't available, but Emma has been giving Bella ibuprofen in hopes of breaking the fever.

Emma opens the door and peeks into the room to see if Bella's awake. "I brought you some rice," Emma says, walking toward Bella and standing at the side of the bed. Emma uses the back of her hand to feel Bella's forehead. She's heating up again, and just this morning her fever was down.

"I'm not hungry," Bella says, whispering. Although Bella had turned 13 a few months ago, Emma thinks her petite frame makes her look much younger.

Emma sets the plate on the nightstand and walks to the bathroom, where she runs four washcloths under cold water and wrings them out. She then walks over to Bella and places one washcloth on her forehead, one on the crook of each arm, and one across her stomach—something her own mother had done for her when she had a fever as a child. She sits on the side of the bed and places her hand on the cloth on Bella's forehead. She hates the thought of Bella being quarantined from all the others by herself in the dark. It seems that since the vanishings, Bella has had to fight too often to survive—first inside the church where Brandon and Emma found her, and now with this virus. Bella uses one of the washcloths to cover her face as she coughs, and Emma winces at the sound. "I'm so sorry, Bella."

Bella removes the washcloth from her mouth and looks up at Emma. "Don't be. I'm okay. I'm ready, Emma. Just like the others." The virus has already claimed three lives from their home church.

Bella's words grip Emma's throat. "What do you…? Don't say that, Bella. All those who died were older. You're so young. You're strong. Everything's going to be okay."

Bella puts her hand on top of Emma's. "I love you, Emma."

Emma puts her other hand on top of Bella's. "I love you, sweet Bella."

"I'm tired."

Emma nods, patting Bella's hand. "I'll let you sleep. Get some good rest, okay?" She squeezes Bella's hand and walks to the window, opening it for some fresh air before washing her hands. She keeps the flashlight low, just enough to see Bella's face, praying aloud that she'll be healed, then picks up the plate of rice to take it back downstairs.

Kennisha is handing the last couple of plates of food to the children when Emma hands Bella's plate to her. "She can't eat?" Kennisha asks. Emma shakes her head. "Is her fever still down?"

"No," Emma says, keeping her voice low. "It's back. And her cough is worse. But she'll turn a corner, right? She's so young. The virus keeps killing older people who aren't in good health already. Bella's been healthy and strong up until two days ago."

A knock at the door makes everyone jump, and Emma wonders if it's someone dropping off another baby or child. She picks up the gas lantern and makes her way through the children sitting on the kitchen floor eating, heading for the front door.

"Who is it?" she asks, keeping the door locked and latched.

"I hear you take in children," a man says on the darkened porch. He's using a flashlight so she can see his face.

"Do you have a child?" Emma asks.

"I'm a pastor," he says. "*Was* a pastor. Can I come in and talk to you?" Emma leaves the door latched as she opens it partway, straining to see the man. "My name is Jamie," he says. "I'm a believer. I follow Jesus."

Emma unlatches the door and opens it. "Come on in," she says. Kennisha hears his voice and walks into the living room, carrying a candle.

"This is my friend Kennisha," says Emma.

"I'm Jamie," he says, reaching to shake Kennisha's hand.

Emma and Kennisha both look at Jamie, and even in the pale light they are struck by the man's appearance. He looks as if he had once taken great pride in his body and spent a great deal of time at the gym. But today, he looks gaunt, tired, and spent.

"You were a pastor?" Emma asks, beckoning for him to sit on the sofa. She sits down next to him, and Kennisha sits in the chair opposite them.

He nods. "I have the degrees on my wall to prove it." He looks at their faces lit with the amber glow of the gas lantern and candle. "I know what you're thinking. How am I still here? What was I teaching?"

The quiet stretches out between them for a moment before Emma asks, "Were you teaching Jesus?"

He rubs his hands together, nodding sadly. "I was teaching Jesus. The agreeable, convenient Jesus. Buddy Jesus. The he-is-who-you-want-him-to-be Jesus. The he-was-a-great-prophet-but-so-were-a-lot-of-other-people Jesus."

"Did you know that he was coming back?" Kennisha asks.

He closes his eyes, thinking. "In my head, yes."

A sad smile crosses Emma's face. "But not in your heart?"

Jamie's eyes fill with tears. "I liked the good, kind verses of the Bible. Not the confusing or what I felt were the judgmental, scary, or offensive parts."

"And what about the people in your church?" Kennisha asks.

"I don't know about some, but many of them are still here because I never..." he says, his voice breaking.

"You have a wedding ring," Emma says. "Are your wife and family here?"

"My wife left me shortly after Jesus called his followers. She took our two kids and moved in with a man from the church." He laughs at the irony. "What a mess, right?" He looks up at them through watery eyes. "I've been trying to get them back. I go see my kids, but I can tell the world is getting to them. They hate me. My wife hates me." Emma and Kennisha look at each other, searching for the right thing to say, but come up short.

"The church I pastored is still standing," he says, straightening. "I've been living there along with several people who lost their homes. Every day I hear of more kids being taken and sold. The Coffee Shop District is filled day and night with people buying and selling children." He rubs his head. "Parents are selling their kids into prostitution for money. How sick is that?" He looks up at the ceiling and shakes his head, then turns to look at Emma and Kennisha. "I want you to use the church for all the kids you're rescuing." Emma and Kennisha's mouths drop open.

"The building is paid for. There's a full kitchen. Bigger than what you have here."

"They're destroying churches around the world," Kennisha says. "They just pulled the steeple down from the church a few blocks from here."

"The building doesn't look like a church," Jamie says. "The sign in front says, 'The Rescue.' That was the name of the church." He scoffs, shaking his head. "What a pompous name! We didn't rescue anybody from anything at that church." He buries his head in his hands and sighs, using his palms to wipe his face. "It looks like a regular building and it's yours, if you'll take it. It's got some structural damage from the attack on the city, but it's still standing. I'll do everything I can to work and make sure that you have food to feed the kids and that they have something to sleep on. You're doing more inside this home than I ever did inside that church. This is a true place of rescue. I just can't let the building sit there and not be of use."

Emma looks at Kennisha, fumbling for words. "We have been trying to figure out how to get out of the city. It's so dangerous for Christians now. I don't think..."

"I understand," Jamie says, not letting her finish. He listens to the sound of the children inside the kitchen. "But there's no way out for kids." He lets his words hang in the air before continuing. "And time is short. I've been reading all those parts of the Bible that I ignored for so many years. I know what's up ahead." He looks at them. "You do too." Emma and Kennisha are silent. Yes, they know what's ahead as well. "As hard as it is to believe," says Jamie, "it will get a lot darker than it is now."

"But we'll have the light of the world," Kennisha says, her candle's flame shining in waves across her face. "Just as we do now."

Jamie smiles as Micah and three of the children walk into the living room, sitting next to Emma and Kennisha or standing in the kitchen doorway. "We can rescue as many kids as we can in what time we have," he says. "The time is coming when we won't be able to buy and sell anything anymore."

Emma and Kennisha nod; they'd had this conversation many times. They know from the Bible that a worldwide system for marking people is coming, a system that will align many people with the leadership of the Antichrist. Those who don't take the mark won't be able to buy or sell anything. They will not be able to pay for food, clothes, cell phones, medical supplies, gas, or any other essentials. And refusal of the mark means death.

"When that day comes," Jamie says, "we won't be able to stay in the building any longer because we won't be able to pay for water, or taxes, or even electricity if it's ever restored to the city again. And we need to prepare for those days. It will take lots of us to prepare." Emma and Kennisha exchange glances. "Things will get worse," Jamie says, "but we can save as many kids as possible and lead them to Jesus. I'll need your help." His eyes search theirs in the silence. "Will you help me?"

To discover more about the biblical facts behind the story, read Where in the Word? *on page 261, or continue reading the novel.*

CHAPTER 22

Brooklyn, NY

The next day, Emma is relieved to wake to the first hint of dawn seeping under Kennisha's bedroom door. The plague of darkness has ended! She and Kennisha had slept outside the door in the hallway so they could check on Bella throughout the night. Her fever was still up, and Emma and Kennisha kept cool washcloths on her, praying the fever would break.

Emma flings off the blanket and quietly opens the door, tiptoeing to the bed to see Bella, whose body looks small and still. Kennisha steps into the room beside Emma, looking down at Bella. Emma gasps and sits on the edge of the bed, taking Bella's hand in hers. "She died all alone in the dark," she whispers, her voice breaking.

"She wasn't alone, Em," Kennisha says, wiping her cheeks and moving to the other side of the bed to sit next to Bella. "I don't believe for a second that she was alone. And she's in the light now." Kennisha looks at Emma. "She knew she was loved here, Emma. We all loved her."

Emma nods as her face becomes wet with tears. "I honestly thought she would get better," she says, stroking Bella's hair. "She said she was ready to go."

Kennisha takes hold of Bella's hand. "We all are, Bella." They sit with her for several minutes before Kennisha stands, walking around the bed to hug Emma. "I'll get Brandon to track down the death wagon.

We'll need to strip the bed and clean the room before any other kids can come in here."

"She's number four," Emma says, patting Bella's hand.

Kennisha stands in the doorway. "I know," she responds, her voice just above a whisper. Neither of them speak it, but they both wonder how many more from their own church group will die from this.

More than fifty home church members will be here in less than an hour, and Emma needs to get busy. "I'll see you soon, Bella," she whispers, wiping tears from her face. "I miss you already, but I'm so glad you're with Jesus and not here anymore."

Even though there's a crackdown on Christians gathering together, house churches are springing up all over the city and country. Each time the number of people attending their home church gets this big, Brandon makes sure new churches are started, and it's time to do that again. This fellowship spends each day reading Scripture aloud and praying for one another. Some of them still have their jobs in hospitals and doctor's offices, the sanitation department or some other part of the city government, while others who worked for restaurants, retail stores, or other businesses that were destroyed in the attack are looking for ways to earn income. If someone comes upon extra food, they bring it, sharing it with the group. They know that they are in this together and need one another.

Emma understands from her reading of Scripture that they are much like the early New Testament church, and this realization often overwhelms her. It's her desire that they stay in the Word and follow Jesus closely, but she knows that makes them vulnerable to persecution, and she wonders who among them will lose their homes, their jobs, or even their lives for following Jesus. The group has been responsible for adopting or finding homes for nearly 150 children so far, and Bella is the first to die.

Emma is ushering the last of the members inside when she sees a man outside the house looking at her.

"Hi, Emma," he says, stepping closer.

She steps out onto the porch. "Lerenzo?" He nods as she walks down the steps to him. "How did you get here?" He points to a child's bike in the front yard. "You rode that from Queens?"

"It wasn't comfortable," he says in his soft Spanish accent. "You mentioned this morning meeting when I saw you at Marine Park and I thought I'd come, if that's all right." She nods, leading him inside. He notices the look of concern on her face and asks, "Are you okay?"

"One of our children died," she says, her voice breaking with emotion. "We're waiting for the death wagon." She points to an open spot on the floor for him to sit.

Lerenzo listens as the group talks about Bella and praises God for her life. They mention the latest children who have been rescued and how to get them to their families or into another one. They discuss how they can help the ones struggling with sickness within the group, and then they sing—as they always do. After that they read the Scriptures aloud, and then pray at length together, even the children.

In a world full of killer viruses, death wagons, and spiraling global conditions, Emma is so grateful that she has these people around her. She catches Lerenzo's eye and tries to smile.

CHAPTER 23

Rome, Italy

President Banes walks into the Palace of Justice with his security detail and steps in front of a face scanner.

"Welcome back, Mr. Banes," the woman at the front desk says when the door unlocks to allow him entrance.

President Banes pauses, looking at her. "I'm still President Banes," he says, smiling.

"I'm sorry, sir. Mr. Quade has asked that each member of the E10 be referred to as Mr. or Ms. He said that because you're one unified body, no one should be individualized or separated by titles."

He nods. "I see. Thank you." President Banes is quiet as he enters the elevator. After the never-ending sorrow of losing his wife and two young children in the disappearances, he realizes deep inside that he should not be provoked by Victor's petty actions, but he is. As counsel secretary, Victor is continually making decisions on his own rather than deferring to the rest of the E10, and his face constantly fills screens around the world on behalf of the governmental body.

Upon returning from the United States, once again President Banes feels broken and disheartened. The entire country is still reeling from the mass disappearances. The cities that were bombed in the days following the vanishings still look like war zones and will likely never pull up from the rubble of destruction, though he doesn't say that publicly.

Four months ago, an earthquake chewed up the coastline from California to Washington, causing enormous devastation. At 9.0 on the Richter scale, it wasn't as large as scientists had been predicting for decades and has left them saying that the Big One is still on its way.

This happened after the massive earthquake that had split the country in two, which has proven disastrous for transportation. It is impossible to transport everything by air, and the constant churning of the seas with massive waves has made movement by ship hazardous and life-threatening. Millions of immigrants continue to pour over the US borders, increasing the burden on medical care, education, housing, safety, and food production. Racial strife continues to tear apart major cities with multiple thousands of lives lost. After losing such a large part of its population, as well as the power grids in most of the major cities, the country has been floundering, going backward instead of forward. But it's no longer his country—it's gone mad like the rest of the world.

News stories overwhelm the airwaves daily from every corner of the earth with accounts of people slaughtering one another and death tolls rising into the hundreds of millions. That staggering number alone makes President Banes terrified at the thought of how many more will die. Among the victims are Jews who have become Christ followers since the vanishings, and they are losing their lives like no other time in history around the globe.

As President Banes walks to his office, he hears someone calling to him and turns to see Prime Minister Sophia Clattenberg. Nearly a year ago Sophia looked to be in her fifties with dark brown hair, milk-like skin, and bright blue eyes, but the turmoil since the disappearances has aged her by ten years.

"Good morning, Thomas. How are things in the States?" His face is grim, and she stops, clutching the files she's carrying. "I'm terribly sorry. I've seen the images. Devastating. No country is exempt. Did you see your granddaughter?"

Through his daughter from his first marriage, President Banes had become a grandfather for the first time just weeks after the vanishings. "She died when she was two months old," he says, his tiredness clearly evident in his voice.

"I'm sorry, Thomas," Sophia says. "I didn't know."

He sighs. "You wouldn't. This is not really the place to talk about personal matters." He purses his lips, looking at her. "It was measles. I thought we eradicated that decades ago."

"I thought we eradicated a lot of things," Sophia says. She glances at the security detail surrounding President Banes and leans in, whispering. "Could I have a word?"

"Of course," he says, holding his arm in front of her to lead the way. She steps into her office and he closes the door behind them. The television is on, revealing Victor standing at the podium a couple of floors below them. They watch as Victor speaks:

"It has come to our attention that crosswinds are steadily over forty-five knots per hour at airports throughout the world, cancelling all flights for a second day. Please check with your local airport to find out when flights will resume in your area. We believe the crosswinds will stop later today." Victor then ignores questions from reporters wondering if he believes the two old men in Jerusalem really did summon the crosswinds, as revealed by video clips. But Victor clears his throat to move on to his next topic.

"Looks like you returned just in time," Sophia says, turning down the volume.

President Banes watches video images of the two witnesses in Jerusalem as they continue to preach. From the beginning, the world has thought they were lunatics; their archaic way of speaking sounds ludicrous and their sackcloth wardrobe is considered absurd, but their power is undeniable—at least to him it is. Yet the more they reveal their power, the greater the hatred the world directs at them.

As they continue watching images of the wars, droughts, and famine conditions from around the world on TV, Sophia observes, "It seems we've learned nothing from history. We continue to kill each other and walk past the starving. And what about disease control? Prior to the disappearances, cholera killed 120,000 people each year. Will that number now be doubled, tripled, six times as many? And how is it even possible that bubonic plague has never been fully eradicated since the fourteenth century? It killed over 50 million people then. How many has it already claimed since the disappearances?" She scoffs. "We thought we were so intelligent, so savvy," she says, sarcasm dripping in her voice. "It's like the Middle Ages again. There still isn't enough medication to help patients in the pandemic. How many has it killed already? How many new viruses are out there? And why are they increasing?" She clicks the television off and motions to a chair for him to sit.

"How are you, prime minister?" President Banes asks before suddenly remembering Victor's new directive. "I mean *Ms. Clattenberg*."

She smiles and sits down. "I didn't think you would like that very much."

He sighs. "I'm still in office. When US presidents leave office, they are still referred to as president." He's careful not to reveal his aggravation. "But that was another era. It feels like a lifetime ago, doesn't it?"

She takes a deep breath, looking at him. "You'll find the file in your inbox with the proposal for the universal cashless system."

"From Bruno?"

She nods. "Yes, he put this together with Victor. It's from Victor's work with the European Union a few years back. It's solid. I see no other choice."

"I don't either," he says, scratching his head. "So many countries are in upheaval since that awful day, the US among them. I see no other way around it, and it's the only way we can all survive." He puts his hands on the chair arms, getting ready to stand. "I'll look over the file before our meeting."

"Ah," she says, reaching her hand out for him to stay and keeping her voice at a whisper. "Please tell me if I'm overstepping my bounds here, but your wife and young children. Were they followers of Jesus?"

He settles back into the chair, puzzled by her question. "Yes. Why?"

She raises her eyebrows, whispering. "My oldest daughter contacted me a few days ago. One of those men—you know, the Jewish men who are out preaching around the world? One of them was in Trafalgar Square, and Lindsey and her family stopped to listen to him. She said that he used the Bible and proved that all the people who disappeared were followers of Jesus."

He remains quiet, waiting for her to continue.

"She actually used the word *proved.* My Lindsey is the most headstrong woman you'll ever meet. When she was in second grade, she told me that there was no God. She set a path for herself and she has lived it, and no one and nothing has gotten in her way—least of all, religion of any sort. So when she told me that she stopped to listen to this man..." she fumbles for words. "I was stunned. Then when she told me that she and her family believed this man...I was speechless. I mean, she was a no-holds-barred atheist. Then when she told me that she declared Jesus her Savior, I was completely astounded."

Sophia leans forward, looking President Banes in the eyes and whispering even lower. "Thomas, do you believe that all those people were followers of Jesus?"

President Banes is uncomfortable with this conversation. He can't share his innermost thoughts with anyone here. This is the E10, the governing body of the entire world! "Everyone needs something to believe, Sophia. We've never seen anything like this in the history of the world. We all need something to believe in." She smiles, nodding. Eager to change the subject, President Banes stands up. "I should go read that file and all the others that have piled up on my desk in my absence. I'll get back to you later," he says as he exits the room.

President Banes sits at his desk and taps the computer keyboard, waking his computer. Clicking the mouse a couple times, he finds the file marked *House refurb notes* and opens it. His eyes fill with tears as he reads again one of the last emails he received from his wife.

> *Dear Tom,*
>
> *Just sending you a note to let you know that the children and I already miss you. This big house just isn't the same without you in it. I can't imagine how Harry Truman clunked around in here without his Bess. Although given the toxicity of DC, I certainly understand her reason for choosing to live mostly in Missouri over this. I'm praying for you as you travel today. I pray every day that God will give you the wisdom you need for the presidency and for this time. I pray that one day you*

will come to know him as Ethan, Ellie, and I know him. I pray that Jesus will be real to you and not just a historical figure. BTW…Ethan wants to have a family movie night when you get home. ☺

I love you,

Peg

Jesus answered, "I am the way and the truth and the life. No one comes to the Father except through me." John 14:6

He reads the same words he's read at least a hundred times since Peg and the children disappeared, and tears fill his eyes again as he closes the file on his computer.

CHAPTER 24

Rome, Italy

Get him out of here!"

At what sounds like gunfire, President Banes rises from his desk and hurries to the door. Shouting is coming from down the hallway and he reaches for the doorknob.

"Do not move!" a guard's voice can be heard saying outside President Banes's door.

"Come out of your offices and listen to me," a man says. "I am unarmed. I am not here to hurt you."

President Banes starts to open his door, but two security personnel hold him back. "Please step aside," he says to them.

"No, sir," one says.

"Is the man unarmed?" President Banes asks, trying to see around them.

"Stay where you are, sir," the guard commands.

"Answer my question. Is he unarmed?"

"We believe he is, sir."

"Out of my way," President Banes says to the guards, pushing through them and facing a young man with dark hair and eyes and a small frame. He is wearing blue jeans and a hoodie and is altogether unimpressive looking.

"Stay back, sir," says a guard who seems to be in charge, stepping in front of the president.

Sophia, Bruno, and the members of the E10 step into the hallway, along with Victor Quade and all their aides and personnel.

"Lift up your shirt and turn around," President Banes instructs the young man.

The guards train their weapons on the young man as he lifts his shirt high to his chest, revealing a slim build with his ribs prominently visible. President Banes reaches forward and pats down the man's arms and legs. "He's unarmed," he says. "Let him speak. What is your name?"

"Zerah. I came from Israel."

"You mean you're originally from Israel?"

Zerah shakes his head. "I just arrived from Israel."

"How?" George Albrecht snaps. "All flights are cancelled because of the crosswinds."

Zerah turns his attention to him. "The Lord my God brought me here."

"You're one of *them*," President Banes says, whispering.

"What can we do for you, Zerah?" Sophia asks.

"I'm here to tell you of Jesus, who died and rose again."

"Get him out of here!" George says. None of the security guards move. "Now!" George shouts.

"Sir, we opened fire on him when he walked past the entrance, but we couldn't stop him," the head guard says. "The bullets injured one of our own men, and there are too many people in here to open fire." As the guard is speaking, Victor pushes his way to the front of the now-crowded hallway.

Zerah looks at everyone around him. "Jesus said, 'I am the way and the truth and the life. No one comes to the Father except through me.'" As Zerah says this, the president's heart thumps frantically. That is the verse his wife put at the end of her last email to him.

More security guards rush into the hallway, their guns drawn. "Take him down!" Bruno barks.

"No!" urges the head guard. "Hold your fire. Opening fire will only harm others. Not him."

The voices in the hallway grow louder and more strident, and Sophia shouts to be heard above everyone. "Let him speak! This body exists to lead and listen."

"We don't listen to tripe, Sophia," Maria snaps.

"He is a citizen in this world, and he has a voice," Sophia says. "Let him speak." She nods at Zerah, and he smiles at her.

"Jesus said, 'Let not your hearts be troubled. Believe in God; believe also in me. In my Father's house are many rooms. If it were not so, would I have told you that I go to prepare a place for you? And if I go and prepare a place for you, I will come again and will take you to myself, that where I am you may be also...I am the way, and the truth, and the life. No one comes to the Father except through me.'"

"There is no father," Victor says. "There is no Jesus."

Zerah steps in front of Victor, looking at him. "The fool says in his heart, 'There is no God.' They are corrupt, they do abominable deeds; the LORD looks down from heaven on the children of man, to see if there are any who understand, who seek after God...Have they no knowledge, all the evildoers who eat up my people as they eat bread and do not call upon the LORD? They are in great terror, for God is with the generation of the righteous."

"The righteous?" George asks. "Is that what you call all those dead bodies you leave behind at the places where you preach? This body will determine what god people worship. Not you."

Zerah walks up to George. He stands so close that George steps back, uncomfortable. "There is no God but one, God, the Father, from whom are all things and for whom we exist, and one Lord, Jesus Christ, through whom are all things and through whom we exist."

Zerah turns to look at all of them. "But not everyone possesses this knowledge. Some people are still so accustomed to false gods that their conscience is weak; it is defiled. Salvation is found in no one else but Jesus, for there is no other name under heaven given to mankind by which we must be saved. If you confess with your mouth that Jesus is Lord and believe in your heart that God raised him from the dead, you will be saved."

"Saved from what?" Sophia asks.

"Death," Zerah says to her. "A death that will eternally separate you from God and his presence and blessings. God's Word tells us that."

"God has no say here," Adrien says.

Zerah looks at Adrien. "Our God is in the heavens; he does whatever he pleases. Power and might are in his hand so that no one can stand against him. His plan cannot be hindered or stopped. Jesus will come to rule over the earth. He said, 'Behold, I am coming soon!'"

"Coming soon?" Bruno says, laughing. "Who? Jesus?" He looks to the others and many of them laugh and curse, but President Banes remains intent on watching Zerah, who is unaffected by their jeers. "Enough of this," Bruno says. "We've been patient long enough. Remove him."

"But..." the head guard says.

"Now!" Bruno and some others shout. The guards step toward Zerah, but are unable to get any closer. Adrien swears as he pushes past some others, heading for Zerah, but something knocks him to the ground. He blurts out expletives as Victor reaches for a gun holstered at the side of one of the security guards.

"Sir! Don't!" the head guard shouts. Victor opens fire and a security guard and aide fall to the floor. Others kneel beside them, putting pressure on their bleeding wounds and shouting for Victor to stop. "Sir!" the head guard yells.

"Fascinating," Victor says, lowering the gun and staring at Zerah. "What a strange and delightful power you have."

"Power belongs to the Lord God Jehovah. It is not mine."

Victor cocks his head, looking Zerah up and down. "You are not a god then? A savior?"

"I serve the risen Savior, Jesus Christ the Messiah."

Laughing, Victor claps his hands as if watching a mesmerizing magic act. "So many names! Lord God Jehovah. Savior, Jesus Christ, Messiah. So confusing, yet you are fascinating, Zerah. So simple and so sold out to this hidden Messiah of yours. A true Messiah, a true Savior is seen for all to witness his greatness. Your Messiah is invisible and weak." Victor draws closer to Zerah's face, but Zerah is not intimidated or frightened.

"The Lord God is abundant in power. He can do all things, and no purpose of his can be thwarted," Zerah says to Victor. He turns to all the others in the hallway. "Satan has determined to have you. He is sifting you like wheat." Zerah walks past each one of them, looking them in the eyes. "Jesus Christ is coming again, and every eye will see him. He will cut off all those who don't belong to him and cast them into utter darkness, forever separating them from him."

"Pity," Adrien says, prompting several people to laugh.

"Call on the name of the Lord Jesus while he may be found. Today is the day of salvation," Zerah says as he walks down the hallway to the stairs. His voice echoes off the walls as he makes his way down the stairwell. "Repent! For the kingdom of heaven is at hand."

His voice becomes more distant as he exits the main doors and can be heard shouting in front of the building. While medics rush in to help the two who have been shot, members of the E10 move to the windows and are rattled, angry, or dismayed as they watch the young man walk away. The high winds continue to blow, causing pedestrians to lose their footing, but Zerah strolls without the winds touching him, continuing to shout what George calls "myth and fairytales." President Banes can barely catch his breath from what he's just seen, and doesn't realize Victor is watching him.

CHAPTER 25

Brooklyn, NY
One Month Later

Several children sit on the floor as Emma and Kennisha cut their hair close to their scalp. Then two other adults follow up with razors to shave off the rest of the hair. During the next few minutes, more than 40 children will become bald.

"This is the finger of God," the First Witness said in Jerusalem two days ago as dust from the streets throughout the world flitted upward, becoming lice and crawling on humans and animals and burrowing deep into their hair and coats of fur. There is not enough lice-killing medicine for such an outbreak, nor is their enough petroleum jelly or olive oil, which is far too costly, to smother the lice and their eggs.

Emma watches as Lerenzo shaves his own head. He shows up here each morning at 5:00 to pray and help in any way he can before leaving to drive a truck for the day. Emma finds herself looking forward to seeing him each morning but resists any thoughts beyond that.

Kennisha runs a comb through Emma's hair, meticulously searching for lice. For everyone within the building, there is only one choice to combat the plague. "It's okay," Emma says, watching Lerenzo shave his head. "You just have to cut it off." Kennisha groans softly, hating the thought. "They can strike the earth with any plague they want, as often as they want," Emma says, reciting the verse in Revelation about the power of the two witnesses.

"God's purpose for the plagues is to get us to turn our eyes off ourselves and onto him," Kennisha says, using a pair of scissors to cut off a handful of Emma's hair. "It's about keeping us focused on the return of Jesus."

"We sure aren't going to want to keep our eyes on each other after this," Emma says, watching her long hair fall into a dark puddle around her. "We'll look like brown and white thumbs walking around." Kennisha chuckles, and Emma joins her. There are so few opportunities for laughter that they both bend over and laugh all the louder.

As soon as Jamie told them about the church building, Emma, Brandon, Kennisha, and the children moved out of Mrs. Ramos's house, taking only what they absolutely needed. They took down the church sign and, for their own purposes, call the building Salus, a Latin term meaning "safety" and "salvation." Inside these walls they've struggled with the same plagues the world has and have watched as 23 friends and children have been carried away in death wagons after battling something as simple as the flu or strep throat, or worse ailments like the bubonic plague.

With each loss Emma is overcome by sadness, and her eyes fill with tears at unexpected moments as she remembers those who had grown dear to her. The number of children who have needed help has increased; more and more babies and young ones are being left to die or sold into prostitution or trafficking rings. Emma and the church members have their hands full trying to save children, finding them homes or bringing them here. It is dangerous work, and Emma still grieves the recent loss of three more members who were shot and killed when they dared to attempt a sex trafficking ring rescue. They've even had to fight off assailants who have come to the building to try to kidnap children. Vigilance and fear consume them as they go out into the streets looking for children and safeguard those inside Salus.

True to his word, Jamie and some teams of men travel throughout New York and the surrounding states looking for supplies. Each day, they pool together their money so a team can go out to find canned goods, bedding, clothing, produce seeds, and anything that can be stored for the years ahead, sometimes traveling more than 100 miles in search of what is affordable. This is not an easy task, as the prices of everything from eggs to flour to gasoline have skyrocketed since the plague of blood waters and the destruction caused by the locusts. They have planted a garden at a farmhouse in New Jersey, owned by relatives of a family in their home church, and hope it will provide some produce in the weeks ahead. Emma's stomach rumbles. She's been hungry for two days now. They're usually able to serve one small meal a day to everyone in the building, but the cupboards are now empty and there won't be any more food until the teams show up again.

It takes everyone working around the clock to feed, clothe, and teach the children, and they do it willingly. No one can bear the thought of any one of these children going back out on the streets, which are more and more becoming breeding grounds for violence. They don't meet as a church within this building, but in each other's homes, in small groups, so they won't draw attention to themselves.

Each morning at five, several adult volunteers show up to help with the kids, and Jamie, Brandon, Emma, or Kennisha begin the day with Bible reading and prayer. There still isn't electricity in the city and probably never will be, so gas lanterns are used early in the morning and late at night to help them see.

They use Bibles to teach the children, but the Bibles bear the covers of *Huckleberry Finn*, *Treasure Island*, *The Three Musketeers*, and *The Lord of the Rings*. The children are taught in groups of no bigger than three so that if an outsider unexpectedly walks into the building, they would assume that the children are reading ordinary books. Pages from the actual books are left inside so that Emma, Kennisha, or anyone else reading Bible passages to the children can quickly switch over to reading about Huck and Jim on the raft or Frodo and Sam's trek to Mordor. If the city leaders knew that the gospel of Jesus was being taught here, they would all be imprisoned or killed, children included.

Emma loves every one of these kids and prays for them throughout the day. A few of the older ones have run away from the safety of these walls and their faces still haunt her as she wonders why they would leave the shelter of this place. But the world is filled with temptations that are hard to resist. People can marry whoever or whatever they want now; restrictions are no longer in place. Underage drinking is allowed, and drugs are available on every corner. More abortions are performed in the city than ever before, and prostitution is no longer a crime. The money people can make by selling their bodies in a time of great depression is a narcotic that is sometimes too hard to fight.

Emma knows they will have to move out of the city eventually; it's only a matter of time before people realize this makeshift orphanage is also a haven for believers. Though the command from the E10 to hand over anyone assembling in the name of Jesus is proclaimed often, new believers meet here each morning until they can be put into a different home church. The doors are always locked, men are constantly on guard, and everyone keeps their voices low as they read the Bible and pray together, fully aware of what will happen to them if they are caught.

Emma's thoughts are disrupted as Kennisha finishes by rubbing vinegar over Emma's head to cleanse her scalp of any traces of lice eggs. Emma then cuts and shaves Kennisha's beautiful black hair. After everyone's head has been shaved, they look at each other and laugh before collecting the cut hair and burning it. Then they scour and scrub by hand the entire building, everyone's clothes, and all the bedding.

The next morning, as Jamie reads from the Bible to the volunteers, new believers, and children, Emma notices the shadow of someone running past the curtained window. She beckons to Kennisha, and they both go to the door. Emma cautiously opens it, looking outside, and sees no one. But her breath is taken away by the purple and pink colors dancing and swirling in the early morning sky. As she marvels at the sight, a soft noise catches her attention. She looks down and sees a box on the stoop. Picking it up, she hands it to Kennisha, then closes and locks the door.

Kennisha sets the box on a table near the door and carefully lifts the flaps. She and Emma lean over and discover a sleeping newborn inside, along with a note. This is common now; since moving into the building, babies and children have been left here at all hours of the day and night. Emma picks up the note and they read it together: *I heard that you take in children. Please help him. I named him Max.*

"There's no formula left," Kennisha says. Milk has been impossible to get lately, for dairy farms across the country were left shorthanded after the disappearances, and in many places no refrigeration is available to help keep the milk fresh. And formula had become too expensive to buy.

"What about Estela?" Emma whispers, looking at the young woman sitting among the volunteers. "Her baby is five months old now. She's still breastfeeding. Maybe she could help feed him."

"She's so thin," Kennisha says. "Would she have enough milk to feed two babies?"

Emma stands up straighter. "I don't know, but we have to try." Looking down at the baby again, she says, "I'm so glad you're here, Max." The thought overwhelms her: Max's mother had chosen life in a time of great darkness. This now makes more than 300 children who have been rescued from the streets by this home church. She walks quietly over to Estela and whispers in her ear. Estela follows her to the box and looks inside at the baby, who is now awake. "If you don't think you'll have the milk for him..." Emma begins.

"He needs to eat," Estela says, cutting her off. She takes the new baby and tucks herself away on a chair at the back of the room. She is 18 and has an infant of her own, but she can't let this child die. The love of Christ compels her and all the others who come here to volunteer each day. She shows the infant what he is now screaming for and prays that Max will latch on, smiling when he does. She pats his back and bends to kiss his head, a young woman barely entering adulthood, caring for a child not her own.

Brandon moves to the front of the room and opens his Bible. "John chapter three," he says, reading: "Now there was a man of the Pharisees named Nicodemus, a ruler of the Jews. This man came to Jesus by night and said to him, 'Rabbi, we know that you are a teacher come from God, for no one can do these signs that you do unless God is with him.' Jesus answered him, 'Truly, truly, I say to you, unless one is born again he cannot see the kingdom of God.'" Brandon looks up at everyone and rubs his bald head. "Do you know what God's Word says? We are not born right the first time. There is a wrongness in each one of us, from birth, that has to be made right. We have to be born again." He watches as Estela continues to feed the baby.

"This little baby," he says, indicating Max at the back of the auditorium, "who has just been delivered to us, was born into sin. We are all like this baby. We were not born the right way and have to be born again so that we can be right before God. I clung to my sins for years. I would be the first one to tell you loud and proud that God made me who I was, and God don't make no junk. But God's Word says we are all born in sin, and we must be born again. We don't become a new creation until we are in Christ Jesus, and only then can we live in him! That is our message to this dying world."

Others, even the children, pipe in with a praise, a word from Scripture, a short teaching, or a prayer for those among them who are sick. They pray for nearly two hours, asking for strong backs, obedience, protection, and God's mercy. In a world of uncertainty, fear, and tumult, Emma and the others feel safe, loved, cared for, and closer to God than at any other time in their lives.

Emma turns as she hears a knock at the door. She unlocks and opens it to see forty-something Umberto and his wife, Aleta, outside with Jordan. The couple has provided a home for Jordan since Emma and Brandon rescued her, Taylor, and Bella from Mrs. Ramos's church.

Umberto and Aleta step inside, and Emma notices the distress on their faces. "What's wrong?" she asks. Then she sees large, bulbous nodules on Jordan's neck. "Bubonic plague?" Emma has seen this several times already on church members who have died. Umberto nods and his eyes fill. Bella springs to Emma's mind and she can't handle the thought of losing Jordan, the fireball who saved Bella's life inside that church months ago. She puts her hand on Jordan's beautiful face, her long black hair now gone. "Antibiotics?"

Umberto's voice is shaky. "We waited in line to see a doctor for six hours. There are no more antibiotics in the city. The CDC said there isn't enough available for reported cases around the country."

"We'll pray," Emma says, nodding at Kennisha as they both put their hands on Jordan's shoulders.

Jordan grabs their hands off her shoulders, holding on to each one of them. "Don't pray that I'll be healed, Emma." Emma begins to shake her head. "I won't be here long, and I'm happy. I know where I'm going, Emma. I'll be healed like Bella, and I'll be loved like I've always wanted. I'll see Jesus face to face." Emma and Kennisha are unable to hold back their tears. "That will be my healing. Let me pray for you." She squeezes Emma's and Kennisha's hands and prays, "Thank you, Jesus, for sending Emma and Brandon into that church to save me, Taylor, and Bella. Thank you for this place that saves kids' lives every day. Please use it to save thousands more."

Emma could not know that in the days ahead, Jordan and baby Max would both be carried away in a death wagon, and that other plagues would soon ravage the world. But as shouts from the street are heard from under the doors, Jordan's sweet voice continues to rise in prayer.

To discover more about the biblical facts behind the story, read Where in the Word? *on page 269, or continue reading the novel.*

CHAPTER 26

Newark, NJ
Two Months Later

The E10's call for a unified global religion, eradication of Bibles, churches, and Christian material and the flood of fake videos the E10 produced has increased hatred against the two witnesses in Jerusalem and the 144,000 Jewish men who are preaching the gospel throughout the world. Under protection of the peace covenant, Jews may be safe inside Israel, but hatred against them rises all over the globe as the ICC, the International Criminal Court in the Hague, breathes out murderous hatred for the Jews, blaming them for the worldwide spread of pandemics, crimes against humanity, war crimes, and genocide. There is no peace covenant to protect them in Paris, Toronto, Ukraine, Buenos Aires, New York City, São Paulo, Berlin, and other cities. Countless synagogues have already been burned or destroyed and Jews murdered. Immigration to Israel is at an all-time high as Jews flee unrest around the globe for the safety and protection of Israel.

For this reason, Elliott has been concerned for his parents and his brother Ben. Following the snatching up of Jesus's followers, when Washington, DC, was struck with a nuclear warhead, President Banes directed the people in all major cities to evacuate. Elliott's family had fled to southern Ohio and have been living at his Uncle Harold's house for more than a year now. With the use of a satellite phone he acquired through a man whom he led to Jesus, he has been able to touch base with his family many times. They continue to reject his message about Jesus, but at least they are speaking to him again. Although they haven't felt directly threatened in southern Ohio, they have seen and heard the news and have not attended synagogue since the vanishings.

Elliott is exhausted. He has been up since 3:00, preaching throughout the city of Newark. When Jesus sealed him for this work, he was told to stay in New York City, and he did, until God called him to nearby cities as well. God often instantly translates him to those cities, but today he walks into the bus terminal to get a ticket to Philadelphia, and the terminal is packed full of others who are making their way out of the city in search of food and safety.

Countless thousands have come to Christ as a result of Elliott's bold message of salvation. But many of those who have listened to him and received Christ as their Savior have been badly wounded or killed. Believers have become targets all over the globe, making gathering together increasingly dangerous. Yet even with the E10's crackdown on Bibles, churches, and events where the gospel message is preached, people still come, risking their lives. House churches have sprouted all across the country, with groups of ten to fifteen people gathering in a home, apartment, basement, or back room of a business to encourage one another and read the Word of God. The E10 has tried to wipe the Internet clean, but people still find ways to get the message uploaded and sent throughout the globe.

Machetes, knives, or swords are held to believers' throats, and guns are held to their heads in a final effort to make them deny Christ. Reports and videos make the daily news as groups of five or ten or as many as fifty Christians are killed at one time.

Elliott steps onto the bus and it's packed; some are sitting three to a seat. Many passengers are still bald following the plague of lice, while others have sprouts of hair that make them look like comical baby birds. Elliott's hair is still full and thick and many cast wayward glances at him, wondering if he could be plagued with lice, putting them at danger once again. They all look weary, troubled, or tormented by the horrors they are facing.

Elliott finds a seat and looks out the window, watching as red, blue, and green auroras dance and swirl across the sky and the moon glows with a deep red color. The incredible sights in the nighttime sky each evening take his breath away.

"Look," a young man behind Elliott says to his girlfriend. "Aliens are communicating again."

"They're auroras," Elliott says, turning to them.

"Auroras are around the Arctic or Antarctic," the young man says.

"God gave them to us as a sign so we would look up," Elliott says, "and know that he is God."

The young man narrows his eyes. "We already know they're aliens communicating. Scientists said that."

Elliott looks at the young man earnestly and smiles. "God said in the Bible that, in the last days, 'I will show wonders in the heavens above and signs on the earth below.' "

The young man is getting angry. "You're one of them, aren't you? A Jesus freak. You're not allowed on here."

Elliott lets several people attempt to remove him as he begins to preach and read to them from Revelation. But when they discover they cannot do anything to him, they eventually settle into their seats, a defeated and fuming yet captive audience for the next couple of hours.

Philadelphia, PA

"Go and make disciples," Elliott says to those who have turned to Jesus as they get off the bus in Philadelphia.

Stepping into the darkened bus station lit only by gas lamps, he hopes to find a spot to rest. Philadelphia was one of the cities targeted by Russia after the vanishings, and its power grid has been decimated since the attack. With the exception of gas lamps and torches here and there, the city is plagued with darkness. He finds a bench to sleep on when the satellite phone rings inside his jacket pocket. He looks at his watch: it's a little after two in the morning. "Hello," he says.

"Elliott!"

It's his father, and Elliott can tell this is urgent. "Dad! What is it?"

"Elliott! You're all over the Internet! You and other Jews like you."

Elliott smiles, thinking of the E10's attempt to end God's Word on the Internet; God's Word will never be stopped. He can hear his mother, his brother Ben, Uncle Harold, and Aunt Lillian in the background, yelling and whooping.

"We saw a video of you saying that women were only good for raping and that you hated homosexuals and transgenders," his father says. Elliott starts to speak, but his father presses on.

"It was you, Elliott! Your voice, your mannerisms, everything. You were spewing hate, but we knew it wasn't you. You would never say those things or talk that way. We knew that someone was trying to destroy you, and we kept digging until we found other videos in which you talk about Yeshua." Elliott's breath is coming in quick, short bursts.

"We've all been up for hours watching and listening. We've sent the links to all of our family members!" Elliott still can't get a word in edgewise. "Elliott! We believe! We believe in Yeshua!"

Tears fill Elliott's eyes. "Thank you, Father," he says, looking upward.

"Those fake videos are condemning, Elliott," his father says.

"You didn't believe them," Elliott says. "Hashem says when you seek me with all your heart, you'll find me. You kept seeking, Dad. You found him!"

"Elliott," his father says, nearly breathless. "Just think of how many people who can't hear you or the others preach in person. Think of how many are seeing you online, just like us. When they find the real videos, they'll think that you are either crazy or you are telling the truth—the truth of Yeshua! Forgive me, Elliott! Forgive me for saying that you were dead to me those many months ago."

Elliott laughs as he cries. The bus terminal is dark and crowded but filled at this moment with the light of God. "Of course, Dad! I love you! I love all of you so much!"

"We love you, Elliott!" his mother screams into the phone. "We can't wait to see more of you and the other 144,000 around the world preaching and bringing people to Yeshua. Yes, I read Revelation like you asked me to, so I know you're one of the 144,000!" Elliott grins, listening to his mother. He had asked her to read Revelation chapter 11, but at first she was afraid to. She did it anyway, thank God.

"We'll see you soon, Elliott," his father yells into the phone.

Elliott smiles. His father has just said what he himself always tells people. "Yes, Dad. See you soon."

When they hang up, Elliott is no longer tired. He is eager to hit the streets of Philadelphia even during the early morning hours and share the gospel with everyone he sees.

CHAPTER 27

Jerusalem, Israel

The First Witness walks through the Shuk, the Machane Yehuda market, where his voice can be heard above those of the vendors. "Yeshua has said, 'See that no one leads you astray. For many will come in my name, saying, "I am the Christ," and they will lead many astray… And because lawlessness will be increased, the love of many will grow cold. But the one who endures to the end will be saved. And this gospel of the kingdom will be proclaimed throughout the whole world as a testimony to all nations, and then the end will come.'"

"What end, old man?" a young man in his twenties asks, confronting the witnesses. "It's been over two thousand years of people talking about the end. Look at us! The world is still here."

The First Witness smiles at him. "Hashem is calling you, Joseph. He doesn't want you or Lydia to die without him. He wants you to forsake your sexual immorality with Lydia and your lust for money and come to him." Joseph doesn't ask how the old man knows anything about his private life, but slinks away into the crowd, dumbfounded.

The Second Witness walks through the Arab Souk in the Old City of Jerusalem as people haggle over the prices of vegetables, necklaces, luggage, souvenirs, shirts, and shawls. He begins to preach, saying, "Hear these words of Yeshua! 'When you see the abomination of desolation spoken of by the prophet Daniel, standing in the holy place…

then let those who are in Judea flee to the mountains. Let the one who is on the housetop not go down to take what is in his house, and let the one who is in the field not turn back to take his cloak...If those days had not been cut short, no human being would be saved. But for the sake of the elect those days will be cut short...For as the lightning comes from the east and shines as far as the west, so will be the coming of the Son of Man. Wherever the corpse is, there the vultures will gather.'"

A girl around twelve or so stops and looks at him. "What does that mean? What is the corpse?" she asks, her brown eyes sincere and full of questions. Her mother yanks on her arm but the young girl stands firm, looking at the Second Witness.

He bends down to look her in the eyes. "The corpse is the one who does not have life in Yeshua. They are dead without him. It means that Yeshua loves you so much, Seleta, that he doesn't want you to die without him."

The mother furiously pulls on Seleta. "Come now!"

The girl yanks her arm away. "He knows my name, Mother! Listen to him!"

The Second Witness looks at the mother. "Shira, Yeshua is calling you and Seleta and Reuben and Z'ev to him. Today is the day of salvation. How shall you escape if you neglect so great a salvation?"

The mother begins to tremble, and the Second Witness puts his hand on the back of her head, just like her own father does to her and his grandchildren. She and Seleta believe, hugging him as passersby jeer at them or yell obscenities.

"What is the abomination of desolation?" Seleta asks, holding the Second Witness's hand.

"An abomination of revolting idolatry will be set up inside the temple."

"And that will be dangerous for us," Seleta says.

"So we are to get out of the city," Shira says, looking at him and understanding.

The Second Witness pats her cheek, a half-smile crossing his face. She hugs him, and he turns to continue his way through the marketplace. As the witnesses walk through the market areas, they call out individual sins, urging people to come clean before Yeshua.

From Rome, Victor Quade watches as the old men walk the streets of Jerusalem urging people to bow before holy Hashem, and his blood boils listening to them. No one is free from their torment as each witness looks at passersby, saying:

"You cannot store up wealth for yourself before holy Hashem!"

"You defile yourself when you become one flesh with another woman who is not your wife before holy Hashem!"

"You must not steal before holy Hashem!"

"You must not cheat or swindle anyone before holy Hashem!"

"Repent of your idolatry. You must not worship anything besides Adonai!"

"You must never defile a child before holy Hashem!"

"You must not hate someone because of their skin color. We are all made in the image of Adonai!"

"You must not look on or commit acts of perversion before holy Hashem!"

"You must never kill before Adonai!"

"You must not practice homosexuality before holy Hashem!"

"Repent of your drunkenness and gluttony before Adonai!"

And to all each witness urges, "The kingdom of Hashem is near. Repent and believe on Yeshua Hamashiach!"

Victor pounds his desk in disgust, his face turning dark with rage. He watches where one person may fall to their knees, there are many others who swear and scream, their loathing for the witnesses coming unhinged. The uproar these men continue to cause is immeasurable and disgust toward them accelerates around the globe, where their words haven't ceased to be heard. It is this bigotry and vile hate speech that must compel the E10 to call for the imprisonments and deaths of Christ followers all over the world. This cannot be tolerated any longer.

"Repent!" The First Witness urges. "Repent before holy Hashem!"

Violence breaks out as people try yet again to harm the witnesses. Victor leans closer to the screen as the First Witness stomps his foot and the earth comes alive with scorpions crawling beneath the mob and stinging them, causing everyone to flee. "They don't have that kind of power!" Victor shouts at the screen.

"Do you not yet perceive or understand?" the First Witness says. "Are your hearts still so hardened? Having eyes do you not see, and having ears do you not yet hear? Our holy Hashem says, 'For this purpose I have raised up my witnesses, to show you my power, so that my name may be proclaimed in all the earth. You are still exalting yourself and not Adonai. Behold, I will cause very heavy hail to fall, such as never has been in the world from the day it was created until now.'"

Victor scoffs at their words and social media sites ignite with rants and jeers, and news anchors mock the old men as deplorable and deranged, saying their diatribe has become "pathetic and laughable."

The First Witness stretches out his hand, and thunder booms all over the world, startling Victor. "So that you may know there is no one like Hashem in all the earth. The E10 will not save you. Only holy Hashem is mighty to save!"

Victor Quade yells in fury at the screen inside his office and jumps as great hail, more enormous than anyone has ever seen, pounds against his window. He runs from his chair to the window and watches as lightning strikes the ground and tongues of fire leap from the earth.

"Hashem alone is God," the First Witness says into the storm. "There is no other!"

Victor's eyes are as cold as steel as the hail continues to batter his window and shatters it.

CHAPTER 28

Brooklyn, NY

As the hail begins to fall, Emma, Lerenzo, Linda, and three others comb the streets in search of children or teens who have been abandoned or prostituted. Emma screams as Lerenzo grabs her hand and leaps for an abandoned restaurant. The door is locked and he shoves her against the door and wraps his arms around her, protecting her. The hail falls to the street as fire flashes brilliantly through it all; each massive stone sounds like a grenade exploding as it hits the ground or vehicles parked at the curb. People hurl themselves under cars, inside dumpsters or doorways, or break windows of businesses and homes for safety, while others fall where they are struck. Rooftops are set ablaze as lightning bolts strike and fire leaps off the street, scorching anything in its path, causing all those hiding to shout out in fear. Emma can feel the heat of the flames from the lightning that struck just inches from them and holds tighter to Lerenzo as hail shatters the restaurant windows. Shouts and screams pierce the air around them, drowning out her voice.

The unceasing pounding and fire continues for what feels like hours, but it stops as quickly as it started. Lerenzo turns to see the damage and Emma steps away from the door, her mind reeling at what she's seeing. The street looks decimated: trees are devastated, vehicles are destroyed, as if pounded with a large sledgehammer, and the pavement, buildings, and cars are scorched black. Five people are dead, crumpled on the nearby sidewalk and the road.

"Where are the others?" Emma says, her head swiveling as she tries to find her friends. They are nowhere in sight.

"Let's go," Lerenzo says, grabbing her hand as they run back through the streets to Salus.

When they are three blocks away, Emma is relieved to see Linda ahead of them near Salus, but gasps when she sees Linda dart across the street after two men, one of them dragging Lia by the arm toward a van. "Lia!" Emma shouts, running faster toward her. Lerenzo bolts in front of her when he realizes what is happening. Emma isn't breathing as Linda grabs for Lia, putting her body between Lia and the man. The other man pulls out a gun and shoots Linda in the head, her body falling to the pavement as Emma screams in horror. Lerenzo's legs burn as he runs for Lia who falls on top of Linda, holding on as one of the men tries to pull her away. He fires a bullet into her body before the two men dash into a van. Emma's knees buckle and she drops to the ground less than half a block away as Lerenzo runs ahead and falls next to Linda and Lia, turning Lia over and pulling her body to him, her head and arms dangling lifeless. He looks up at Emma as her face twists up in agony.

To discover more about the biblical facts behind the story, read Where in the Word? *on page 275, or continue reading the novel.*

CHAPTER 29

Rome, Italy
Six Months Later

Several members of the E10 and their aides, along with Counsel Secretary Victor Quade and generals from the Global Union Forces, get out of their vehicles at the Palace of Justice. Sophia Clattenberg steps gingerly to avoid the frogs covering the pavement and stairs leading to the building. Adrien Moreau and Bruno Neri use a mixture of profanities as the vexing amphibians hop onto their shoes. President Banes hurries up the stairs, trying to avoid the raucous, jumping horde that seems to condemn the arriving members of the E10 with every croak.

Days earlier, the two witnesses said from Jerusalem, "Thus says Hashem, 'I will plague all your lands with frogs. Rivers shall swarm with frogs that shall come up into your house and into your bedroom and on your bed and into your ovens and your kneading bowls, and into your businesses and temple. Repent and believe on Yeshua.'" Throughout the world, frogs came out of rivers, canals, lakes, ponds, and streams and covered the land.

Everyone finds their seat at the conference table and aides capture the frogs that have made their way into the room, running them outside. As always, the E10 is watching screens at the front of the room, assessing situations from around the world. They look tired and weary, and all of them bear scars on their faces, necks, or arms from the boils that broke out on their bodies just three months earlier, another plague inflicted by the witnesses.

Day after day, Victor Quade or one of the E10 members addresses the world, relaying information about the zones that are in place in regions throughout the globe, with promises of food, safety, security, and peace. Each day they watch these screens featuring satellite or drone images or live TV shots from across the continents. The coverage of wars and conflicts, drought and famine, diseases and illnesses, ever-escalating violence, and strange plagues is never-ending.

The Jewish men who are traversing the globe and the two witnesses in Jerusalem continue to preach their message of Jesus, which leaves most members of the E10 infuriated. Somehow, despite the crackdown on Christians and churches and the thousands of fake videos the E10 produced of the Jewish men and of the two witnesses via artificial intelligence, the message of their Christ persists, even growing in some of the areas where the persecution of believers is harshest. The screens turn from footage of prisons swelling with Christians to footage of men, women, and children lined up in locations throughout the world with executioners holding swords or machetes and beheading them.

"My God!" Sophia gasps, turning from the screens.

"They live by the sword and die by the sword," Maria says.

"What's happening with those people?" Adrien asks, pointing at different screens. "Why are they lined up that way?"

"These are the auctions," an aide replies.

"What sort of auctions?" President Banes asks, his tone wary.

"Servitude auctions," the aide says.

Sophia looks up at the screens. "We are seeing mostly women and children!" she says with anger. "Servitude?" She stands, raising her arms in alarm. "They're being sold for sex!"

"We don't know that," Adrien says.

She turns on him. "We *do* know that, Adrien! We're not blind. The world had more than forty million slaves prior to the disappearances, and the majority of those were women and children who were sold for sex. What could that number possibly be now?"

"They need to work, Sophia," George says. "Many of these people are no doubt providing for their families."

Sophia marches to the front of the room, pointing to a screen showing a child of nine or so. "This child right here, George? She's providing for her family?"

"She is most likely providing income to her family," George says. "Yes."

"She is being sold for sex! Sex with a child! All these women and young girls," Sophia says, sweeping her hand over the images, "are being sold for sex!" She glares at the members of the E10, her breath coming in ragged spurts. "And we yawn."

"It's business," Victor says. "Everyone is making money to provide for their families."

"It's children, Victor," Sophia shouts. "Children!"

"Why haven't we seen these images before?" President Banes asks.

"We weren't aware of them, sir," an aide says.

President Banes nods. "So, these areas of business, as Victor calls them, were just set up? They look like they're well operated. As if they've been in business for ages."

Sophia slumps into her seat, lowering her head into her hands. "We women fought so many battles over the years…our right to vote, equal rights, our right to choose, but this one we left mostly alone. There were some groups who battled sex trafficking, but that was an issue we didn't want to know about. We cried 'Safety!' when it came to women's healthcare and abortion, but for the most part, pretended these women and children didn't exist. What about their safety? We are letting children and young girls and women all over the world become slaves in the most horrific circumstances."

"Sophia…" Maria says.

"Don't say my name!" Sophia shouts. "All those children have names. All of them. But no one will ever know their names. They're just numbers and bodies. And money for sex. That's it."

Everyone in the room sits in silence for several moments before Bruno clears his throat. "What can we do about this?" No one offers a suggestion. "Can we stop this or at least curb it?"

"As Sophia stated," George says, "it was a catastrophic problem before the vanishings. Very little was accomplished to rein it in. This is beyond us now."

President Banes rubs his forehead, too stunned to speak. He feels powerless, and this governing body has proven to be ineffective and weak, incapable of keeping up with what's going on and making changes. How brazen they all were to believe that they had the answers for a world that's reeling in hopelessness.

CHAPTER 30

Tel Aviv, Israel
Seven Months Later

Yeshua is coming back!" Zerah says from the stage inside a crowded nightclub. "He says, 'Look, I am coming soon! I come like a thief in the night.' The time for your salvation is now."

Bouncers and members of a band had tried to remove Zerah as he jumped onto the platform, but their instruments were silenced as Zerah spoke. He looks out over the people in the dimly lit club, then resumes speaking.

"Yeshua says, 'I am the Alpha and the Omega, the first and the last, the beginning and the end. Blessed are those who wash their robes, so that they may have the right to the tree of life and that they may enter the city by the gates. Outside are the dogs and sorcerers and the sexually immoral and murderers and idolaters, and everyone who loves and practices falsehood.' If Yeshua isn't Lord of your life, you will be a dog outside the gates of heaven. He is the only way!" Many storm out of the club disgusted and angry, cursing and shouting at Zerah, but he preaches on.

"If you declare with your mouth 'Yeshua is Lord,' and believe in your heart that Hashem raised him from the dead, you will be saved. Confess your sins before Hashem, repent, and call on Yeshua as your Savior." Zerah hears a man cursing and pushing his way through the crowd, then sees him jump onto the stage. His face is twisted in rage as he shouts expletives at Zerah. Zerah walks up to Amir, his brother-in-law, and tries to embrace him.

Amir swings at Zerah but misses, and he begins to laugh. "What sort of freak are you, Zerah?" He looks out over the crowd, many who are baffled by what they've seen and heard. "What sort of circus is this?"

"You know who I am, Amir. I am a normal man. This is Hashem's power."

Amir gets close to Zerah's face, screaming. "There is no Hashem, you fool!"

Zerah shakes his head sadly. "The fool says in his heart there is no Adonai."

Amir raises his fists to the ceiling, shouting. "What are you doing? You are ruining our nation! We are finally free of Muslim terrorism, and now you travel through the country spewing your own terrorism. You and those old men in Jerusalem!" Enraged, Amir beats his chest. "You have destroyed our family! Your own father disowned you. You have ruined me and my family!"

Words of kindness pour from Zerah to his brother-in-law. "You are a wonderful husband and father, Amir. Go home to Rada. Go home to the children. They need you. You're their father, and they love you."

Amir begins to cry. "You have poisoned their minds. You won't poison me, Zerah!" He raises his fists in fury again toward the ceiling. "You and your Hashem will not poison me!"

Zerah's eyes are full of compassion and Amir turns away, unable to look at him. "I pray the time will come that you will realize your need, Amir, and when that happens, you will call on the name of Yeshua."

Amir wipes tears from his face, cursing, then pulls a gun from inside his jacket and opens fire on Zerah. But Zerah is unharmed, and instead, others on the stage are shot, falling wounded or dead. People run, screaming in terror. A bouncer quickly reaches for his gun and aims it at Amir, pulling the trigger three times.

"Call on Yeshua as your Savior," Zerah shouts over the horrified crowd, looking down at Amir, now still in death. "Hell is demanding your life! Give your life to Yeshua and live."

Baltimore, MD

When Elliott sees his Uncle Harold's phone number from Ohio on the satellite phone, he looks up into the darkness of night, where the planets are lined up in a row and stars are falling, creating cascading streaks of light across the sky. The sight inspires awe, and he answers the phone call with joy. "Hello!"

"They're all gone, Elliott!" a woman's voice screams hysterically.

"Aunt Lillian!" he says, stopping outside a bar in Baltimore. His heart pounds at the fear in her voice. "What's happened?"

"They're all gone! Your mom and dad, Ben, Harold, five members of our synagogue. All dead! They burst into our home and killed them. Only Petra, a young girl, survived."

Elliott can feel the blood draining from his head and slumps down to the sidewalk, yet he praises God through the shock and grief. "Thank you, Father. They're with you," he says in a voice that's barely above a whisper.

Aunt Lillian begins to wail, and Elliott tries to talk over her, but she can't hear him. "I had gone to get Joel, an elderly member of our synagogue. We've been showing everyone your preaching online. We've been reading Scripture to them and leading them to Yeshua. I was gone for fifteen minutes. Fifteen minutes! We never hurt anyone. Why would they do this, Elliott?"

"Because Yeshua said we would hate and kill each other. We've been killing each other for thousands of years, and now, nothing is holding us back. But Jesus says, 'Look up'..."

"Redemption is near," his aunt whispers through tears.

CHAPTER 31

Rome, Italy
Four Months Later

Images of the drought, which is now approaching its third year, appear on screens for members of the E10. In a world that was once filled with plenty, including excess food, nearly three billion people are now suffering from famine. In the years prior to the mass vanishings, famine was predominately limited to portions of Africa and Asia. But now, famine has spread across the globe, touching countries that had long been able to provide food and water for their people.

Where at one time insurgents and warring parties would block humanitarian aid workers from delivering relief where it was needed, that is no longer an issue, as there are no longer workers who even attempt to deliver aid. Even if there were, it would be too dangerous to get inside many of the war-ridden countries. Where food is available, it is priced beyond the means of what most people can afford, even in formerly prosperous countries. Meteorologists appear on the screens with predictions that many crops will fail again for the third year in a row.

Sophia pushes the plate of Roman artichokes and pasta away from her. "Take this, please," she says to an aide. "I can't finish it."

"Such drama, Sophia," Maria says.

Sophia scowls, looking at her. "You can eat? This table is filled with food as countless others starve."

"It only proves that food is available," Maria says.

"It's available for some, not for all," Sophia says. "Famine was once a preventable catastrophe!" She looks at President Banes. "Thomas, the United States used to be the number one contributor of humanitarian aid in the world!"

President Banes shakes his head, watching the grim images on the screens. "Those days are gone," he says, his voice hazy with the memories of his country's former glory. "We should be doing more," he says, searching the faces of the other members.

"Food zones are in place," George says.

"But we can't get to many of those food zones because of insurgents and warring factions," Sophia says, exasperated.

George shrugs. "We are doing all that we can to get food into the zones. The cashless monetary system is making it easier than ever to obtain food. We are all interdependent, helping one another."

Sophia opens her mouth in dismay. "But there isn't enough food, production, or transportation!"

Victor speaks over her. "It is as it should be. The universe continues to purge itself." President Banes sighs. He's so sick of hearing Quade repeat these words. "Did I say something wrong, Thomas?"

President Banes bristles at hearing Victor call him by his first name. "Wars, famine, exorbitant prices, disease, droughts, plagues, pandemics, beheadings, women and children sold as slaves—this is all as it should be?"

"I think we've seen that the universe is purging the weakest among us," Victor says. "Many are being eliminated, and the strong are thriving. This is our truth."

"We've seen it time and again, Thomas," Adrien adds. "The universe rejected the hate among us and took all those away who were filling our world with revulsion and disease. They were made weak by their cruelty, bigotry, and hatred, and the universe had to expel them from our lands. Once again, the weak are being expelled."

An aide switches images on the screens to reveal cities and towns throughout the globe besieged by conflict, showing pictures of decimated streets and gutted-out buildings looking more like grim jack-o-lanterns than hubs of business. Brown, torn earth and towns coated in ash stand in stark contrast to the shiny blue sky and glistening streets in Rome.

President Banes looks at the grim results of war and says in a tone that is sarcastic and strained, "Apparently our message of peace and security is still not being understood."

"With every conflict comes the prospect of peace," Maria says.

"How do you come to that conclusion?" Sophia asks.

"The ones who are victorious will reside in peace," Maria replies.

"Peace according to the victors," Sophia says, pointing to the screens. "What *they* want is not peace. They want power and control and death for their opponent."

"And that makes us more interdependent," Maria says. Sophia throws her hands in the air, exasperated. "Don't you see?" Maria continues. "Those who die aren't looking for interdependence, but independence. That's no longer the world we live in. We are connected. These conflicts will make it possible to connect us further."

"And our promise of peace and security?" President Banes asks.

"It's coming, Thomas," George says. "Many in the Middle East are experiencing tremendous peace. What we have done there is unmatched in history. Look at Israel."

"It is not because of the peace covenant," President Banes says. Several of the E10 members raise objections against him. "It's not!" President Banes exclaims. "It was the fire and brimstone and hail and deluge of water that fell from the sky that has kept every radical jihadist from stepping foot near Israel. That piece of paper did nothing!" Victor rises to speak, but President Banes continues. "Quade, you can fill every television and computer screen with your affirming rhetoric and false promises on behalf of this governing body, but it doesn't mean that it's true. Not for a moment."

Victor's face is hard and red, but his voice is quiet. "I simply pass on to the citizens of the world what this body would have me say. Our new world is thirsty for peace, and I know that all of you are doing your best to bring it to them. It is my highest honor to be a voice of peace for this body...for you, Thomas. Have we achieved perfect peace yet? No, but we will. The earth is groaning as it tries to get us there. The universe is expelling the unbelievers, those who are standing in the way of peace, and we must encourage the new world citizens to be patient and to trust the universe's process." He smiles at President Banes and President Banes nods, wondering for a moment if Victor is right.

"No one believed that a new world could be ordered in just a few months," Bruno says. "We all have to be patient and wait."

"*We* have to be unified," Victor says. "Just as we are asking the world to be unified. We must remember that we are the voice of truth and reason for our new world. There are lies and there is truth."

"And are they lying or telling the truth?" Sophia asks, pointing to a screen showing the two witnesses in Jerusalem. "Is this drought a lie? The locusts that chewed up all the crops? Was that a lie? Or when they said that our water would be turned into blood. Was that a lie? Because the dead fish coming out of those bloody waters proved otherwise. The dead livestock that drank from those waters and littered pasturelands painted a different picture from your version of truth. The cholera and waterborne diseases that spread from those plagued waters. Another lie? The lice? The darkness? The boils? Being mute for days. The hail. These blasted frogs? All lies?"

"We've been through all this," George says, "There are scientific explanations behind all these things, and..."

"They're clearly the most gifted sorcerers I've ever seen," Victor says, cutting him off. "And they're giving citizens of the world more reason to hate them," he says, opening the door to discuss once again what to do with the witnesses.

"We've tried to kill their message, yet that hasn't been effective," Bruno says, taking Victor's lead. "Some of those men claiming to be a savior have been killed..."

"Are you serious, Bruno?" Sophia says. "Are you proposing that we kill them? Just because you don't like their message? What world are we living in?"

"The entire world hates them," George says. "I think Bruno is saying there must be something that can be done."

"Like murder?" President Banes asks.

"Hatred isn't merely toward those two old men," Adrien says. "The outcry against Israel and Jerusalem is tremendous. That's actually an understatement. I've spoken with representatives in countless regions around the world who find this covenant completely biased and excessive."

Unfortunately, this ends the discussion of what to do about the witnesses for today, but Victor will bring it up again until something is done.

Some members nod in agreement that the seven-year covenant is biased. Of all the cities in the world, Jerusalem is constantly in the news. First it was the war, then the supernatural unprecedented intervention that saved Israel from her enemies. Then came news of the peace covenant and the rebuilding of the temple, which left no room for Muslim holy sites. That was followed by the grandiose temple dedication and Israel's rise as the world's superpower. Add to that the old men in Jerusalem and the Jewish evangelists around the world and people have grown sick and tired of all things Israel.

"Although I think parts of the covenant went too far," Bruno says, "such as letting the Jewish people rebuild their temple, which has invited hostility and war, the covenant does seem to be keeping Israel's enemies quiet for the moment. Which is why we have something akin to peace in the Middle East."

Victor remains silent, listening.

"But for how long?" Sophia asks. "Tensions are rising. We all know it. A Jew isn't safe anywhere in the world because of this covenant."

"The covenant remains in place," Bruno says. "If we break that covenant, what does that say about this body?"

"But how can we abide by it?" George asks. "The Middle East is a ticking time bomb. A shock wave was sent through the Middle East after the war with Israel that left Russia, Turkey, Syria, Libya, and the others obliterated. No country dared to raise a finger against Israel then.

"But time has marched on, and much of the world is reeling from the drought, famine, wars, diseases, and natural disasters that are coming against us on every side. When they look at Israel, which is prospering and has an abundance of water due to their osmosis plants, they get angry." Many members of the E10 nod in agreement. "Israel is in much better shape compared to the other countries in the Middle East. Their high-tech companies are pulling in billions of dollars from other countries that are desperate for their inventions to help them maintain a decent standard of living. Israel's oil and gas are being shipped around the world, while other oil-producing countries have been devastated by war."

George pauses for effect. "We've reached the point where the countries surrounding Israel aren't remembering that invasion. They're only remembering the images they're seeing on the news coming out of Israel each day. They're only seeing that temple stand where their Muslim holy sites once were, and they're only hearing those outrageous, hate-filled old men in Jerusalem who won't shut up. The Middle East will not put up with this much longer. We can only hold off the inevitable for so long."

They sit in uncomfortable silence before Maria says, "We haven't even mentioned what's happening in China." Prior to the vanishings, China made it known that they were actively engaged in a battle for global supremacy. "Their military might is staggering," Maria says, looking at the images on the screens. "And from what we can tell, Japan, North Korea, India, and Singapore are meeting with China. These are pictures from last week, with the military leaders from each of these nations visiting Beijing," she says, pointing to the screens.

Bruno shakes his head, looking at the pictures and videos. "What are they doing? What are these meetings for?"

"Why would a country like India want to be under someone else's rule again?" President Banes asks. "You didn't mention Pakistan, but they also struggled for independence from European rule, and I can't imagine they're toeing the line either. Just think of the size army that India, Pakistan, and the other nations could create. It could be one-hundred million or more strong. China wants world supremacy. Why would they give up their power or military might to the ten people around this table?"

"Because you are the world's governing body," Victor says. "We are one world now. There is no room for any nation to think independently of this body."

President Banes watches the military exercises in China and points to a screen. "I don't think Israel is our biggest concern right now."

At that moment the room seems to become dim, and President Banes looks upward at the lights. Others do the same, wondering aloud if the lights within the building are fading.

Sophia realizes what is happening and points to a screen showing the two witnesses in Jerusalem. An aide turns up the volume as the First Witness says, "Woe to those who are wise in their own eyes and clever in their own sight. And now, behold, thus says Hashem, you will be blind and unable to see the sun for a time so that you may have ears to hear."

Immediately, mist and darkness fall upon the eyes of the E10 and on all throughout the world, leaving people to grope about in search of someone—anyone—to lead them.

CHAPTER 32

Jerusalem, Israel
Seven Months Later

The two witnesses walk to the temple and stand on the stairs as onlookers groan or curse at the sight of them.

"Thus says Adonai," the First Witness says. "'I send my plagues so that you may know that there is none like me in all the earth. I strike you with pestilence to show you my power, so that my name may be proclaimed in all the earth. You are still exalting yourself and not looking to me.'"

He raises his hand, motioning upward, and the world waits.

Rome, Italy

Members of the E10, along with their aides and generals with the Global Union Forces, gather in their conference room once again for the afternoon briefing. A fly buzzes in front of Maria Willems's face and she swats at it as she takes her seat. Another fly grazes Bruno Neri's forehead and he slaps his hand in the air in front of him.

George Albrecht uses the files in his hands to wave away the annoying insects landing on the tabletop in front of him. Cursing, he looks around the room. "Is there a window open?"

Several aides check the windows, and all of them are closed. George swats flies off his jacket and from his hair, and Bruno begins to chuckle. "Looks like you're lord of the flies, George," Bruno jokes.

George isn't amused. "Get something to kill these things!" he snaps at no one in particular. "They're blowflies. Disgusting."

"What exactly is a blowfly?" Adrien Moreau asks, feigning slight interest.

"They lay their eggs on dead or decaying matter," George says matter-of-factly.

"Lovely image," Maria says.

The remaining members file in and take their seats, looking to the screens at the front of the room when suddenly swarms of flies swoop out of the air and heating vents, through the light fixtures, and underneath the windows and doors, creating a black cyclone of droning noise. Sophia screams as several alight on her face, Victor swears when a cluster of them land on his mouth, and members jump from their seats, batting away at the whirring pests. The room darkens as thousands of flies land on the windows and lights. Everyone rushes into the hallway, only to be met with a great buzzing tornado that wings into their ears, up their noses, and into their mouths. They flail and fumble their way through the hallway, down the stairs, and out the doors, but it's no better outside. The sky is dark with smoke-like columns of the swarming and harassing menace and people try to outrun them, slapping and swiping at the air in desperate attempts to free themselves from these terrorizing pests.

President Banes runs down the street, stopping at a building to catch his breath. He leans against the building, covering his mouth and nose and screams inside his throat. "This is you, isn't it? God, I know this is you. I know that you sent them. I know. I know that it's you." Tears leak their way through his fingers as the flies continue to swarm.

*

Brooklyn, NY

Emma, Lerenzo, Brandon, Kennisha, Jamie, and some of the other adults who help at Salus sit at a table in the kitchen area discussing who will search the streets today for children. To date, they've helped more than 1,000 children by either finding them homes to live in or providing shelter for them inside Salus. Twelve volunteers have lost their lives in rescue attempts, and Emma and all of her friends know they are in a deadly business, taking a risk each time they set out to find children or release them from bondage.

A fly lands on the table in front of Brandon and he swats it away. He watches as another fly buzzes Kennisha's head, and suddenly the room grows darker. They all turn and see black splotches on the windows, blocking out the sunlight.

"Flies!" Brandon shouts, jumping to his feet.

"The food!" Lerenzo yells, running to the kitchen, where the swarming insects are already pulsating their way into sealed bins of rice and crackers on the countertop.

The children can be heard screaming throughout the building as Jamie bolts to the supply closet, grabbing whatever packing or duct tape he can find, and throwing each of them a roll. They seal the tops of bins, boxes, and packages as the flies swarm and dive, landing on their mouths and whirring around their eyes.

To discover more about the biblical facts behind the story, read Where in the Word? *on page 279, or continue reading the novel.*

CHAPTER 33

Rome, Italy
Four Months Later

Most members of the E10 watch in outrage as the screens in front of them fill with images of the two old men in Jerusalem and the Jewish male missionaries canvassing the world with their message of Christ.

"How is it possible that those men," Adrien Moreau says as he points to the screens of the Jewish men preaching around the world, "and those men," he says, pointing to the two witnesses, "are still getting news coverage? Every time these men sneeze, it's uploaded millions and millions of times. We have instructed that everything be blocked!"

"There are countless computer experts in the world, Adrien," President Banes says. "They're going to know their way around a computer better than anybody here." President Banes looks at the aide standing near the screens. "Turn it up," he says. The aide turns up the volume so they can listen to the witnesses.

"Enter by the narrow gate," the Second Witness says as he walks through West Jerusalem. "For the gate is wide and the way is easy that leads to destruction, and those who enter by it are many. For the gate is narrow and the way is hard that leads to life, and those who find it are few."

The First Witness shouts, "Yeshua says, 'Do not fear those who kill the body but cannot kill the soul. Rather fear him who can destroy both soul and body in hell…Whoever finds his life will lose it, and whoever loses his life for my sake will find it.'" The witness pauses to look at the people in the crowd. "Yeshua says, 'The time is fulfilled, and the kingdom of God is at hand; repent and believe in the gospel.' Yeshua came not to call the righteous, but sinners. Do not fear the days ahead. Only believe on Yeshua, and you shall be saved!"

"You're for this?" Adrien says to President Banes. "You're for them being able to be seen and heard all over the world with this rhetoric?"

President Banes nods. "People need information. All of it. So they can come to their own conclusions. We have done nothing with all those around the world who claim to be a savior yet continue to focus on these men."

"Because those who are claiming to be a savior are harmless," Maria Willems says. "Their ideology isn't killing anyone. Their rhetoric isn't hate speech." She points to the screens. "Those men are vile, bigoted, and dangerous sorcerers!"

"Sorcerers who called up days of darkness and intense heat?" Sophia Clattenberg asks. "Sorcerers who killed livestock throughout the world and created flies and lice all over the earth?"

Maria and George scoff. "There were dead animals! Of course there were flies!" George says.

Sophia turns slowly, looking at them. "We didn't have dead livestock inside or around this building, but we had flies. So many of them that we were driven from our offices. They were so thick they looked like carpeting on the floor! We have experienced every affliction those men called for!" Sophia says sternly, getting louder. "We all broke out in boils that needed treatment for weeks and we still have the scars to prove it, yet each time those men say something we dismiss them as frauds or kooks. But everything they've commanded to happen has come true."

The room is quiet for a moment before Victor says, "And it appears that we can't destroy their message so…" He's leaving this statement open-ended.

"If we can't destroy the message or any of these men, why aren't we destroying their followers?" Adrien asks.

"Christ followers are being killed all over the world," President Banes says.

"Not because the E10 ordered it done," Adrien says.

Sophia raises her hand. "Are you recommending a Holocaust-level roundup of everyone who believes the message of Christ?" she asks, incredulous at the thought.

"That message is hostile," Maria says, shrieking at Sophia. "It isn't tolerant. No one feels safe listening to the words of those men. It's not a message of love and unity and acceptance."

"It does seem that the world is making us aware," Victor says, who has been biding his time.

"Aware of what?" President Banes asks.

"That we need to do something more," Bruno says. "We can't have our new world torn apart like this. We need peace and security. We need to offer that."

"These men say they know the one who offers that peace and security," President Banes says, looking at the screens. "As the governing body of the world we cannot mandate the killing of anyone! How will that provide peace and security to anyone?" The other members are quiet, and President Banes feels confident he and Sophia have quelled this horrific idea.

"You say the old men in Jerusalem offer peace and security," Bruno says, pointing to a screen filled with the presence of a man in his mid-forties and wearing a pure white robe. "So does that man."

"Who is he?" Sophia asks.

"Intelligence isn't in yet, but he is espousing a new faith," Bruno says. "One of peace, unity, and love. Turn him up," he says to the aide.

"We have entered a new age of spiritual consciousness," the man says in front of the Fountain of Apollo at the Palace of Versailles. "Our peace comes from within, and we share that peace with others. We know the way that is true and right from within, and we share that way with others. The divine is within us, and we share that divinity with others. We hold within us the power for the earth to thrive, and we share that power with the earth. We are being led by the great and honorable members of the E10 as they create a new world order, and we offer our energy and light to them." He bends down and moves his hand through the fountain's water and it turns red.

Victor leans forward. "Incredible."

"Just like the old men in Jerusalem," Maria says, gasping.

"Except this is a fountain, not waters throughout the entire world," President Banes says.

"He has the same power!" Maria snaps.

"But you have never credited the old men in Jerusalem with that power," Sophia says. "You have constantly called them sorcerers. How is this man not a sorcerer?"

"He is speaking kindness," George says. "And peace."

Victor watches as throngs of people gather closer to touch the man and view the waters. They're looking at him as if he's a god, hoping his touch will make all things new in their lives. "Mesmerizing," Victor whispers.

"His message is what people want to hear," Maria says. "That is the message that needs to be heard throughout the world. Not theirs." She points to the two witnesses and the Jewish men preaching on several screens.

"Then we must make that man heard and others like him," George says.

An aide turns up the volume on the two witnesses at President Banes's request, and both of the old men are looking up at the sky. The Second Witness begins to speak as if he is choking back tears.

"Adonai says, 'How long will you refuse to humble yourself before me? Oh, that you would have ears to hear and eyes to see!' Yeshua says, 'O Jerusalem, Jerusalem, the city that kills the prophets and stones those who are sent to it! How often would I have gathered your children together as a hen gathers her brood under her wings, and you were not willing! See, your house is left to you desolate. For I tell you, you will not see me again, until you say, "Blessed is he who comes in the name of the Lord." ' "

The Second Witness stops, looking out at all those too busy or too angry to listen as they shuffle by. "Adonai says, 'Repent. The day of salvation is now, for tomorrow the earth shall know death, from the family of kings to the family of the slave, even among your livestock. There will be loud wailing throughout the world, greater than the earth has ever known. Repent now! The kingdom of God is at hand.'"

As most members of the E10 scoff and shake their heads, a chill runs down President Banes's spine.

CHAPTER 34

Rome, Italy

Victor Quade stands atop the staircase inside the lobby of the Palace of Justice, looking grim and dark with rage. "We do not know how the men in Jerusalem were able to call destruction on so many lives throughout our beloved world, but we must face the reality that there is no scientific explanation for so many fatalities at once. Within our own body we lost sisters, mothers, grandfathers, and sons. General Voss with the Global Union Forces has died, a man whose guidance we depended on daily, and my own father has perished at the hands of these madmen and murderers. Precious livestock has died at a time that we grapple with food shortages and famine across the globe."

Victor glances down, gripping the podium tighter before looking into the camera again.

"You have my word that these men will be destroyed. I will personally bring an end to them. And our beautiful world will breathe freely and finally be at peace."

He refuses questions, turns his back, and walks away.

Brooklyn, NY: Ten Days Later

One child and two volunteers lay dead inside Salus the day after the witnesses said every family would experience death. Many more of Emma's friends were found dead among the home churches, and in a way, Emma envies all of them. They are home. Free. The plague of death was inflicted to turn the hearts of all throughout the earth to repent before a holy God, but the outcry against the witnesses and God has only grown more vicious.

"A man from the city came to see me yesterday," Jamie says, breaking Emma's thoughts at their morning meeting. "The city says we owe back income tax."

Emma looks as confused as everyone else. "What is our income? We don't make anything here."

Jamie shakes his head. "The city says we are acting as a hotel."

Their voices rise together. "A hotel?" Lerenzo asks. "We're a shelter. Everybody knows that we take kids in from off the street."

Jamie nods. "Grant...the man who came here, is for us. He's a Christ follower." He points to the shelves of books behind them. "He picked up *Jane Eyre*, flipping through the pages and reading aloud from the Psalms; he said his family has done the same thing with their Bibles. It's only a matter of time before the city or anybody on the street realizes that we're not a shelter but a church, and they'll arrest us and the kids...or worse."

"How much time do you think we have before the city comes back?" Emma asks.

Jamie shrugs. "A few days? Weeks? I don't know."

At the end of the meeting and prayer time together, Emma moves to a window and looks out on the street, where a duststorm rages. It began last night, forcing them to stay inside as dust blew thick and dark across the city. She is so tired and hungry and the thought of moving everyone out of New York seems overwhelming right now. She can hear Lerenzo saying goodbye to everyone behind her as he heads off to work. He gives nearly all of his paycheck to the work at Salus and the rest to his family to help them survive. He has been a constant, faithful presence for Emma and she can't imagine what she would do without him, Kennisha, Brandon, or Jamie.

"Are you okay?"

Emma turns to see Lerenzo and nods. "It's hard to keep up. Changes every day."

He steps in beside her. "We always said we would know when it was time to get out of the city."

She keeps her gaze out the window, watching the tempest of dust swirl feverishly a few feet from her. "I know. I know it's time."

Lerenzo has never seen Emma quite like this and is uncertain what to say to her. "Well, I need to get to work," he says, heading for the door. "I'll see you soon."

"I'm sorry, Lerenzo," she says turning to him, the words blurting out faster than her mind can stop them.

He turns back to her. "For wha…?"

Emma talks over him. "I've been so scared that I couldn't..." She looks out over the hundred or so kids gathering so Jamie can read the Bible to them. "But when I watch these kids and I see more of them come through the door every day, I know that I can't be scared." She looks at him. "*We* can't be scared." Lerenzo searches her eyes, trying to understand. "I just know that when you're with me…I'm not as scared." She feels stupid and shakes her head.

"No, no, no!" he says moving to her and clasping her shoulders. "Don't shake your head! Don't even think about shaking your head." He pauses, looking at her. "I don't know what today holds, but I know I don't want to face it without you. I know I love you and want to marry you, Emma. I've known that for months now."

Tears spring to her eyes. "But how? We can't…"

"Yes we can! We *can*, Emma! I know you're scared. But we live by faith, not by fear. That would've sounded stupid to all of us before the world was turned upside down, but now it's our strength." He takes her hands into his. "Would you be my wife, Emma?"

She nods and whispers, "Yes."

For the first time since he met her, Lerenzo kisses the woman he loves.

*

Four Days Later

Jamie officiated Lerenzo and Emma's wedding on the day Lerenzo asked for her hand in marriage, and the children cheered and applauded, making Emma forget for a moment the world they all lived in. Today, along with Brandon, Kennisha, and two other adults from Salus, they finish combing the streets in groups of three for children or teens.

After much prayer, and with the attacks against Christians becoming more frequent, Emma and the rest of the leaders at Salus have determined to move out of the building and relocate to the farmhouse in New Jersey. Some members of their home church have lived there since the vanishings; it's the farm that has provided some food for them over the last three-plus years and the place they've been using to store supplies for the future. Most of the children have already been moved there during the past two days, and the remaining five will leave this morning when a van from New Jersey returns for them. The home will be a roof over their heads—for now.

Jamie told the group yesterday that he's not leaving the city. "I can't go," he said. "My kids are still here. They need to know Jesus. And I can't leave this church because that's what it is—a church. I got a lot of things wrong when I was pastor here. But this building really became a church with all of us here. It was a sanctuary for kids on the street. It has been a place of rest for Elliott when he travels through. I can't close the doors and walk away. The doors have to stay open, and people need to know they can come here to find Jesus."

The thought of leaving Jamie behind still breaks Emma's heart, but she knows that he may be the only light shining to those who live in this part of the city.

A little after nine o'clock, Emma and the group head back toward Salus after finding a ten-year-old boy looking for food near to where the 316 Deli used to be, and a girl aged thirteen looking for work. Normally the teams from Salus stay on the streets for much longer each morning, but a van is expected to pick them up in thirty minutes. With a car already loaded at Salus, they'll have to split their group between it and the van and be on their way.

They walk the few blocks back to the building and, as they approach it, Emma notices that the door is ajar; they always keep it closed and locked. As she pushes the door open and looks inside, her knees buckle beneath her. She can't scream or moan; her mouth is open, but she's unable to make a sound.

"He said he'll see you soon," Elliott says, standing near Jamie's body. Jamie's head has been severed and the bodies of the five children lie strewn in a bloody circle, Ines and Signe among them. Kennisha moans, slumping to the floor.

Lerenzo is trembling as he bends over, trying to pick up Emma. "We have to get out of here." He looks at Elliott. "How?"

"I was about a block or so away when I saw Jamie outside loading something into a car," Elliott says. "A man walked up to him and I heard Jamie call him Grant."

"The guy from the city," Brandon says, breathless, his arms around the new boy and girl they've just found on the streets. The children are horribly frightened, and he pulls them closer to him. "He told Jamie he was a believer." The thought strikes Brandon and he says, "He lied so he could come back with more men and do this."

"I'm sure he thought more of you would be here," Elliott says. "Jamie was leading him into the building. I saw the man signal over his shoulder, and a group of men got out of cars and ran toward the building, but Jamie was already inside."

Emma is groaning, her forehead touching the floor.

"I ran down the block, but when I got in here, the children were gone."

Emma can't lift herself from the floor, and Kennisha falls next to her, sobbing.

"Was Jamie alive when you got here?" Lerenzo asks, his voice breaking.

Elliott nods. "I shouted his name, and some of the men tried to get to me. Jamie looked at me and yelled, 'Tell them I'll see them soon.'" Lerenzo and Brandon begin to wail alongside Emma and Kennisha. "Jamie said, 'The children weren't afraid, Elliott! They knew where they were going, and they were ready.'" Elliott moves to Brandon and touches his arm. "That's because of you and Jamie and all of you here." Brandon weeps, and Elliott wraps his arms around him.

Emma raises herself up to her knees, looking at Elliott. "Did you see it, Elliott? Did you see Jamie die?"

Tears fill Elliott's eyes as he nods, and she shakes her head. "I'm so sorry, Elliott. I'm so sorry for everything you've seen."

"Come on!" Lerenzo says. "We need to leave!"

"I didn't get to say goodbye this morning," Emma says, her voice failing.

"It wasn't goodbye anyway," Elliott says, helping Lerenzo get her up off the floor.

They rush to the street as the van from New Jersey pulls to the curb, and Emma looks at Elliott through her tears. "We'll see you soon."

He nods as they drive away, then heads down the street to find Jamie's kids so he can fulfill Jamie's last request: *Tell my kids about Jesus.*

CHAPTER 35

Rome, Italy
Five Months Later

Prime Minister Sophia Clattenberg steps inside President Banes's office, looking exhausted and drawn out. "Good morning, Thomas. How was your trip to the States?"

President Banes stands to greet her. "It was the same, prime minister. I did get to see my children."

Sophia nods. "How is your son?"

He shakes his head. "Not well. We said our goodbyes through a pane of glass. Security wouldn't let me near him." His voice catches and he clears his throat. "Another casualty of this new pandemic—whatever it is."

Knowing he doesn't want to dwell on his sorrow, Sophia hands him a file to change the subject. "For your review before our next meeting," she says, opening it and pointing to a note inside. She looks at him, urging him with her eyes to read it now.

He reads the hand-scribbled note: *I know you believe, Thomas. I know you believe that those old men in Jerusalem and the Jewish preachers around the world are from God. I believe too.* He glances up at her.

"Where is your daughter living now?" Sophia asks.

President Banes realizes she does not want to draw anyone's attention to their conversation by any sort of silence in the office. They are both aware that their conversations, cell phones, and computers are now monitored.

"Both of my children are in Illinois," he says.

She continues to talk more about her children to give him time to read her note.

> *My daughter told me to read Revelation in the Bible, but I don't have a Bible, and I can't look it up online. We took care of that, didn't we? She's been sending me handwritten letters that comprise the entire book. Instead of writing the name of Jesus she replaces it with my dad's name. The old men in Jerusalem are in Revelation along with the drought, the blood waters, and the plagues that they strike upon the earth. The wars and the deaths that follow, people killing each other, the diseases, famine. The Jewish men throughout the world. An evil leader. A false religious figure. Natural disasters. A great earthquake is coming. It seems the universe itself will actually shake. Too much to cover here. It will get worse, Thomas, if you can imagine it. You must read it. We have to do something.*

He looks over the file at her, interrupting her one-sided conversation about her children. "That's good to hear," he says. "It sounds like they're doing as well as any of us."

Sophia turns to the door. They can't talk too long without rousing suspicion. "We're all glad that you're back and are healthy, Thomas."

"Thank you, Sophia."

She closes the door as she leaves, and he opens a desk drawer to place the file in it. As he does so, he removes the small note and crumples it out of view of the security cameras, then shoves it into his sock.

Inside his apartment that evening President Banes heads for the bathroom and turns on the shower. He undresses and steps inside, working at removing a tile high on the wall that holds the built-in shelf for the soap. He removes the tile and reaches his hand inside the hole, pulling out a small New Testament. His wife Peggy gave this to him shortly before she and their two young children disappeared.

Fearing that his security detail would find the small book following the crackdown on Bibles and all things related to Jesus, he hid it in what started as a loose tile in the shower wall. He steps away from the cascading water to the back of the shower, opens the Bible, and goes directly to Revelation.

As he reads chapter after chapter, his heart thumps wildly. "All of this is you," he whispers. "It's you, God." He ends up reading Revelation in its entirety before putting the New Testament back in its secret spot. He doesn't dare read it through again, knowing that his movements inside the apartment are being recorded.

President Banes puts on his robe and walks to the living room, turning on the TV, where footage of Victor Quade speaking on behalf of the E10 earlier today is being played. He can see Victor's mouth move, but despite the volume being turned up loud, can't hear a word he's saying.

CHAPTER 36

Beer Sheba, Israel

Zerah stands outside the Jewish National Fund Amphitheater, where he has been preaching for the last four days. A few residents of Beer Sheba had heard him speak in Ashdod and asked him to come here. At first he thought he would preach once in the amphitheater and then take the gospel to the streets, but the 12,500 seats have been filled repeatedly throughout each day as Jews have come from all across Israel to this historically sleepy, dusty town to hear him.

The Israel Defense Forces have tried to remove Zerah to the delight and wonder of all who have been in attendance, and the harder they try, the more people are eager to come, hanging on Zerah's every word as the Bible he holds in his hand comes to life. Today, soldiers with the IDF use a weaponized drone against Zerah, but it merely destroys the ground around him and he enters the amphitheater unharmed.

Zerah walks to the stage, opens his Bible, and reads, "There will be great distress upon the earth and wrath against this people. They will fall by the edge of the sword and be led captive among all nations, and Jerusalem will be trampled underfoot by the Gentiles, until the times of the Gentiles are fulfilled."

The IDF surround the amphitheater, trying to keep more people from entering. But the crowd pushes inward against them, clamoring to find a spot to stand. In spite of the noise from the IDF, the audience is quiet, listening, full of concern but eager to hear more.

"And there will be signs in the sun and moon and stars," Zerah reads. Many people cast their gaze upward where what looks to be fire flashes through the clouds, turning them red and making the sky look electric. "And on the earth distress of nations in perplexity because of the roaring of the sea and the waves, people fainting with fear and with foreboding of what is coming on the world. For the powers of the heavens will be shaken. And then they will see the Son of Man coming in a cloud with power and great glory. Now *when these things begin to take place*," he says, emphasizing these words, "straighten up and raise your heads, because your redemption is drawing near."

Zerah looks into the stands, and many nod or wipe their eyes. "Truly, I say to you, this generation will not pass away until all has taken place. Heaven and earth will pass away, but my words will not pass away...that day...will come upon all who dwell on the face of the whole earth." He looks up at everyone again, repeating the words. "Stay awake at all times, praying that you may have strength to escape all these things that are going to take place, and to stand before the Son of Man."

He can tell his listeners are anxious to hear more and continues reading. "So when you see the abomination of desolation spoken of by the prophet Daniel, standing in the holy place (let the reader understand), then let those who are in Judea flee to the mountains. Let the one who is on the housetop not go down to take what is in his house, and let the one who is in the field not turn back to take his cloak. And alas for women who are pregnant and for those who are nursing infants in those days! Pray that your flight may not be in winter or on a Sabbath. For then there will be great tribulation, such as has not been from the beginning of the world until now, no, and never will be. And if those days had not been cut short, no human being would be saved. But for the sake of the elect those days will be cut short."

Zerah stops reading and glances up. "The day is coming, my friends, when every one of you will have to flee. Victor Quade will set himself up as god inside the temple and will have all of you killed."

This throng of Jews, like the others before them, knows. They recognize the signs in the sky and on the earth. They know what's ahead and are spreading the word.

And Zerah will stay here as long as the crowds continue to come.

To discover more about the biblical facts behind the story, read Where in the Word? *on page 285, or continue reading the novel.*

CHAPTER 37

Rome, Italy

As the members of the E10 finish lunch inside the conference room, they go over the worldwide reports being fed via the screens in front of them. President Banes reads through the information on one screen and his face registers confusion.

"What is this?" he asks, pointing to the screen and looking over his glasses at the other members. "Is that a graph, by country, of how many Christ followers have been exterminated?"

Prime Minister Sophia Clattenberg looks at the screen with horror. "Who put this chart together?"

"I did," Victor Quade says.

"Are those guillotines?" President Banes asks, appalled at the images on the screen as more than twenty Christ followers are praying and preaching as they are led to kneel before guillotines, where they are beheaded for the world to witness.

"The E10 has confirmed the production of and use of the guillotine as a method of global punishment for crimes against the global union," George says.

President Banes can't believe what he is seeing. "And one of those crimes includes following Christ?" The other members sit staring at him and his mind reels as he struggles to put words together. "We've talked within this body about dealing with the messengers, but how did that translate to the murder of innocent people?" he asks.

"We mentioned months ago that something needed to be done," Bruno says.

"We never agreed to murder," President Banes says.

"For months, people have been killing these followers on their own," Bruno says. "It hasn't been dictated—until now."

President Banes opens his mouth, but Victor talks over him. "We all know that suppressing the message is not enough, Thom," he says, making President Banes wince. "And you know people have tried killing these Jewish men around the world and the old men in Jerusalem, but without success. There is no peace, no safety, no tolerance, and no open-mindedness with these Christ followers in the world."

President Banes's face turns flush with anger. "Are *you* the one who ordered the murder of Christ followers around the world?" Victor doesn't respond. President Banes stands to his feet. "You don't have that authority."

"We gave him the authority," Adrien says.

President Banes is speechless.

"The scourge of Jesus vermin won't follow this governing body," Victor says. "You say turn in your Bibles, and they hide their Bibles. You say don't gather together as a church, and they gather together as a church. You say that the ideology they follow is dangerous and violent and intolerant, and they prove that it is by defying this body. Those two old men in Jerusalem call this body wicked and evil, and you sit here and do nothing about them. They tell people how to be victorious and wear a victor's crown. My crown!"

"They aren't talking about you," President Banes says, slumping back into his chair, grieved by what he's hearing.

"Quiet!" Victor shouts. "Those two old men are telling people how to wear my crown!"

Sophia notices President Banes's muscles tightening.

"They stood in Jerusalem and..." Victor looks at an aide close to the screens and commands, "Play it."

Footage of the two witnesses appears. "Be faithful unto death, and you will receive the victor's crown of life," the First Witness says.

"He said the victor's crown *of life*, Victor," President Banes says. "Not your personal crown."

The other members of the E10 hiss at him to shut up.

"The one who conquers, I will make him a pillar in the temple of Adonai," the First Witness says. "I will grant him to sit with me on my throne, as I also conquered and sat down with my Father on his throne. To the one who conquers and who keeps my work until the end, to him I will give authority over the nations, and he will rule them with a rod of iron, as when earthen pots are broken in pieces.'"

Victor asks the aide to turn down the volume. "They are agitating the crowds to violence, to be conquerors, and rule with a rod of iron," he says, his voice calm. "The Jews are being hypnotized, and along with Christ followers around the world, are all part of a resistance against us—against all of us." Bruno opens his mouth to speak, but Victor won't allow it. "You heard them. They are calling for a revolution and will be rising up to *dash us to pieces*. Those Jewish men around the world, which we now believe number well over one-hundred thousand, repeatedly tell their followers how to overcome. Overcome what? Overcome us! They are inciting rebellion against us and against our world."

"That's not what they mean," President Banes says.

The conference room erupts in anger, voices shouting against the two witnesses, the Jewish preachers, and all Christ followers.

Sophia stands, raising her hands in the air. "I agree with Thomas. Those men in Jerusalem and the Jewish preachers are not raising up a resistance. They are telling people to put their hope in Jesus Christ."

"Who is the leader of their rebellion," Adrien says. "We must silence these people and remove their energy from our planet. The IDF tried again yesterday to kill the 'blight of Jerusalem.' They were unsuccessful. Show them," he says, nodding at an aide. The aide plays footage of a drone flying near Independence Park in Jerusalem. "This drone was equipped for a targeted kill to minimize collateral damage. Watch."

They all watch the screen as a missile strike hits the two witnesses and several people fall to the ground, engulfed by a cloud of dust mushrooming to the height of the surrounding trees. The two witnesses emerge from the ash preaching; their clothes are without scorch marks and the hairs of their beards unsinged.

"Time and again they have escaped death, but we must find a way," Adrien says.

"We do not kill people!" Sophia exclaims. "That is not what this governing body is about! We are supposed to lead and help and create a world where people can live in peace without fear of being murdered because of what they believe."

"We *are* leading," Maria says. "Each day we come to this room and determine what is the next right thing to do."

"I don't recall any meeting where we discussed killing Christ followers," President Banes says with controlled anger.

"We had the meeting without you and Sophia," Bruno says.

Sophia collapses into her chair. "You what?"

Bruno raises his hands to calm her. "It has become obvious during the last several months that neither of you are thinking rationally." President Banes and Sophia begin to talk over him, but he waves at them dismissively, talking louder. "You are both strong, powerful leaders, but we knew you would not be for this. We also knew that we are the majority and you are only two voices. We had to do something," he says, looking at them. "No matter how tightly we are clamping down, this message of Christ is still spreading."

"The message of Islam is still spreading," Sophia says. "Or have you not noticed how many people have died at their hands? That message is spreading, but none of you are concerned. Yet you have this myopic concern for this group of people who aren't killing anyone!"

"Their message is killing us," Bruno says. "It's killing our world by spreading a hate that cannot be contained."

"The Word of God cannot be stopped," President Banes says, just above a whisper. "My wife told me that. The Word of the Lord endures forever." He looks at them. "You suppress the Word, and it spreads. You attempt to destroy the Word, and it thrives. You kill people of the Word, and it lives on still." He and Sophia sit in silence, feeling sickened by what they've heard from the others. "This must stop," he says.

"There is no stopping it, Thomas," George says.

"I will find a way," President Banes says.

"There is no way," Victor says.

CHAPTER 38

Rome, Italy

Hours later, President Banes pulls together his things for home. He's leaving early today; he is still sickened by what happened at the meeting and he feels like he's coming down with something. He's been fighting chills for the last couple hours, and now he's nauseated and burning up. Sophia indicated earlier she was concerned that something she ate during lunch was making her ill. He'll check on her before he leaves. As he reaches for his computer, his cell phone rings. It's Sophia.

"Hi Sophia," he says, putting his computer in its case.

"It's Victor. I have her phone."

President Banes continues to gather his things. "Why do you...?"

"The nausea and the sweats are the last stage, Thomas."

President Banes stops what he's doing.

"Your heart will stop, and that's it. It will all be over."

President Banes slumps to his chair, unfastening the top two buttons on his shirt. "What are you saying, Quade?"

"Do you think that you and Sophia are clever enough to outsmart me?"

President Banes stands and realizes he's losing control of his legs. He stumbles for the door and out into the hallway for Sophia's office.

He opens her door and she's slumped in her chair. He rushes over and reaches for her head to lift it, but can see by her face that she's dead.

"She's already dead, Thom," Victor says on the other end of the phone.

President Banes turns back to the door, wondering where everyone is. "Why?"

"The three of you will never let me lead like the others will."

President Banes staggers into the hallway, holding himself up against the wall. "Three?"

Victor sighs. "Bruno, of course."

President Banes heads for Bruno's office.

"He's too strong. Or *was* too strong," Victor says.

President Banes opens Bruno's door to find him sprawled dead on the floor.

"Sorry that no one is there to help you, Thom. The E10 was called downstairs for an unscheduled press photo. By the time they realize the three of you aren't there and send someone to find you, you'll all be gone. Sadly, the three of you were the only ones to eat the soup. The others will soon know how fortunate they are to be alive."

"You'll be destroyed, Victor," President Banes says, his voice coming out in gasps. "Jesus is coming, and you'll be cast alive into the lake of fire. Your end is already written."

"So is yours," Victor says, hanging up.

President Banes tries to get to his office but falls to the floor in the hallway. His breath is ragged and thin as he opens the photos on his phone, clicking on the one of Peg and his two young children at one of Ryan's Little League baseball games. He holds his eyes open as long as he can, looking at them.

CHAPTER 39

Jerusalem, Israel
Two Months Later

Zerah breaks through the throng of Global Union and Israel Defense Forces soldiers surrounding Jerusalem. Several try to stop him, but it is no use. He runs through the streets, pursued by soldiers armed to the hilt. He bounds up the temple stairs, where the two witnesses are preaching, and every soldier's gun is trained on them.

Victor Quade is standing at the bottom of the stairs, looking at the witnesses in amusement. Following the deaths of President Banes, Prime Minister Sophia Clattenberg, and Bruno Neri, Victor took leadership of the E10 and called Prime Minister Ari, convincing him he had a plan to rid the world of the two old men in Jerusalem. For the last 60 days, soldiers have attempted to kill the witnesses by firing on them or using biological or chemical weapons. The entire world has stood on edge each day, watching the drama play out live on screens around the globe.

Yet each time an assassination attempt is made, the two witnesses deter or destroy more soldiers—sometimes with fire from their mouths, and on other occasions with thousands of deadly Mediterranean recluse spiders crawling over them, hordes of flying black beetles infesting them, blinding sunlight, biting scorpions, powerful winds, poisonous vipers, and crevices opening in the earth. With each attack on the witnesses, more Jews come to Yeshua.

"Turn from your sins, O Israel!" the First Witness says. "Hear the word of the Lord! You are the apple of his eye. The man of sin is here with you, longing for your souls and the soul of Israel. Adonai loves you and longs for you. Today is the day of salvation. Repent and follow Yeshua!"

Zerah prays and opens his arms wide. "Repent and follow Yeshua!" he shouts to the crowd and the soldiers surrounding the temple.

"Repent and follow Yeshua!" the two witnesses shout together.

Victor raises an arm in the air, just as he's done dozens of times each day over the last 60 days, and every soldier opens fire, this time riddling the witnesses with bullet holes. The witnesses fall to the ground, the First Witness tumbling down several stairs and breaking his neck. The Second Witness is splayed across the stairs, his eyes fixed to the skies. The soldiers and many onlookers pause for a long moment before breaking into cheers. Others in the crowd fall to their knees, weeping.

Zerah stands alone at the bottom of the stairs looking at their bodies. When people realize that the two men are actually dead, they begin to celebrate—first in Jerusalem, then around the world as the news about them goes viral.

Victor walks up the stairs, stands next to the fallen witnesses, bends over each one to take a closer look, and then rises up, smiling and stringing together a slew of curses. "It is finished!" he says, pumping his fist into the air to shouts and cheers. "They are *dead*!"

The crowd erupts again, and Victor raises his arms to quiet them. "As a reward for how they've plagued our world, let's leave their bodies here to rot until everyone around the globe has been able to see them. And we can all celebrate their deaths together in unity." The crowd screams in delight, and Victor continues: "Our world will finally know peace!"

Zerah looks at Victor and slowly ascends the stairs. Soldiers try in vain to keep him away from Victor but cannot. Zerah steps right up to Victor, looking him in the eye.

"You're next," Victor sneers. "You, and all the parasites like you."

"All that God has purposed, he will do," Zerah says. "The Word of God endures forever."

Victor smiles. "Those were Thomas Banes's last feeble words before he died."

Zerah shakes his head. "You can kill the body, but you cannot kill the soul." He stands next to the body of the Second Witness and turns to the crowd. "Today is the day of salvation! The kingdom of Hashem is at hand. Repent of your sins and follow Yeshua!"

For three days straight, news from around the world has provided nonstop footage of the two witnesses dead in Jerusalem. People have held parties and exchanged gifts because, in the words of Victor Quade on a newscast, "Our global nightmare has ended." Prime Minister Ari has been celebrating with Victor in Israel, but it is Victor alone who has stood in front of the witnesses's dead bodies for countless interviews.

Zerah has stayed in Jerusalem, preaching as Jews have been celebrating in the streets, urging them to flee the city. "Víctor Quade will set himself up as the holy one inside the temple. Yeshua told us that when this happens to 'flee to the mountains.' He told us that great tribulation is coming. Worse than what we've already seen. Get out of the country—get out now! Repent and believe in the gospel of Yeshua. My fellow Jews, Hashem loves you. Repent and believe on Yeshua."

Hours later, Zerah remains on the temple steps, where birds pick away at the decaying flesh of the two witnesses and dogs tear them to pieces, the rotting odor of their corpses permeating the temple area. He stands at the bottom of the stairs, still imploring sinners to believe in Yeshua. Out of the corner of his eye he sees a finger on the hand of the Second Witness tremble. He stops, holding his breath, turning to look.

In a sudden and noisy migration, the birds fly away from the bodies. Decomposing, white flesh on the two witnesses is being renewed with smooth, healthy skin, alive with color. Eyes appear in their pecked-out sockets, bones fuse together, and muscles form in the bodies of both men, making their limbs strong. Onlookers scream in terror, and surveillance cameras instantly feed the images worldwide. Victor Quade shouts in anger as he watches this live on television in his plush hotel room nearby. Horrified viewers around the globe caterwaul at the sight.

"Praise you, Adonai!" Zerah says, watching the breath of God raise the two witnesses to their feet. "Praise you, Adonai!" he shouts louder as the men rise upward into the clouds. Zerah continues to shout praises as the crowd, struck with terror, wails. Shock and unbelief ricochet around the world.

Victor curses and shouts, running from his hotel room for the temple when the floor beneath him shakes violently. The hotel ceiling and walls fold on top of him like a paper napkin and a steel beam gouges his head, crushing it beneath the weight. His lifeless body lays bloody and pinned beneath the girders as a tenth of the city crumbles during the massive earthquake.

The entire universe shudders, trembling at what is coming. Buildings, roads, homes, and lives crumple in the severe shaking, more violent than anything the earth has ever known, triggering volcanic eruptions around the globe and filling the skies with ash. The heavens shake and meteors are knocked loose from their orbits in the galaxy, falling like stars to the earth and scorching the land beneath them. The skies recoil as if in fear, rolling up like a scroll, and mountains and islands tremble and shift as people sob and scream, trying to hide from the unyielding calamity.

"It is the wrath of Hashem!" Prime Minister Ari wails, hiding in the tunnels beneath Jerusalem.

"God's wrath has come!" Adrien Moreau cries inside the Palace of Justice seconds before the building collapses on top of him and the remaining members of the E10.

Emma, Lerenzo, Brandon, Kennisha, and the 30-plus children inside the farm home in New Jersey scramble beneath the four cafeteria tables they brought from Salus. Those who can't get under the tables drop to their knees, covering their heads as the house rattles like a child's toy. They cry out together in prayer and, on the other side of the world, the screams of many of the terrified survivors in Jerusalem turn to praise as they give glory to Adonai. Those who realize they should heed the words of the two witnesses and Zerah forsake their homes and run for their lives, out of the city and away from their beloved country.

The earth grows darker as thick layers of volcanic ash block the sun and people cry out in terror, pleading for the mountains to fall on them, or at the very least, hide them from the wrath of God. And Zerah, Elliott, and their fellow Jewish evangelists continue to preach salvation in Jesus as meteors, which bring catastrophic destruction, fall around them.

To discover more about the biblical facts behind the story, read Where in the Word? *on page 291, or continue reading the novel.*

WHERE IN THE WORD?

WHERE IN THE WORD?

THRASHING TIME

Our friend Carolyn Arends is a brilliant songwriter and author who lives in Canada. She tells the story of being a young girl in church and listening to a missionary couple from a steamy jungle one Sunday morning. Her interest was piqued when the couple told about an enormous snake, much longer than a man's body, that slithered its way into their home. She says,

> Terrified, they ran outside and searched frantically for a local who might know what to do. A machete-wielding neighbor came to the rescue, calmly marching into their house and decapitating the snake with one clean chop. The neighbor reemerged triumphant and assured the missionaries that the reptile had been defeated. But there was a catch, he warned: It was going to take a while for the snake to realize it was dead. A snake's neurology and blood flow are such that it can take considerable time for it to stop moving even after decapitation. For the next several hours, the missionaries were forced to wait outside while the snake thrashed about, smashing furniture and flailing against walls and windows, wreaking havoc until its body finally understood that it no longer had a head.

> Sweating in the heat, they had felt frustrated and a little sickened but also grateful that the snake's rampage wouldn't last forever. And at some point in their waiting, they told us, they had a mutual epiphany. I leaned in with the rest of the congregation, queasy and fascinated. "Do you see it?" asked the husband. "Satan is a lot like that big old snake. He's already been defeated. He just doesn't know it yet. In the meantime, he's going to do some damage. But never forget that he's a goner."[1]

When it seems that the world has gone mad, when it's difficult to hear one more story of genocide, sex trafficking, violence in the streets, fighting in Congress, the COVID-19 pandemic that shut down our country and much of the world, or vitriol in social media, remember that it's thrashing time. Satan knows his time is short and he's going to do major damage and claim many lives as he thrashes about, but as it is written in the Bible, Jesus has already crushed that great serpent's head (Genesis 3:15).

As I did in *The Time of Jacob's Trouble*, I will take you into the pages of the Bible to discover where I gathered the plotline for *The Day of Ezekiel's Hope*. Quite honestly, I don't think I'm capable of writing how the end of days will play out on earth. I can't fully comprehend how Satan will thrash about in those days, but I believe they will be far worse and far more supernatural than any fiction story could ever tell. God will pull out all the stops to bring people to Him; He will dispatch the 144,000 Jewish evangelists like Elliott and Zerah around the world to spread the gospel of Jesus, and the two witnesses will preach for three-and-a-half years in Jerusalem. Even so, Jesus says that wickedness will increase (Matthew 24:12) and if those days hadn't been cut short, no human being would survive (verse 22). Those will be "perilous times" (2 Timothy 3:1 KJV). The definition of the Greek New Testament word translated "perilous" is "dangerous, furious, fierce."

We're also told that during these days "evil men and seducers shall wax worse and worse, deceiving, and being deceived" (2 Timothy 3:13 KJV), with "men's hearts failing them for fear" (Luke 21:26 KJV).

The Greek word translated "failing" means "to expire." That time will be so horrifying that people's hearts will literally stop from fear. No, I haven't done an adequate job in portraying those coming days.

THE LAST HOUR

The apostle John said, "Children, it is the last hour" (1 John 2:18). If John was in "the last hour" in the first century, then surely we who are alive today must be in the last milliseconds before Christ's return. In an interview, Billy Graham said, "We're coming toward the end of the age, not the end of the world or the earth but the end of the age—the period that God has set aside for this particular time. There's a great deal to say in the Bible about the signs to watch for in the time prior to Christ's return [Matthew 24; Mark 13; Luke 21; Acts 2:17; 2 Peter 3:3; 1 Timothy 4:1; 2 Timothy 3:1-7; etc.], and when these signs all converge at once, we can be sure that we're close to the end of the age."[2] And those signs, in my judgment, are converging now for the first time in history.

The prophecies of Jesus's first coming are well known and are often thought of in connection with the angels, shepherds, and animals that make up each of our nativity scenes. But at the time of Christ's birth, there were few who actually knew the signs of His coming and who recognized who He was. For example, Mary's cousin Elizabeth recognizes that Mary is carrying the Christ child, and even John the Baptist leaps inside his mother's womb when Mary was nearby (Luke 1:39-45). Simeon and Anna know that the baby Jesus is the Messiah (Luke 2:25-38), and the magi know to follow the star that leads to where He is (Matthew 2:1-12). And as Jesus fulfilled prophecies during His time of ministry on earth, how many people recognized who He was, and how many refused to believe? How many today still refuse to believe? How many recognize the signs of His second coming?

In *Things to Come,* Dr. J. Dwight Pentecost wrote, "God, the architect of the ages, has seen fit to take us into His confidence concerning His plans for the future, and has revealed His purpose and program in detail in the Word." When we look at today's headlines in light of Bible prophecy, "we're investigating the case of current events with secret intelligence provided by the God of time and eternity."[3] In other words, the signs God has given us are intel in advance!

WATCH THE SIGNS AND STAY AWAKE

God has given us the signs to recognize that the second coming of Christ is drawing near, and as you may have heard, He has done so to prepare us, not to scare us. The signs are there to keep us looking up!

Several years ago, I was driving to an out-of-state event and was talking to my mom on the phone. She said, "Be sure you pay attention to the map and watch the signs." Her advice rings true for Bible prophecy. Throughout Scripture, God gives us signs and warnings before He sends judgment. Just like signs on a highway, God's signs become more frequent as we get closer to the destination, and the destination here is the second coming of Christ.

Like the sons of Issachar, we need to be discerners of the times (1 Chronicles 12:32 NIV). The Pharisees and Sadducees were *not* like the sons of Issachar. Matthew 16:2-3 says they came to Jesus and tested Him by asking Him to show them a sign from heaven. He replied, "When evening comes, you say, 'It will be fair weather, for the sky is red,' and in the morning, 'Today it will be stormy, for the sky is red and overcast.' You know how to interpret the appearance of the sky, *but you cannot interpret the signs of the times*" (NIV).

In Mark's account of the same encounter, it says that Jesus "sighed deeply" (8:12). I bet He did. Jesus had already done miracle after miracle: casting out demons, healing the sick, calming storms, feeding thousands of people from the lunch the little boy brought, and raising Lazarus from the dead, yet that wasn't enough. Their hearts were so hardened that no sign could have persuaded them to believe, and sadly, that is how it is for many in the world today.

There are signs every day that things are looking up, that we are getting closer and closer to the return of Jesus, but many people, even in the church, yawn or bury their head in the sand. Soon after the release of *The Time of Jacob's Trouble* I received a message from a reader who was angry that it wasn't all fiction but included a nonfiction section as well. The reader asked, "Why did you include so much from the Bible?" Another reader said the book was too "scriptured" for her. They had no interest in what the Bible has to tell us about "the end of the age" (Matthew 28:20) and stopped reading. Five hundred of the Bible's prophecies have already been fulfilled with 100 percent accuracy; with that kind of track record, shouldn't we *want* to know the prophecies that God has given us about the end?

NOT SO FAST

The Bible tells us that we *can* know the signs that will precede Christ's return, but we *cannot* know the hour of His return. Jesus said that even He and the angels don't know—only the Father (Matthew 24:36). Jesus said in Matthew 24 that there will be a generation that will see all the signs take place prior to His return and that "this generation will not pass away until all these things take place" (verse 34).

We may not know the specific date Jesus will come back, but we are instructed to be aware of the *season* we're living in. We are supposed to be alert to what's happening around the world. When Jesus described the events and signs of the end of the age to His disciples in Mark 13 (a parallel account of Matthew 24 and Luke 21), He repeatedly urged them as follows:

- "See that no one leads you astray" (verse 5).
- "Be on your guard" (verse 9).
- "Be on guard; I have told you all things beforehand" (verse 23).
- "Be on guard, keep awake! Be alert! For you do not know when the time will come" (verse 33).
- "Stay awake—for you do not know when the master of the house will come" (verse 35).
- "...lest he come suddenly and find you asleep" (verse 36).
- "What I say to you I say to all: Stay awake" (verse 37).

We shouldn't force a news headline to be a sign as some people tend to do, but Jesus says we should be awake, on guard, and be aware of what the Bible says about the return of Jesus so that we recognize a clear sign when we see one.

WHAT WE UNDERSTAND NOW

The Bible says there are certain end-time prophecies that will not be understood until the time comes for us to understand them. Daniel had been given prophecies that he didn't understand:

> I heard, but I did not understand. Then I said, "O my lord, what shall be the outcome of these things?" He said, "Go your way, Daniel, for *the words are shut up and sealed until the time of the end*. Many shall purify themselves and make themselves white and be refined, but the wicked shall act wickedly. And none of the wicked shall understand, but those who are wise shall understand" (Daniel 12:8-10).

Daniel was told that the words of the prophecy he had been given would be sealed "until the time of the end," and those who are wise will understand! Today, we are in "the time of the end" as written in Daniel, and we are understanding prophecies that no other generation in all of recorded history has understood. They are unfolding before us. In the chapters ahead, I will share with you a few prophecies from the Bible that people have not understood until now, until this generation.

WHERE IN THE WORD?

THE COALITION AGAINST ISRAEL

The opening chapter of this book presents a fictional account of the future Ezekiel 38–39 invasion of Israel. That invasion will be very real, and it will happen someday. Let's look at some key Bible verses and see how they're relevant to what is happening today. I encourage you to read these chapters in their entirety so that you can gain a better understanding of what they say.

> Now the word of the LORD came to me, saying, "Son of man, set your face against Gog, of the land of Magog, the prince of Rosh, Meshech, and Tubal, and prophesy against him, and say, 'Thus says the Lord GOD: "Behold, I am against you, O Gog, the prince of Rosh, Meshech, and Tubal. *I will turn you around, put hooks into your jaws, and lead you out*, with all your army, horses, and horsemen, all splendidly clothed, a great company with bucklers and shields, all of them handling swords. Persia, Ethiopia, and Libya are with them, all of them with shield and helmet; Gomer and all its troops; the house of Togarmah from the far north and all its troops—many people are with you.'"
> ...Thus says the Lord GOD: 'On that day it shall come to pass that *thoughts will arise in your mind*, and you will make an evil plan'" (Ezekiel 38:1-6, 10 NKJV).

> Therefore, son of man, prophesy, and say to Gog, "Thus says the Lord God: 'On that day when my people Israel are dwelling securely, will you not know it? *You will come from your place out of the uttermost parts of the north,* you and many peoples with you, all of them riding on horses, a great host, a mighty army. You will come up against my people Israel, like a cloud covering the land. *In the latter days I will bring you against my land,* that the nations may know me, when through you, O Gog, I vindicate my holiness before their eyes'" (Ezekiel 38:14-16).

WHO IS GOG, WHERE IS HE FROM, AND WHEN WILL HE ATTACK?

Gog is mentioned 11 times in Ezekiel 38–39, and he's obviously a person. We know this because:

- He's called "the chief prince" (38:2-3).
- Thoughts arise in his mind and he makes an evil plan (verse 10).
- He is referred to as "him" (verses 2, 22), "he" (verse 17), and "his" (39:11).
- He has a "hand" to hold weapons (verse 3).

So we know that Gog is a person—specifically a man, and not a land. But where is he from? Ezekiel 38:15 tells us that he and many peoples with him will come from the "uttermost parts of the north." If you look at a map of Israel and draw a line straight north, you will land in the uttermost parts of the north, which is Russia. In the study of how ancient words came into modern languages, it is said that it's quite common for the vowels to be changed but the consonants to stay the same. In the case of the word Rosh in Ezekiel 38:2, the letter *o* was changed to *u* as in Rush—Russia, the country "from the uttermost parts of the north."

The prophet Daniel also describes a ruler who would lead an attack against Israel in the latter days and describes him as the "king of the north" (Daniel 11:40). Ezekiel calls this king Gog. There are some who say that Rosh isn't Russia, but today we do see Russia moving into place alongside Iran (their ancient name of Persia is mentioned in Ezekiel 38:5) and Turkey (identified as Togarmah) on the northernmost border of Israel. Ezekiel tells us a Russian leader with "a mighty army" (verse 15) will come against Israel in "the latter days" (verse 16) or "the latter years" (verse 8). In the Old Testament, the latter days and the latter years refer to end time events. This invasion has not happened in previous history, but will happen someday.

HOW DO WE KNOW THIS PASSAGE REFERS TO END-TIME EVENTS?

In 538 BC, when the Jews began their return to Israel after 70 years of captivity in Babylon, they returned from *just one single nation*, not from "the nations" (38:12) or from "many peoples" (verse 8). After the destruction of Jerusalem in AD 70, the Jewish people scattered throughout the world into many nations. Not until the late nineteenth century did Jewish people start returning to their ancient homeland, and since 1948, when Israel became a nation again, the Jews have been regathering earnestly from *many nations* around the world, just as Ezekiel prophesied.

The prophecy of a future coalition invading Israel in Ezekiel 38–39 didn't make sense for previous generations because Israel didn't exist, nor was it restored. But we are the generation that "gets it" because Israel became a nation again in 1948, and since that time, more than 3.3 million Jews have immigrated from other nations to Israel.[1] The Jewish people have to be back in their own land in order for this invasion to occur.

WHAT SOME OF THE PLAYERS ARE UP TO

Russia occupies great portions of Georgia, which is strategically located between Eastern Europe and Western Asia, and built a military base just north of Israel in Syria in 2015. Iran and Turkey also have military forces inside Syria.[2] The presidents of Russia, Turkey, and Iran have been meeting.[3] At one such get-together in February 2019, they discussed in part "the situation in the north-east of Syria and agreed to coordinate their activities to ensure security, safety and stability in this area."[4]

In this way we see the coalition of Ezekiel 38 and 39 coming together. When you think about the meetings that have been taking place between the presidents of Russia, Iran, and Turkey, keep in mind that 90 percent of the Islamic world identifies as Sunni Muslims. Turkey is predominantly Sunni Muslim, and Iran is Shiite Muslim. A Shiite president isn't just going to step aside and take orders from a Sunni president or vice versa. Russia is the only non-Muslim nation listed among the countries of Ezekiel 38, and in a strange, geopolitical way, it makes sense that these two differing Muslim nations will allow Russia to be the leader of this coalition; Russia's leader will act as a buffer between them. Their endgame is ultimately the same: destroy Israel and take the spoils.

WHY THE COALITION WILL ATTACK ISRAEL

In Ezekiel 38:12-13 we read why the invaders will attack Israel: "to seize spoil and carry off plunder...to carry away silver and gold, to take away livestock and goods." The plan for this coalition of nations is to invade the land of Israel, kill the people, and steal their goods. Israel, which is roughly the size of New Jersey, has the seventh strongest economy in the Middle East, ahead of Turkey, Iran, Egypt, and others.[5] Since Israel was reestablished in 1948, it has become a very wealthy nation. In a country of 8.5 million people, Israel is home to 21 billionaires[6] and more than 131,000 millionaires[7] and is now being called the new Silicon Valley, with the largest numbers of startup companies per capita in the entire world.[8]

Oil reserves have been discovered in Israel in the Golan Heights, at the Syrian border.[9] And the Leviathan Reservoir is "one of the world's largest offshore gas finds of the 21st century" and is considered Israel's "newest and most valuable energy asset." It is estimated to hold 500-800 billion cubit meters of natural gas, enough to supply 100 percent of Israel's electricity needs for 40 years and provide exports as well, and is almost entirely in Israeli territorial waters.[10] Approximately 2.7 trillion cubic feet of natural gas is present within the Karish and Tanin gas deposits, which were originally discovered in 2009 and 2010 offshore Israel in the Mediterranean Sea.[11]

On January 2, 2020, Israel inked a deal with Greece to pump between 9 to 12 billion cubic meters of natural gas 1,200 miles to Greece each year, and then on to Italy and other southeastern European countries, creating a huge boost in Israel's economy. Turkey's President Erdogan is not pleased with this deal; he envisioned a joint operation between Turkey and Libya in that area,[12] and this deal will reduce reliance on Russian gas, taking money out of Russia's pocket.[13] Russia's economy is shaky and the nation can't afford to lose customers, especially to the tiny nation of Israel. This gas pipeline poses a lucrative spoil for the Ezekiel 38 coalition.

Israel's exports of goods and services broke another record in 2019 as revenues neared $114 billion.[14] Keep in mind that Israel is the forty-eighth smallest country in the world with an area of 8,019 square miles, and yet in 2017 it ranked the forty-ninth top exporting country in the world.[15] All of this has happened since Israel was recognized by the United Nations as a country in 1948.

Greed will be the motivating factor among the Ezekiel 38–39 coalition against Israel—greed for the goods and the land. Iran has dreamed of a world without Zionism and has been screaming since 1979 that Israel must be wiped off the map,[16] and Russia's economy has been on shaky ground for some time. The land of Israel and her goods will prove extremely valuable to this coalition.

WHERE IN THE WORD?

Is Israel Dwelling Securely?

As we keep looking at the Ezekiel 38–39 invasion, we read these statements about a day when the people of Israel will dwell in security:

- "Its people were brought out from the peoples and *now dwell securely*, all of them" (verse 8).
- "I will go up against the land of *unwalled villages*. I will fall upon the quiet *people who dwell securely*, all of them *dwelling without walls, and having no bars or gates"* (verse 11).
- "Thus says the Lord God: On that day when my people Israel *are dwelling securely*, will you not know it?" (verse 14).

Many would say that the nation is not dwelling securely because Israel has fought a war nearly every decade since its statehood in 1948, and it remains under constant threat from warring nations. Yet despite attacks and conflicts that come against the country, more than 4.5 million tourists visited Israel in 2019[1] and citizens feel safe even while walking alone at night because they are well protected.[2]

According to the *New York Post*, Israel has

> one of the most technologically-advanced militaries in the world that is changing the way wars are fought and is a high-tech superpower and one of the world's top weapons exporters with approximately $6.5 billion in annual arms sales. Since 1985, for example, Israel is the world's largest exporter of drones, responsible for about 60 percent of the global market, trailed by the US, whose market share is under 25 percent. Its customers are everywhere—Russia, South Korea, Australia, France, Germany and Brazil.[3]

Israel is a satellite superpower with eight spy satellites in space. In 2000, the Arrow antimissile program went into operation with the capability to intercept incoming long-range enemy missiles. David's Sling intercepts medium-range enemy missiles, and the Iron Dome Weapon System detects and intercepts incoming rockets, mortars, and artillery. Barrier walls along the West Bank and Gaza protect Israelis from neighboring enemies and, according to Ezekiel 38, these walls will not be in place someday. In the fiction portion of this book, I suggest that they'll come down during the great earthquake that takes place at the time of the Ezekiel 38–39 invasion.

At the time of this writing, Israel has signed a peace treaty called the Abraham Accords Peace Agreement with the United Arab Emirates and Bahrain, recognizing "each state's right to sovereignty and to live in peace and security."[4] According to President Trump, there are at least five other countries seeking peace with Israel as well. In President Trump's words, these are "warring countries" that are "tired of fighting."[5] There isn't space here to cover the peace covenant that the Antichrist will confirm in Daniel 9:27, but the Abraham Accords Peace Agreement certainly brings more security to Israel and could be the precursor to this final biblical peace covenant.

So yes, the Jews are dwelling safely in the land.

HAS THE EZEKIEL 38–39 INVASION ALREADY HAPPENED?

There has never been an invasion against Israel as described in Ezekiel 38–39. Some authors and pastors believe this invasion has already happened, but that is contrary to what we read in the following passage:

> In my jealousy and in my blazing wrath I declare, On that day there shall be a great earthquake in the land of Israel. The fish of the sea and the birds of the heavens and the beasts of the field and all creeping things that creep on the ground, and all the people who are on the face of the earth, shall quake at my presence. And the mountains shall be thrown down, and the cliffs shall fall, and every wall shall tumble to the ground. I will summon a sword against Gog on all my mountains, declares the Lord God. Every man's sword will be against his brother. With pestilence and bloodshed I will enter into judgment with him, and I will rain upon him and his hordes and the many peoples who are with him torrential rains and hailstones, fire and sulfur. So I will show my greatness and my holiness and make myself known in the eyes of many nations. Then they will know that I am the Lord (Ezekiel 38:19-23).

Never in the history of conflicts and wars against Israel has there been

- a great earthquake (verse 19)
- that has thrown down mountains or caused cliffs and walls to tumble to the ground (verse 20), along with
- torrential rains, hailstones, and fire and sulfur rained down upon Israel's enemies (verse 22).

In this future invasion of Israel, God Himself will intervene and show His greatness and holiness (verse 23) in a supernatural way that has never been seen before. There will be no doubt who won this war for Israel. That is the great hope of Ezekiel 38!

In the novel portion of *The Day of Ezekiel's Hope*, I wrote that this invasion occurs days after Jesus seizes His followers and takes them to be with Him. I suggested that not until this coalition is out of the way and the governments of their countries are in turmoil does the "Architect of Peace" (Victor Quade in the novel) "confirm a covenant" (the Hebrew word translated "confirm" here means "to make stronger") of peace with Israel (Daniel 9:27 NIV). Could this invasion happen later? Absolutely. The Antichrist could confirm the covenant with Israel, and this could anger the coalition of Russia, Iran, Turkey, etc., causing them to strike against the Jewish nation. For the purpose of the novel, I think it can be proposed that the confusion caused by the disappearances around the world would provide a catalyst for this coalition to first disable the United States. Once Israel's greatest ally and military superpower in the world has been hobbled, then the coalition would go after Israel in the hopes of bringing about complete annihilation.

THE COALITION OF NATIONS

I mentioned earlier that the presidents of Russia, Iran, and Turkey have been meeting. Historically, Russia and Iran have been enemies, but for the last several decades they have been fighting on the same side, so to speak. This is important because they are key players in the Ezekiel 38–39 coalition against Israel. The nations listed in Ezekiel 38 are Magog, Meshech and Tubal, Persia, Ethiopia, Put, Gomer, and Beth-togarmah. Your Bible translation may name "Rosh" within that list, while other translations use "chief of Rosh," which we covered earlier.

Mark Hitchcock explains that "Ezekiel used ancient place names familiar to the people of his day. The names have changed many times throughout history, but the geographical territory remains the same."[6] Concerning the other nations listed, author and Bible scholar Ron Rhodes says,

> *Magog* refers to the geographical area in the southern portion of the former Soviet Union—probably including the former Soviet republics of Kazakhstan, Krygyzstan, Uzbekistan, Turkmenistan, Tajikstan, and possibly even northern parts of modern Afghanistan. Significantly, this

entire area is Muslim dominated, with more than enough religious motivation to move against Israel.

Meshech and Tubal refer to the geographical territory to the south of the Black and Caspian Seas of Ezekiel's day—what is today modern Turkey.[7]

Persia became Iran in 1935.

Ethiopia refers to the geographical territory to the south of Egypt on the Nile River—what is today known as Sudan. Sudan is a hardline Islamic nation that is a kindred spirit with Iran in its venomous hatred of Israel.

Put is modern-day Libya. Put is larger than the Libya that exists today, and hence the boundaries of Put as referenced in Ezekiel 38–39 may extend beyond modern Libya, perhaps including portions of Algeria and Tunisia.

Gomer apparently refers to part of the geographical territory in modern Turkey. The ancient historian Josephus said Gomer founded those the Greeks called the Galatians. The Galatians of New Testament times lived in central Turkey.

Beth-togarmah refers to parts of Turkey, just north of Israel.[8]

Again, when we speak of prophesies that did not make sense to previous generations, the list of nations in Ezekiel 38 would have been confusing because many of those countries are not within close geographical distance of another. My grandparents would have wondered, *Why would these nations, separated by many miles, come against Israel?* However, this prophecy makes sense to our generation because we see that the nations of this coalition are predominantly Muslim, and that their leaders have formed alliances. The religion of Islam wasn't in existence when Ezekiel prophesied these passages, and the presidents of Russia, Iran, and Turkey didn't start working together until recently, so there would have been no connecting dots for many generations who read Ezekiel's words. But for our generation, who understands Islam's hatred for Israel and sees the nations in Ezekiel 38 working together, this makes sense.

WHICH ONE OF THESE IS NOT LIKE THE OTHERS?

Russia seems to be the odd country out in Ezekiel 38, but beginning in 1967, Russia's inclusion in the list has made sense. In 1967, the Soviet Union mobilized warships, submarines, and fighter jets ready to attack Israel. US President Lyndon Johnson sent the US Sixth Fleet to intimidate the Russians, and it worked.[9] In 1973, Russia provided weapons, military training, intelligence, and ammunition to Egypt and Syria as they attacked Israel.[10] In 1989, Moscow and Tehran negotiated their first arms deal, with Russia becoming Iran's main supplier of conventional arms.[11] These arms have been used to supply terrorist groups like Hezbollah in Lebanon.

According to The Washington Institute,

> Western diplomats and analysts in Lebanon estimated Hezbollah receives close to $200 million a year from Iran. The increase is likely due to Iran's keen interest in undermining prospects for Israeli-Palestinian peace (and, in general, further destabilizing the Israeli-Palestinian conflict), and Hezbollah's growing role as Iran's proxy to achieve this goal.[12]

The Middle East's appetite for weapons has increased, and Russia is a formidable presence in the region; its engagement with the Middle East has been steadily on the rise, and its share of the defense market has doubled in three years.[13]

Russia is not a Muslim country, but the Russian government's motives are seen in today's headlines. In an interview on *60 Minutes*, John Carlin, the Assistant Attorney General for National Security during the Obama administration, said of Russia, "...the thing that matters the most is that you do what the don wants; what the head of the crime family wants, and here the head of the crime family is Putin."

Correspondent Lesley Stahl asked, "The Russian government is running a criminal syndicate. Is that going too far?"

"No," Carlin replied. "I think increasingly today the Russian government is a criminal syndicate...It's causing harm to countries, companies, and people throughout the world."[14]

I'm not suggesting that Vladimir Putin is Ezekiel 38's Gog, but he certainly is Gog-like. Recent headlines say he conquered the Middle East[15] and call him the "New King" of the Middle East,[16] the "New King of Syria,"[17] and "Middle East kingmaker,"[18] among other titles. And in 2020, Russian voters paved the way for Putin to remain in power until 2036.[19] Ezekiel 38:10 tells us this about whoever the leader of Russia is at the time of the Ezekiel 38 invasion: "On that day, thoughts will come into your mind and you will devise an evil scheme." Thoughts will come into Gog's mind and he will devise an evil scheme against Israel.

Remarkably, Ezekiel prophesied Russia as the bad guy 2,500 years ago.

WHERE IN THE WORD?

THE TWO WITNESSES

"God never leaves Himself without a witness." That's what I heard J. Vernon McGee say years ago on his radio program *Thru the Bible*. After Jesus snatches away all those who are in Christ (please refer to *The Time of Jacob's Trouble*, pages 224-227 for this teaching), God is not going to leave the world in darkness. Bibles, Christian books, Christian programming on the Internet (I suggest in the novel that the time will come when Bibles and Christian information will be blocked on the Internet) will still be available as a witness to His great love. God will also raise up 144,000 Jewish missionaries who will travel the earth preaching His Word, and He will raise up two witnesses in Jerusalem, "the holy city" (Revelation 11:2). The Lord refers to them as "My two witnesses" (verse 3) so there is no doubt that these two have been sent by God to fulfill His purposes. God will grant them authority (some Bible translations say power), and they will prophesy for 1,260 days (verse 3), or three-and-a-half years. And they will prophesy in sackcloth, the garment for mourning and repentance.

I recently watched an Internet video of a man explaining who the two witnesses are, and he read Revelation 11:4 several times: "These are the two olive trees and the two lampstands that stand before the Lord of the earth." He then took several minutes to explain that the two witnesses are an actual olive tree and a lampstand. He failed to explain how a lampstand or an olive tree could prophesy (verse 3), pour fire from their mouths that consumes their foes (verse 5), and have the power to perform miracles (verse 6), and he certainly didn't explain how they have bodies (verse 7) and rise from the dead (verse 12). Again, Revelation is not an allegory; we're told repeatedly within Revelation that it is a book of prophecy (Revelation 1:3; 11:6; 19:10; 22:7; 22:10; 22:18; 22:19). The two witnesses aren't characters in an allegory, but real people.

A wonderful thing about reading Revelation, and to further clarify that the book isn't allegory, is that John often explains the seemingly mysterious passages within a few verses of stating them. For example, in Revelation 1:12 the apostle John saw seven golden lampstands, and in verse 16 he saw seven stars within the hand of Jesus. Verse 20 tells us what they are: "As for the mystery of the seven stars that you saw in my right hand, and the seven golden lampstands, the seven stars are the angels of the seven churches, and the seven lampstands are the seven churches."

My 19-year-old daughter, Gracie, recently told me that she was reading Revelation but found it confusing because of all the symbolism. I told her that reading Revelation is much like reading any book—you have to have read the previous chapters in order to understand the ending. Revelation draws heavily on the Old Testament. I have heard there are between 800 and 1,000 references to the Old Testament within the 22 chapters of Revelation, so reading the previous books before reading Revelation is crucial.

In the first century AD, when John wrote Revelation, his readers would have easily understood the symbols used. They would have known that the two witnesses of Revelation 11 are men. In Zechariah 4, the prophet Zechariah has a vision of a golden lampstand with seven lamps and an olive tree on its left and right. Verse 14 says, "These are the two anointed ones who stand by the Lord of the whole earth." These two men in Zechariah's vision did God's work "not by might, nor by power, but by my Spirit" (verse 6). John's readers would have readily appreciated that these two witnesses were God's anointed ones, testifying in His power.

David Jeremiah says,

> In biblical times, God often used two witnesses to validate a truth. Two angels testify to the resurrection of the Savior. Two men in white testify to His Ascension. God often dispatches His people into twos as well. Think of Moses and Aaron, Joshua and Caleb, Zerubbabel and Joshua, Peter and John, Paul and Silas, Timothy and Titus. The disciples were sent out two by two, and the seventy were also told to travel in pairs. These two witnesses will follow that pattern as they proclaim one of the most important calls to repentance of all time.[1]

WHAT THE TWO WITNESSES CAN DO

God will give the two witnesses power to consume their foes with fire from their mouths:

> If anyone would harm them, fire pours from their mouth and consumes their foes. If anyone would harm them, this is how he is doomed to be killed (Revelation 11:5).

These men will capture the world's attention because God will give them the power to perform miracles, including a three-and-a-half-year drought and striking the earth with *every kind of plague* (just think about that!) and turning the waters to blood: "They have the power to shut the sky, that no rain may fall during the days of their prophesying, and they have power over the waters to turn them into blood and to strike the earth with every kind of plague, as often as they desire" (Revelation 11:6).

Why would God enable them to perform such miracles? Remember the plagues of Egypt in Exodus 7–12? The waters became blood, frogs covered the land, there was lice and then flies, pestilence tormented livestock and all the Egyptian cattle died, there were boils on humans and animals, hail mixed with fire, locusts, three days of total darkness, and then the death of every firstborn human and animal.

Only those millions of Hebrews who were held in slavery, with the blood of a lamb smeared over their doorposts, would survive that final plague of death.

Imagine the torment and suffering as each plague fell. After each plague, Moses, speaking for the Lord, beseeched the Pharaoh to "Let my people go," but each time, Pharaoh hardened his heart and refused to release them. In the same way, the two witnesses will stop the rain and turn the waters to blood and call down every plague to cover the earth for the purpose of beseeching people to soften their hardened hearts, to repent, and turn to Jesus. They will have the power to inflict plague after plague as often as they want! I can't fully imagine what life will be like at that time, but it's not hard to figure out why these men will be hated by the entire world.

WHO WILL KILL THEM?

When the two witnesses are finished prophesying, then and only then will anyone be able to kill them: "When they have finished their testimony, *the beast that rises from the bottomless pit* will make war on them and conquer them and kill them" (Revelation 11:7).

The beast—the Antichrist—will be responsible for killing the two witnesses. He's called "a beast rising up out of the sea" in Revelation 13:1. He will rise out of the sea of people in the end times—Revelation 17:15 says, "The waters which you saw…are peoples and multitudes and nations and tongues." In Revelation, waters often refer to Gentile nations, so this beast is a person, not a diabolical sea monster, as suggested by those who want to make Revelation a myth. There isn't space to study about the Antichrist in this book, so we'll study about him in the next and final book.

The Antichrist will be hailed a hero for killing the two witnesses because they will be hated around the world. We know this because when they are killed,

> their dead bodies will lie in the street of the great city that symbolically is called Sodom and Egypt, where their Lord was

> crucified. For three and a half days some from the peoples and tribes and languages and nations will *gaze at their dead bodies and refuse to let them be placed in a tomb* (Revelation 11:8-9).

A three-and-a-half-year drought, waters of blood, and plagues of any kind on the earth will mean great destruction, sorrow, and suffering on the earth, so when these men are finally killed, the world will want to gloat over their dead bodies.

I heard a pastor say that Paul and Peter wouldn't last preaching a month of Sundays in today's Western church because their messages would be too bold and too truthful for the itching ears of modern society. If Paul and Peter wouldn't last a month, these two witnesses wouldn't last one service! Their message of repentance will be on a scale the world has never seen. They will tell people that they're more like the devil than Jesus, and they will call out sin day after day, creating such hatred and vitriol that people will try to harm them (Revelation 11:5). These men won't be warm, grandfatherly types (although their message of repentance is about God's jealous love for people), nor will they be politically correct. All the social media and news outlets will be in a constant uproar over them.

The extent to which the two witnesses will be hated is revealed by the worldwide victory party that will take place when they are killed: "Those who dwell on the earth will rejoice over them and make merry and exchange presents, because these two prophets had been a torment to those who dwell on the earth" (Revelation 11:10). The world will heave a sigh of relief because these wicked witnesses have finally been silenced. Interestingly, this is the only mention of people rejoicing during the entire tribulation period. But the celebration will be short-lived.

THE BREATH OF GOD

"After the three and a half days a breath of life from God entered them, and they stood up on their feet, and great fear fell on those who saw them. Then they heard a loud voice from heaven saying to them, 'Come up here!' And they went up to heaven in a cloud, and their enemies watched them" (Revelation 11:12).

Just imagine this scene: the corpses of the two witnesses will be rotting, with birds and dogs picking away at the putrid flesh. As the smell wafts through the air, people will cover their noses and mouths, appalled, disgusted, yet full of glee. But then in a moment, the ripped flesh will heal back together, life will return as blood begins to pump through the witnesses' veins, and eyes that had been pecked out will form in the sockets once again and each witness will open them, seeing the spectators crowded around them. Bones and muscles will become strong again and each man will stand to his feet as the crowd gasps, with people screaming, running away, or falling to their knees. Then, just as in Revelation 4:1 when John was called heavenward with these same words, the crowd will hear a loud voice say, "Come up here!," and the two witnesses will ascend into heaven in a cloud as their enemies watch (Revelation 11:12).

This prophecy would have been confusing to my parents or grandparents. How would it be possible for people from all over the earth to see two dead men on the streets of Jerusalem for three-and a half days? Neither of my parents had a TV in their homes growing up; all they had was a radio. It's no longer a question as to how the world will see these men because of the Internet and satellite technology that exists today.

Following the murders of the Lord's anointed ones, we read this: "At that hour there was a great earthquake, and a tenth of the city fell. Seven thousand people were killed in the earthquake, and the rest were terrified and gave glory to the God of heaven" (verse 13). In an instant, 7,000 people will be buried alive, and those left living will be frightened and give glory to God. If only all the earth would come to believe in Christ at this moment, but we know from Revelation that they don't. And as a result, God's judgments will continue to fall.

WHEN WILL THE TWO WITNESSES PROPHESY?

Some scholars believe the witnesses will prophesy during the last three-and-a-half years of the tribulation, and it could be. But there are a good number who say they will prophesy during the first half, as stated in the novel portion of this book. There, I suggest that the Ezekiel 38 invasion of Israel paves the way for the temple to be built. According to Ezekiel 38, enemy armies and their leadership will be completely wiped out by God in that invasion. That will provide a perfect time for the Antichrist to "confirm a covenant" with Israel (Daniel 9:27 NIV). Without enemy intrusion or hostility toward Israel, the timing would be perfect for building the temple.

I placed the two witnesses at the first half of the tribulation period for a few reasons. I suggest that while the temple is being built, they can begin their ministry in Jerusalem. John is told to measure the temple in Revelation 11:1, but then he is also told, "Do not measure the court outside the temple; leave that out, for it is given over to the nations, and they will trample the holy city for forty-two months" (Revelation 11:2). What is the significance of this?

In the same way that Isaiah prophesied the first and second coming of Jesus in one verse (Isaiah 9:6—"a child is born" speaks of the birth of Jesus, and "the government shall be upon his shoulder" speaks of Jesus's millennial reign on earth), I think it can be suggested that Revelation 11:1-3 reveals two time periods for the temple in the tribulation:

1. When the Gentiles tread the holy city for 42 months (verse 2)—this is when the Antichrist will set himself up "in the temple of God, proclaiming himself to be God" (2 Thessalonians 2:4).
2. The time when the two witnesses prophesy for 1,260 days (verse 3).

It's important to remember what Jesus said about the Antichrist setting himself up to be worshipped as God. He said this would occur at the midpoint of the tribulation, and that when it happened, the people were to flee (Matthew 24:15-16). If the two witnesses were present in the second half of the tribulation, as some people suggest, then how would the Antichrist enter the temple, given the power the witnesses have to destroy their enemies? And if Jesus told His people to flee the holy city, wouldn't the witnesses flee as well? Also, if the two witnesses prophesy during the second half of the tribulation, that means several things will have to happen all in rapid succession:

- the Antichrist will have to kill them
- they need to lie dead for three-and-a-half days
- they will need to ascend in a cloud
- the battle of Armageddon will need to begin
- Jesus will need to return from heaven and annihilate His enemies

It seems plausible by what we read in Revelation 11 that the two witnesses have power over the earth during the first half of the tribulation to inflict plagues that cause people to hate them. When the Antichrist kills them, the people of the world will raise him to the level of superstardom, which, in turn, will pave the way for him to become all-powerful and set himself up as God inside the temple.

WHO ARE THE TWO WITNESSES?

Much has been written about the identities of the two witnesses, and some believe that because neither Elijah nor Enoch died but were translated (snatched away) to heaven, that they will return for a time of ministry during the first half of the tribulation. Others say the men are Elijah and Moses because the miracles they performed in the Old Testament mirror those of the two witnesses in Revelation. Still others say that they could be Elijah and John the Baptist, representing prophets from both the Old Testament and the New Testament.

I would agree that any of those men are possibilities. I would also say that the two witnesses could be two godly men whom the Lord chooses to serve as His spokesmen during the first half of the tribulation. Whoever they are, they will be two of the most powerful yet most hated men in the history of the world—not only because they will pronounce judgment upon many millions of people, but because they will warn of God's coming judgment upon sin, point people to Jesus, and preach repentance.

WHERE IN THE WORD?

WHY IS ISRAEL A SIGNIFICANT PART OF THIS BOOK?

Addressing the importance of Israel in the end times could take up an entire book. For now, I'll simply present some key points about Israel by looking at the Bible and the history of the nation. Understanding Israel's significance, former US senator Michelle Bachmann said in a radio interview, "God's plan for humanity goes through Israel and the Jewish people for redemption. We need to understand that they are key to end time prophetic events."[1] The history of the Jewish nation begins in the book of Genesis:

- The creation story takes up two chapters.
- The fall of man is recorded in one chapter.
- The story from Cain to Abram covers eight chapters.
- The accounts about the family line of Abraham, Isaac, and Jacob—the fathers of the Jewish race—take up 39 chapters!

The total word count of Scripture passages about Abraham and his descendants should tell us they are of great significance and importance to God. Rabbi Binyamin Elon said, "I believe that if you do not know how to read the Bible, you cannot understand the daily newspaper. If you do not know the biblical story of Abraham, Isaac, and Jacob, you cannot possibly understand the miracle of the modern state of Israel."[2]

GOD'S COVENANT WITH ABRAHAM

The Bible's central theme is covenant. *Easton's Bible Dictionary* defines *covenant* this way: "A contract or agreement between two parties."[3] The beginning of God's covenant with His chosen people, the Jews, is in Genesis 12, when God called Abram (this is before God changed his name to Abraham, meaning "father of a multitude") to leave his home in Ur, in Mesopotamia, to go to a new land—Canaan (Genesis 11:31). Archaeologists have discovered many idols on the site of what was once Ur and have uncovered a massive ziggurat, a shrine built for the moon god Nanna.[4] This lines up with what we are told in Joshua 24:2-3, which says Abraham and his ancestors "served other gods."

Abraham is among the list of the "they" who served other gods, but God led Abraham out of Ur to Canaan. There, God gave him a son, Isaac. Very early in the Bible we see what a good, gracious God we have, who saves us from our situations, circumstances, past, rebellion, and failures. God is always willing to lead us, but like Abraham, we must have the desire to follow.

Genesis 12:4 tells us that "Abram went, as the Lord had told him, and Lot went with him. Abram was seventy-five years old when he departed from Haran." Abram left his gods and their idols and everything he had known to follow the Lord. That he was 75 years old at the time reveals that we're never too old to begin following the Lord! Abraham's simple act of obedience changed the course of history in incredibly significant ways.

THE BLESSING

In Genesis 12:1-3 we read God's first promise to Abram:

> Now the Lord said to Abram, "Go from your country and your kindred and your father's house to the land that I will

> show you. And I will make you a great nation, and I will bless you and make your name great, so that you will be a blessing. I will bless those who bless you, and him who dishonors you I will curse, and in you all the families of the earth shall be blessed."

This same promise is repeated four more times in Genesis:

- Before the destruction of Sodom and Gomorrah, God said, "Abraham shall surely become a great and mighty nation, and *all the nations of the earth shall be blessed in him*" (18:18).
- After Abraham was willing to sacrifice his son Isaac, the angel of the Lord said, "In your offspring shall *all the nations of the earth be blessed*" (22:18).
- God promised Isaac, "In your offspring *all the nations of the earth shall be blessed*" (26:4).
- God promised Isaac's son, Jacob, "Your offspring shall be like the dust of the earth, and you shall spread abroad to the west and to the east and to the north and to the south, and *in you and your offspring shall all the families of the earth be blessed.*"

Gerald R. McDermott, a professor and author, found it difficult to believe that modern Israel was "a fulfillment of biblical prophecy," and began to study and research the prophecies of the Bible in order to disprove those who did believe that. He writes,

> One of my Aha! moments was the day I started to see a pattern to the biblical story in both Testaments. The pattern moves from the particular to the universal. God uses the particular (a particular person or people) to bring blessing to the universal (the world). In the Old Testament, God uses a particular man (Abraham) and his people (the Jews) to bring blessings to their neighbors and to the world (the

> universal). The pattern is the same in the New Testament. God uses a particular man (Jesus) and His people (Jesus's body, the Church) to bring blessings to the world.[5]

How has Abraham been a blessing to all the nations? From his descendants we have each and every page of the Bible. We have Jesus, Christianity, and the gospel message that has spread throughout the world. These are the greatest blessings the world has ever known!

In Galatians we learn that God preached the gospel to Abraham, saying, "'In you shall all the nations be blessed.' So then, those who are of faith are blessed along with Abraham, the man of faith" (Galatians 3:8-9). I can't imagine being Abraham and receiving this covenant from God. It must have been overwhelming for him to comprehend! The very first gospel message was preached to Abraham, and we're told that he "believed God, and it was counted to him as righteousness" (Galatians 3:6). He believed that through his descendants, God would bring someone who would be a blessing to all the nations—that is, Jesus—and it was counted to him as righteousness.

THE COVENANT IS ANNOUNCED

In Genesis 12:1-4, God told Abram,

> "Go from your country and your kindred and your father's house *to the land that I will show you.* And *I will make of you a great nation*, and I will bless you and make your name great, so that you will be a blessing. I will bless those who bless you, and him who dishonors you I will curse, and *in you all the families of the earth shall be blessed.*" So Abram went, as the LORD had told him, and Lot went with him.

Within this covenant, God promised:

- the land
- a great nation of people
- a blessing to all the earth

In the pages ahead we'll take a closer look at each element of this covenant.

The Land

> Now the LORD said to Abram, "Go from your country and your kindred and your father's house to the land that I will show you" (Genesis 12:1).

There's so much regarding the land that we'll look at this again later in greater detail, but for now, it's important for us to note that when the word "land" is used here, it really does means land. The term isn't used in a symbolic way to mean something else. In the verses we've already read, we learn that God gave the land to Abraham and his descendants, the people of Israel. God specifically told Abraham that this covenant was for him and his son, Isaac, and for Isaac's descendants. This covenant was not for Ishmael, Abraham's son by Hagar:

> Abraham said to God, "Oh that Ishmael might live before you!" God said, "No, but Sarah your wife shall bear you a son, and you shall call his name Isaac. I will establish my covenant with him as an everlasting covenant for his offspring after him. As for Ishmael, I have heard you; behold, I have blessed him and will make him fruitful and multiply him greatly. He shall father twelve princes, and I will make him into a great nation. *But I will establish my covenant with Isaac,* whom Sarah shall bear to you at this time next year" (Genesis 17:18-21).

Abraham loved and cared for his son Ishmael and wanted to see him brought into the covenant, but God said no. That wasn't part of God's design. The covenant God established with Abraham would continue through his son Isaac (who at this point wasn't even born yet) and would be everlasting.

Yet in His goodness and great love, God told Abraham that he *has* blessed (not that He *would bless,* but he *has blessed*—the blessing was already set in motion) Ishmael and would make him fruitful and "multiply him greatly." God has done that. Ishmael is the father of the Arabs. There are 22 Arab countries today, including Egypt, Iraq, Saudi Arabia, Jordan, Lebanon, Morocco, and United Arab Emirates, encompassing more than 5 million square miles of land and a total population of more than 423 million.[6] Five Arab countries—Saudi Arabia, Iraq, the United Arab Emirates, Kuwait, and Qatar—rank among the top petroleum or gas exporters worldwide.[7, 8] Algeria and Libya are significant gas exporters, and Egypt, Bahrain, Tunisia, and Sudan all have smaller but important reserves. Ishmael has been fruitful, and God has lavishly blessed his descendants.

WHERE IN THE WORD?

WHY THE JEWS?

In Deuteronomy 7:6-8 we read this about the Jewish people:

> You are a people holy to the LORD your God. The LORD your God has chosen you to be a people for his treasured possession, out of all the peoples who are on the face of the earth. It was not because you were more in number than any other people that the LORD set his love on you and chose you, for you were the fewest of all peoples, but it is because the LORD loves you and is keeping the oath that he swore to your fathers.

We learn in these verses that God did not choose the Jews because they were greater in number than any other people, because they weren't. God *chose them* as His treasured possession simply because He loved them. David Jeremiah says,

> The Bible tells us that His choice of Israel had nothing to do with merit. It was not because she was more numerous than other people in the world; she was the least (Deut. 7:7). It was not because Israel was more sensitive to God than any other nations. Although God called her by name, Israel did not know Him (Isaiah 45:4). It was not because Israel was more righteous than other nations. When God

later confirmed His promise of land to the Jews, He reminded them that they were a rebellious, stiff-necked people (Deut. 9:6-7).

If God chose to bless the nation of Israel not because she was more populous or spiritually responsive or righteous than other nations, just why did He choose the Jews? The answer: because *it was His sovereign purpose to do so*. His sovereign purpose means He cares what happens to His people and their land. He is not merely a passive observer to all that is taking place in Israel. As He told the people through Moses, theirs was "*a land for which the Lord your God cares; the eyes of the Lord your God are always on it, from the beginning of the year to the very end of the year*" (Deut. 11:12).[1]

A Great Nation of People

In His covenant to Abram, God said, "I will make of you a great nation" (Genesis 12:2).

I recently read an online article about Genesis 12:1-4 in which the author replaced Israel with the church. He said that Israel is not a "great nation," as stated in verse 2, because it is not large by any means, so therefore these verses must refer to the church. However, the church didn't exist in the Old Testament; it wasn't born until Pentecost in Acts 2. The promise in Genesis 12 is specifically for Abraham and his descendants, Israel. The word "great" in verse 2 (Hebrew, *gadowl*) means large in intensity, in importance, or older. The definition is not about the size of the land or the number of people, as the man in the article was proposing, but rather the magnitude, intensity, and importance of the nation. Israel is great because of its historical magnitude, intensity, and importance to the world.

At the time of this writing in 2020, the population of the world is nearly 8 billion people.[2] There are 1.9 billion Muslims in the world, and 50 Muslim-majority countries.[3] In 2018, the population of Jews in the world was just over 14.6 million with only one Jewish country, Israel.[4] Steven L. Pease says in his book *The Golden Age of Jewish Achievement*, "No contemporary culture has achieved or contributed as much, relative to its scant population, as the Jews."[5] Jews are so few in number that out of every 1,000 people, only two would be Jewish. It cannot be doubted that God has blessed the "apple of his eye" (Zechariah 2:8). Here is a sampling of some achievements that don't include what the Jews have accomplished with the land, which we'll cover in the next chapter:

Of the 902 Nobel prizes ever given, 204, or 22.6 percent, have been given to Jews between 1901 and 2019.[6] Twenty-seven percent of those have been awarded since 1946—after the Holocaust destroyed a third of their numbers. In August 2015, *Times Higher Education* ranked Israel the fifth-best performer this century, based on the sheer number of Nobel Prizes won and the significance and prestige of each one.[7] Comparatively speaking, given their small population, Jewish people should have earned only *one* of the 521 Nobels awarded for physics, chemistry, medicine, and physiology through 2007.[8] However, they have won 137. *Times Higher Education* also ranked global universities based on the number of Nobel Prize winners at them, and Technion-Israel Institute of Technology in Haifa, Israel, placed tenth on the list, higher than every British university and Yale.[9]

Encyclopedia Britannica provides its list of great inventions. Of the 267 individual inventors included, at least 15 were Jews, including Paul Zoll (the defibrillator and the pacemaker), Edwin Land (instant photography), Dennis Gabor (holography), and Charles Ginsburg (videotape recorder). Jews are represented on the list 22 times more than one would expect based on their population. Of movie directors who won Oscars, 37 percent are Jewish. Nearly 26 percent of the Kennedy Center honors and 14 percent of the Grammy Lifetime Achievement Awards have gone to them. Since 1917, 16 percent of Supreme Court justices have been Jewish.[10] From August 7, 2010, to September 18, 2020, they made up one-third of the Supreme Court, holding three spots with Ruth Bader Ginsburg, Stephen Breyer, and Elena Kagan.

In 1899, Mark Twain wrote an article for *Harper's* magazine entitled "Concerning the Jews," and he said,

> Properly, the Jews are hardly to be heard of, but he is heard of, has always been heard of. He is as prominent on the planet

> as any other people, and his commercial importance is extravagantly out of proportion to the smallness of his bulk. His contributions to the world's list of great names in literature, science, art, music, finance, medicine, and abstruse learning are also away out of proportion to the weakness of his numbers. He has made a marvelous fight in the world in all ages and he has done it with his hands tied behind him.[11]

A Blessing to All the Earth

The third key aspect of God's covenant had to do with Abraham being a blessing to all the peoples of the earth: "I will bless you and make your name great, so that you will be a blessing. I will bless those who bless you, and him who dishonors you I will curse, and in you all the families of the earth shall be blessed" (Genesis 12:2-3).

God said He would bless Abraham and make his name great. Is there any other name that is widely revered and honored by Jews, Christians, and Muslims alike? As mentioned earlier, there are currently 423 million Arabs in the world today in 22 Arab countries. All of them are descendants of Abraham through Ishmael. But it was through Abraham's son Isaac that all the families of the earth would be blessed—through Jesus, who said in John 12:32, "I, when I am lifted up from the earth, will draw *all* people to myself." In this verse, "all" (Greek, *pas*) means "each, every, any, all, the whole, everyone, all things, everything." In other words, all means *all*. The cross of Jesus is the way for all people to come to the Father.

God also said in Genesis 12:3 that He would bless those who bless Abraham and curse those who curse him. In the Bible, those who have suppressed Israel have faced severe judgment, including Assyria, Babylon, Egypt, and Rome. This book would be entirely too long if we detailed all the ways various countries have blessed or cursed Israel throughout its history. But God's promise still stands true today: "I will bless those who bless you, and him who dishonors you I will curse."

GOD'S COVENANT IS EVERLASTING

In Genesis 17 God changed Abram and Sarai's names to Abraham and Sarah, telling them they would be a "father of many nations" (verse

4 NIV) and a "mother of nations" (verse 16 NIV). God said, "I will establish my covenant between me and you and your offspring after you… *for an everlasting covenant*" (verse 7). Make no mistake: God is the author and creator of this covenant, and He doesn't go back on His word.

- This is an everlasting covenant (verses 7, 13, 19).
- God doesn't lie or change His mind (Numbers 23:19; Titus 1:2; Hebrews 6:18).
- He can't break His covenant or change the word He has spoken: "My covenant I will not break, nor alter the word that has gone out of My lips" (Psalm 89:34 NKJV).
- "The word of the LORD endures forever" (1 Peter 1:25).

Psalm 105:8-11 says this:

> He remembers his covenant forever,
> the word that he commanded, for a thousand generations,
> the covenant that he made with Abraham,
> his sworn promise to Isaac,
> which he confirmed to Jacob as a statute,
> to Israel as *an everlasting covenant*,
> saying, "To you I will give the land of Canaan
> as your portion for an inheritance" (Psalm 105:8-11).

GOD WILL

God uses the words "I will" 12 times in Genesis 17, letting Abraham and all of us after him know that God alone will do this. Despite what Abraham or his descendants did or will do, God *will* fulfill His covenant promise. If God were to break this "everlasting covenant" with Abraham, then we're all doomed because that makes our covenant of salvation with Jesus flimsy at best.

If we couldn't trust God's promise to the Jewish people, then how could we trust any of His promises about salvation in Christ? How could we believe Him when He says, "I will never leave you nor forsake you" (Hebrews 13:5)? How could we believe Romans 8:35-39, where we are told nothing can separate us from Christ's love? And what about Romans 10:9, which says, "If you confess with your mouth that Jesus is Lord and believe in your heart that God raised him from the dead, you will be saved"—how could we know that is really true?

If God can revoke the promises He made to Abraham, then every promise in the Bible is on shaky ground and nothing can be believed. Beginning in Genesis 12 and going all the way to Revelation 22 we read the continuing story of God's faithfulness to fulfill the promises He made to Abraham and his descendants. Many of those promises regarded the land, of which God said, "I will give [it] to you and to your offspring forever" (Genesis 13:15).

HOW WOULD ABRAHAM KNOW?

In Genesis 15:8, Abraham asked God how he was supposed to know that he would possess the land. In the Old Testament, both parties involved in a covenant were to walk between animal pieces that had been cut up in order to ratify the covenant, and God asked Abraham to bring the animals. But in verse 12, we see that Abraham was asleep when it came time to ratify the covenant. We are told in verse 17 that only God passed between the pieces of the sacrifice in the form of a smoking fire pot and flaming torch. This means the covenant was not two-sided, but one-sided—it was all on God. The keeping of this promise wasn't based on Abraham's or his descendants' faithfulness, but on God's.

WHERE IN THE WORD?

THE PROMISED LAND

Gerald R. McDermott, while doing his research about the land of Israel, says,

> I stumbled upon a fact that no one had ever pointed out; the sheer number of references to the land in the Old Testament. It was overwhelming. As the great Old Testament scholar Gerhard von Rad put it, "Of all the promises made to the patriarchs it was that of the land that was the most prominent and decisive." The land appears more than 1000 times in the Jewish Bible and is even more common than the word "covenant," which scholars agree is fundamental to the Bible. In more than 70% of the places where "covenant" appears, it is linked to the land promise.[1]

AN EVERLASTING POSSESSION

Much of the hatred and strife in the Middle East comes down to this question: Who has the right to the land of Israel? The Jewish people insist the land is theirs because God made it clear to Abraham and his descendants that the promise about the land was an everlasting promise. The land would be theirs forever. "Arabs' claims to the land are based on continuous residence in the country for hundreds of years and the fact that they represented the demographic majority. They reject the notion that a biblical-era kingdom constitutes the basis for a valid modern claim."[2]

God clearly states in the Bible that He gave the land to the Jews for an everlasting possession. Despite Israel's disobedience through the ages, God will never renege on His word or His promise. Robert Jeffress says, "Because of Israel's subsequent disobedience and disbelief, some believe that God revoked His promise to Abraham and made the Church the beneficiary of the covenant." He then adds,

> I will admit that such reasoning sounds logical...and even biblical. God made numerous conditional promises to the Israelites. For example, consider Moses's words to the Israelites before they entered into the Promised Land:
>
>> See, I am setting before you today a blessing and a curse: the blessing, if you listen to the commandments of the LORD your God, which I am commanding you today; and the curse, if you do not listen to the commandments of the LORD your God, but turn aside from the way which I am commanding you today, by following other gods you have not known (Deut 11:26-28).
>
> Since that time, Israel's history has been filled with blessings and curses. Obedience has resulted in peace and prosperity; disobedience has resulted in calamity and exile. Yet *such warnings do not negate the unconditional nature of God's promise to Abraham and his descendants.*"[3]

Israel's disobedience brought God's discipline, but as Jeffress said, it didn't negate the unconditional nature of God's promise to Abraham and his descendants. The apostle Paul wrote, "This is what I mean: the law, which came 430 years afterward, *does not annul a covenant previously ratified by God, so as to make the promise void.* For if the inheritance comes by the law, it no longer comes by promise; *but God gave it to Abraham by a promise*" (Galatians 3:17-18). Even when we disobey, God is faithful; He doesn't break His promise.

IF YOU WILL OBEY

As stated earlier, God's covenant with Abraham was full of "I will" promises. His covenant with Moses regarding the land was filled with "you must" requirements. The covenant with Abraham was unconditional and the covenant with Moses was conditional. Blessings from God and enjoyment of the land were conditional on Israel's obedience to God.

In Exodus 19, God introduced to Moses the means by which Israel would occupy the land: "If you will indeed obey my voice and keep my covenant, you shall be my treasured possession among all peoples, for all the earth is mine; and you shall be to me a kingdom of priests and a holy nation" (verses 5-6).

If they failed to obey, God would punish them:

> But if in spite of this you will not listen to me, but walk contrary to me, then I will walk contrary to you in fury, and I myself will discipline you sevenfold for your sins… And *I will scatter you among the nations,* and I will unsheathe the sword after you, and your land shall be a desolation, and your cities shall be a waste (Leviticus 26:27-28, 33).

> The Lord *will scatter you among all peoples,* from one end of the earth to the other, and there you shall serve other gods of wood and stone, which neither you nor your fathers have known. And among these nations you shall find no respite, and there shall be no resting place for the sole of your foot, but the Lord will give you there a trembling heart and failing eyes and a languishing soul (Deuteronomy 28:64-65).

Despite knowing God's conditional "ifs" and His repeated warnings of judgment, Israel disobeyed God time and again, and as a result, God scattered Israel, removing all but a remnant in the land. God told Ezekiel, "Son of man, when the house of Israel lived in their own land, they defiled it by their ways and their deeds…I scattered them among the nations, and they were dispersed through the countries. In accordance with their ways and their deeds I judged them" (Ezekiel 36:17, 19).

THE SCATTERINGS

Jewish people who live outside of Israel live in what is called the Diaspora (from the Greek, "scattering" or "dispersion"). Today, roughly 49 percent of the world's 14 million Jews call Israel home. More than half reside elsewhere. "The Diaspora is the result of a temporarily broken relationship between Israel and God. His desire and intent are to reunite, resurrect, restore, and return His people through repentance."[4] In the first Diaspora, Babylon conquered Judah and destroyed Jerusalem and Solomon's temple resulting in three waves of the Jews being taken into exile and slavery, including Daniel and his three friends. However, God did not forget the covenant He had made with Abraham.

- Jeremiah wrote that the Lord would restore Israel: "I will bring them back to their own land that I gave to their fathers" (Jeremiah 16:15).
- Leviticus 26:44-45 states, "Yet for all that, when they are in the land of their enemies, I will not spurn them, neither will I abhor them so as to destroy them utterly and break my covenant with them, for I am the LORD their God. But I will for their sake remember the covenant with their forefathers, whom I brought out of the land of Egypt in the sight of the nations, that I might be their God: I am the LORD."

God did as He said and brought the Jews back to their land in 538 BC, although after being in Babylon for 70 years, many of the Jews chose to remain there (about 50,000 returned home).[5] Those who went back to Judah built a second temple on the site of the original one, and that temple was destroyed by the Romans in AD 70.

AD 70—THE SECOND DIASPORA

In AD 66, or 607 years after the Jews returned, Gessius Florus, a Roman procurator of Judea who hated the Jews, sent troops into Jerusalem. Some 3,600 people were slaughtered. A Jewish rebellion ensued that had been sizzling for some time and soon all of Galilee was in uproar, with killings numbering into the thousands on both sides. Four years later, in AD 70, superior Roman forces led by Titus were successful in finally conquering Jerusalem. The city was left ruined and desolate except for Herod's three great towers at the northwest corner of the city, and the second temple was razed to the ground in fulfillment of Jesus's words in Matthew 24:2 and Luke 19:41-43. The fires inside the temple caused the gold plating within the structure to melt, and the gold seeped into the cracks between the great marble blocks that held the temple together. In their greed, the Roman soldiers left "not one stone...on another" (NIV), just as Jesus said, in search of the coveted treasure.

The ancient Jewish historian Josephus Flavius, who was taken prisoner, wrote a firsthand account of what happened:

> While the Temple was ablaze, the attackers plundered it, and countless people who were caught by them were slaughtered. There was no pity for age and no regard was accorded rank; children and old men, laymen and priests, alike were butchered; every class was pursued and crushed in the grip of war, whether they cried out for mercy or offered resistance.[6]

According to the Roman senator and historian Tacitus, at that time, there were 600,000 visitors crowding the streets of Jerusalem for the Passover. It is estimated that between those many travelers trapped inside the city and the permanent residents, between 800,000 and one million Jews perished. An estimated 95,000 were taken captive,[7] and countless others fled for safety, including a remnant atop the mount Masada, a fortress complex built by King Herod.

For the next 1,900 years, the Jews would have no authority over Jerusalem during what Jesus said would be the times of the Gentiles: "They will fall by the edge of the sword and be led captive among all nations, and Jerusalem will be trampled underfoot by the Gentiles, until the times of the Gentiles are fulfilled" (Luke 21:24). In 1948, when Israel became a state, it became sovereign over West Jerusalem. During the Six-Day War in 1967, the Jews fought for and won East Jerusalem, including the Temple Mount, where the Jews' beloved temple stood. But control of the Temple Mount itself was ceded to Jordanian authority, meaning it is still under Gentile control.

WHERE IN THE WORD?

The Final Humiliation

In the previous chapter, we looked at how most of the Jews were driven from their land in AD 70 and the remnant who remained were under Roman authority. The final humiliation for the Jews came during the Bar Kokhba revolt, which was their last attempt at liberation. The Roman emperor Hadrian visited Judea in AD 130 and decided to rebuild Jerusalem, changing its name and building a shrine to the god Zeus where the temple once stood. The remnant Jews revolted and, for a while, had some success—until AD 135, when the Romans inflicted their most severe vengeance, laying waste to the land of Judea (as prophesied in Leviticus 26:31-33 and Ezekiel 33:28-29), plowing bare the site of the temple (as prophesied in Micah 3:12), barring Jews from and controlling Jerusalem (Luke 21:24), and forbidding them to enter for the next 200 years.

Elwood McQuaid paints the picture:

> Roman vengeance was not confined to the city of David. Olive groves for miles around were cut down. Galilee, noted for its olive production, had scarcely a tree left standing. Villages were burned. For a time, a scorched-earth policy was rigidly enforced. Slave markets were set

> up at Gaza and Hebron, and, as the words of Christ had predicted, auctioneers sold Jews to foreign slavers who carried them to the far reaches of the world. Others, who had escaped the tyrants' grasp, packed tattered belongings and slipped quietly out of the land to begin the long centuries of enforced exile.[1]

Jerusalem was renamed Aelia Capitolina and rebuilt as a Roman city. Among other things, Emperor Hadrian made the study and practice of Judaism a crime and erected a new temple to the god Jupiter over the Temple Mount. In an attempt to prevent any Jewish rebuilding or association with the land, and to erase the Jewish people's name and memory from the land altogether, Emperor Hadrian renamed Judea (from which the words *Jew* and *Judaism* are derived) to Syria-Palaestina or Palestine, in honor of Israel's two greatest enemies: the Assyrians and Philistines. Hadrian's plan worked perfectly because until 1948, the land was referred to as Palestine.

Psalm 83:2-4 says,

> For behold, your enemies make an uproar;
> those who hate you have raised their heads.
> They lay crafty plans against your people;
> they consult together against your treasured ones.
> They say, "Come, *let us wipe them out as a nation;*
> *let the name of Israel be remembered no more!*"

Even today, many Christians are confused as to what the land is called. A few years ago, we attended a Christmas Eve service and the pastor said, "When Jesus was born in Palestine..." The hair stood on the back of my neck because Jesus had been resurrected and seated at the right hand of the Father for more than 100 years before Hadrian changed the name of the land.

A few days later, an elder at that same church told me that 10,000 people had come for the Christmas Eve services; every one of them heard the incorrect information that Jesus was born in Palestine. Our Lord was *not* born in Palestine. He never walked through Palestine. Jesus was born in Judea and walked through Judea, Samaria, and Israel. A Muslim US congresswoman made the news after she retweeted a tweet from an American Muslim scholar accusing conservative Christians of being ignorant about Jesus's "Palestinian" heritage. The tweet said, in part, "Don't they know Jesus was a Palestinian?" Hours before that tweet, *The New York Times* printed an opinion piece that stated, "Jesus, born in Bethlehem, was most likely a Palestinian man with dark skin."[2]

Author David Brog writes, "Rome's ethnic cleansing of Judea would be the greatest tragedy to befall the Jewish people until the Holocaust."[3] But even in this scorched wasteland, a remnant still remained, a remnant who, remarkably, was still the majority in the land.

THE LAND IS OCCUPIED

Over the centuries, the land was a territory ruled by the Romans, the Byzantine Empire, the Persian Empire, and the Arabs. The Arabs built mosques on major Jewish sites, including the Temple Mount in Jerusalem, yet even Arab historians admit that Muslims were not a majority in the region. The famous Arab geographer al-Maqdisi wrote that Christians and Jews still outnumbered Muslims in Palestine.[4]

There was a period of nearly 90 years during which the Crusaders ruled the land. Journalist Joan Peters wrote that

> although the Crusaders of the eleventh century were "merciless" in their attempts to eradicate the Jews from the Holy Land, they did not succeed, and in Galilee, a number of Jewish villages survived intact. In the fourteenth century, a visiting Christian monk, Jacques of Verona, wrote of "the long-established Jewish community at the foot of Mount Zion in Jerusalem."[5]

The Crusaders ruled the land until the Muslims gained control again in 1187. Jews began to return to the land from parts of Europe, Arab regions, and North Africa. For a span of two years beginning in 1209, 300 rabbis from Europe immigrated to the land. Muslims relied on slaves called the Mamluks as their army, and in 1260, the Mamluks gained control and ruled the land until the Ottomans invaded in 1517. The Ottoman Empire would rule for the next 400 years. Like previous occupiers, the Turks didn't care about the land; it was just a place to gather taxes from the residents there, and they continued to let the region fall into disrepair. More Jews tried to return, but the Turks refused them.

Since AD 70, the Jews had wanted to go back to the land, and every year at their Seder meal during Passover, they would end the meal with these words: "Next year in Jerusalem." Exiled Jews began sneaking in so they would not be thrown out, but the eighteenth century "was a largely bleak expanse of continued decline for Palestine and its Jews. The same familiar hits—both manmade and natural—just kept on coming."[6]

The nineteenth century saw more of the same, with the population dwindling to around 200,000. "Violence, disease, and poverty decimated the population. Waves of immigrants returned to replenish and rebuild. Then man and nature collaborated to tear it all down again."[7] In 1839, the British opened their Jerusalem Consulate, extending protection to the persecuted Jews of Jerusalem, and for the first time in centuries, the Jews had an ally.

A REMNANT REMAINED

Ever since Jerusalem's destruction in AD 70 and the Jewish people were scattered, no matter who ruled the land, there is abundant historical evidence that a remnant of Jews always remained, living in all parts of the region. This has been confirmed by author David Brog, who has done copious research that he provides in his book *Reclaiming Israel's History*, which I recommend. He says that by 1872 there were 5,000 Christians, 5,000 Muslims, and 11,000 Jews in Jerusalem.[8]

During the Ottoman Empire's rule, no one who lived in the land identified as a Palestinian or Arab. Rather, they identified as Ottoman subjects. In his research, Brog discovered that it was in the early 1900s that a tiny group of Arabic-speaking intellectuals studying in Western-run schools first began to see themselves not as Ottomans but as Arabs.[9] Leading Palestinian academics such as Rashid Khalidi identify the Third Palestinian Arab Congress that met in December 1920 as marking the birth of Palestinian nationalism. However, the process by which Palestinian nationalism would trickle down to the average citizen would take decades.[10]

It is important to understand that *this land was not a recognized country* during the nearly 2,000 years that it was ruled by foreign entities. In 1917, Britain conquered the region, ending the Ottoman rule, and in 1920 was granted a mandate by the League of Nations to establish a responsible government. Even then, the land was not an independent country. It remained a British mandate until Great Britain announced its termination of the mandate on May 15, 1948, one day after the state of Israel declared its independence, but more on that later. First, the land needs to come alive.

PROPHESY TO THE MOUNTAINS

The prophet Ezekiel was among the Jews taken into captivity during the Babylonian conquest. While in Babylon, he received prophetic messages from the Lord and shared them with his fellow Jews in exile. The prophecy to the mountains in Ezekiel 36 is astounding, and I urge you to read the entire chapter. I've included the first seven verses here:

> You, son of man, *prophesy to the mountains of Israel*, and say, O mountains of Israel, hear the word of the LORD. Thus says the Lord GOD: Because the enemy said of you, "Aha!" and, "The ancient heights have become our possession," therefore prophesy, and say, *Thus says the Lord GOD: Precisely because they made you desolate and crushed you from all sides, so that you became the possession of the rest of the nations,* and you became the talk and evil gossip of the people, therefore, O mountains of Israel, hear the word of the Lord GOD: Thus says the Lord GOD to the mountains and the hills, the ravines and the valleys, the desolate wastes and the deserted cities, which have become a prey and derision to the rest of the nations all around, therefore thus says the Lord GOD: Surely I have

> spoken in my hot jealousy against the rest of the nations and against all Edom, who gave my land to themselves as a possession with wholehearted joy and utter contempt, that they might make its pasturelands a prey. Therefore prophesy concerning the land of Israel, and say to the mountains and hills, to the ravines and valleys, Thus says the Lord GOD: Behold, I have spoken in my jealous wrath, because you have suffered the reproach of the nations. Therefore thus says the Lord GOD: I swear that the nations that are all around you shall themselves suffer reproach (Ezekiel 36:1-7).

God told Ezekiel to prophesy directly to the land, which would become desolate and be prey to the nations. The nations gave the land to themselves in utter contempt and it suffered greatly at their hands, becoming bleak, wretched, and barren. But God tells Ezekiel to prophesy life to this land that's barely breathing because His people were soon to come home! And look what happens to the land when they do come home:

> You, O mountains of Israel, shall shoot forth your branches and yield your fruit to my people Israel, for they will soon come home. For behold, I am for you, and I will turn to you, and you shall be tilled and sown. And I will multiply people on you, the whole house of Israel, all of it. The cities shall be inhabited and the waste places rebuilt. And I will multiply on you man and beast, and they shall multiply and be fruitful. And I will cause you to be inhabited as in your former times, and will do more good to you than ever before. Then you will know that I am the LORD. I will let people walk on you, even my people Israel. And they shall possess you, and you shall be their inheritance, and you shall no longer bereave them of children (Ezekiel 36:8-12).

God told Ezekiel to prophesy to the land, saying, in essence, "Get ready. I'm bringing my people home and you're going to be inhabited again. You will be beautiful and fruitful, and will do more good than ever before!" The land would come to life again only when God brought the Jews home to it. Until then, the land was worthless and desolate. But when would God bring His people home? How long would they have to wait? And if He drove them from the land, why bring them back at all?

WHERE IN THE WORD?

Why God Brought the Jews Back

In Ezekiel 36, God explains *why* He's going to bring the Jewish people back into the land and make it fruitful. Beginning in verse 20, God speaks of the Jews after they were driven from the land and into the nations of the world:

> When they came to the nations, wherever they came, they profaned my holy name, in that people said of them, "These are the people of the Lord, and yet they had to go out of his land." *But I had concern for my holy name*, which the house of Israel had profaned among the nations to which they came. Therefore say to the house of Israel, Thus says the Lord God: It is not for your sake, O house of Israel, that I am about to act, *but for the sake of my holy name,* which you have profaned among the nations to which you came. And I will vindicate the holiness of my great name, which has been profaned among the nations, and which you have profaned among them. And the nations will know that I am the Lord, declares the Lord God, when through you I vindicate my holiness before their eyes. I

> will take you from the nations and gather you from all the countries and bring you into your own land...It is not for your sake that I will act, declares the Lord God; let that be known to you...Then the nations that are left all around you shall know that I am the Lord; I have rebuilt the ruined places and replanted that which was desolate. I am the Lord; I have spoken, and I will do it" (Ezekiel 36:20-23, 32, 36).

God's name is holy, and He brought the Jews back to the land to vindicate the holiness of His great name. For God to bring the Jewish people back wasn't about their faithfulness. Rather, it was all about His holy name.

IT IS GOD'S LAND

It's important to note that Ezekiel wasn't told to prophesy to any humans but to the mountains, land, ravines, hills, valleys, the desolate wastes, and deserted cities of Israel (Ezekiel 36:1, 3-4, 6). In speaking to Ezekiel, God calls the land

- "my land" (verse 5)
- "their own land" (meaning the house of Israel in verse 17)
- "his land" (verse 20)
- "your own land" (verse 24)
- "the land that I gave" (verse 28)

This land is significant to God. It is His land, which He gave to the Jews as an everlasting possession. Nowhere in these verses does it ever indicate that the other nations who inhabited the land were possessors of the land, and from the history of the land we learn that the invading entities were just that—invading nations and peoples who ruled over the land that belonged to God. He says of these nations in verse 5, "I have spoken in my hot jealousy against the rest of the nations...who gave my land to themselves as a possession with wholehearted joy and utter contempt, that they might make its pasturelands a prey." This land reflects God's promise to Abraham and his descendants, and it would grieve the heart of God to see it mistreated, abused, and trampled on by invading nations, which is exactly what the occupiers did.

GOD'S PROMISE TO THE LAND ITSELF

Note what God said to His land that has been plundered, devastated, crushed, and made desolate after years of occupation:

- "You, O mountains of Israel, shall shoot forth your branches and yield your fruit to my people Israel" (verse 8).
- "You shall be tilled and sown" (verse 9).
- "I will multiply people on you, the whole house of Israel, all of it" (verse 10).
- "I will multiply on you man and beast, and they shall multiply and be fruitful. And I will cause you to be inhabited as in your former times, and will do more good to you than ever before" (verse 11).
- "I will let people walk on you, even my people Israel. And they shall possess you, and you shall be their inheritance, and you shall no longer bereave them of children" (verse 12).

In a word, the land would flourish for both man and animal! It would be an inheritance to God's people Israel and generations of children would grow up there.

FROM DESOLATE TO FLOURISHING

Mark Twain, in his book *The Innocents Abroad*, wrote about his visit to the Holy Land in 1867. His descriptions are those of a desolate country on life support:

> There is not a solitary village throughout its whole extent—not for thirty miles in either direction. There are two or three small clusters of Bedouin tents, but not a single permanent habitation. One may ride ten miles, hereabouts, and not see ten human beings…there is no dew here, nor flowers, nor birds, nor trees. There is a plain and an unshaded lake, and beyond them some barren mountains.[1]

Of his journey south toward Jerusalem, he wrote,

> The further we went the hotter the sun got, and the more rocky and bare, repulsive and dreary the landscape became…there was hardly a tree or a shrub anywhere. Even the olive and the cactus, those fast friends of a worthless soil, had almost deserted the country. No landscape exists that is more tiresome to the eyes then that which abounds the approaches to Jerusalem.[2]

Twain further stated,

> Of all the lands there are for dismal scenery, I think Palestine must be the prince. The hills are barren, they are dull of color, they are unpicturesque in shape. The valleys are unsightly deserts fringed with a feeble vegetation that has an expression about it of being sorrowful and despondent…every outline is harsh, every feature is distinct, there is no perspective—distance works no enchantment here. It is a hopeless, dreary, heartbroken land.[3]

With the exception of the remnant Jews, few were clamoring to live in this desolate wasteland. More than 70 years after Twain's visit, Walter Lowdermilk, who was with the US Soil Conservation Service, traveled to the land in 1938–1939. He described hillsides that were stripped of topsoil after desert Arabs cut down the trees and left the region "a desert land with no one to till the soil." He observed that "the decay of Palestine reached its darkest stage in the four hundred years of Turkish rule, from 1517 to 1918."[4]

My friend Terrie Carswell said, "Who would want to live in a land that was stripped and desolate? God left it stripped and awful so no one would want that land. It makes me believe the prophecies of God all the more because the land had to lie like that until God brought the Jews home. They were the ones who could restore it, and in His timing, they came home, and the land came to life again."

Though the land lay decaying for nearly 2,000 years God fulfilled the promises He gave through Ezekiel. He promised that when the people returned…

> the land will be tilled and sown,
> and it will blossom and produce fruit again
>
> cities will be inhabited
>
> the desolate places will be rebuilt
>
> people and beasts will multiply
>
> children will be born and the population will grow
>
> I will do more good to you than ever before
>
> My people will possess you
>
> (Ezekiel 36:9-12).

And how will this happen? God said, "I will let people walk on you, even my people Israel. And they shall possess you, and you shall be their inheritance" (verse 12). The land would be desolate *until God lets His people Israel back onto it.* When Israel possessed the land, the land would flourish, just as God prophesied.

WHERE IN THE WORD?

GET READY

As we've discovered in Ezekiel 36, God told Ezekiel to prophesy to the land: "Get ready—I'm bringing My people home." In the very next chapter, the hand of the Lord is on the prophet Ezekiel and He takes him out to a valley and tells him to prophesy to dried bones. Ezekiel does, and the bones stand to their feet.

> He said to me: "Son of man, these bones are the people of Israel. They say, 'Our bones are dried up and our hope is gone; we are cut off.' Therefore prophesy and say to them: 'This is what the Sovereign LORD says: My people, I am going to open your graves and bring you up from them; I will bring you back to the land of Israel. Then you, my people, will know that I am the LORD, when I open your graves and bring you up from them. I will put my Spirit in you and you will live, and I will settle you in your own land. Then you will know that I the LORD have spoken, and I have done it, declares the LORD'" (Ezekiel 37:11-14 NIV).

The Jews had been scattered for nearly 2,000 years; their hope was gone, they had been cut off from their homeland. But God breathed life into the bones of Israel and brought the Jews back and settled them in their own land just as He said He would do.

HOMECOMING

Although not the first to conceive the idea of a Jewish state, Theodor Herzl, a journalist and Austrian Jew, wrote a pamphlet called *The Jewish State* in 1896. He organized and became the first president of the World Zionist Organization, which held its first conference in 1897 in Basel, Switzerland. Herzl said this would be "the foundation stone for the house which will become the refuge of the Jewish nation." His efforts helped provide the momentum that would be crucial to the rebirth of Israel in 1948.

Israel's homecoming also can't be told without telling the story of Chaim Weizmann, a Russian Jew who worked as a chemist in England. He was also a leader in the Zionist movement, and he played a major role for the Allied forces in World War I.

During the war, the English armies used gunpowder made from cordite, which didn't blind the British soldiers with smoke or reveal their position to the enemy. However, to make cordite, acetone is needed, and the compound from which it was made came from Germany, the enemy. British prime minister David Lloyd George and the minister of munitions, Winston Churchill, turned to the brilliant chemist Chaim Weizmann for help. They set him up inside a gin distillery, and he developed a biochemical process for producing synthetic acetone. The fact the British could produce their own acetone contributed largely to the Allied victory and, at the war's end, Britain defeated the Ottoman Empire and gained possession of the land of Palestine.

Grateful to Weizmann, the British government issued the Balfour Declaration of 1917, named after Arthur Balfour, who was Britain's foreign secretary. Both Balfour and Prime Minister David Lloyd George were Christians, and they held the biblical belief that Israel was to be restored to the Jews. The Balfour Declaration read in part:

> His Majesty's government views with favor the establishment in Palestine of a national home for the Jewish people, and will use their best endeavors to facilitate the achievements of this object.[1]

The land given to the Jewish people included what was then known as Palestine and Jordan—45,000 square miles, which is roughly the size of Pennsylvania. In 1922, the British realized that the Arabs were discovering oil and lots of it, and to appease them, they gave two-thirds of Palestine to the Arabs, leaving Israel with less than 10,000 square miles, which is roughly the size of New Jersey.

As we learned earlier, Great Britain was given a mandate from the League of Nations over the land of Palestine in 1920. At the end of World War II, as Nazi concentration camps were being liberated, the world was shocked at the gruesome pictures and news footage of prisoners at Auschwitz, Dachau, and other concentration camps. Six million Jews lost their lives as they were murdered in their own towns and homes and in the horrific camps. Great sympathy poured out from around the world in the form of donations, and more than one million displaced Jews returned to their land.

GOD'S TIMING

President Franklin Roosevelt was inaugurated for his fourth term on January 20, 1945, and died less than three months later. It was known among many at the time that his view of the Jewish people was less than favorable. At a wartime White House luncheon with Prime Minister Churchill, he suggested "the best way to settle the Jewish question" was "to spread the Jews thin all over the world." At other times he said that Harvard should institute a quota on the number of Jewish students, that Jews were dominating the economy in Poland and provoking anti-Semitism there, and there were too many federal employees in Oregon who were Jews.[2] At the 1945 Yalta Conference held between Roosevelt, Churchill, and Stalin, Roosevelt indicated to Stalin that as a concession to the king of Saudi Arabia he would "give him the six million Jews in the United States."[3]

In 1939, the US government refused to admit Jews onboard the *S.S. St. Louis* to come to America. There were 937 passengers on the ship, almost all of them Jewish who were fleeing the Third Reich. They were supposed to dock in Cuba until they could enter the United States, but Cuba refused them, and President Roosevelt would not help either. The US had already let in its quota of immigrants that year, and government officials felt that letting the Jews into the country would threaten national security. The ship went back to Europe, and more than one-quarter of the passengers died in the Holocaust.[4]

PRESIDENT TRUMAN

In 1933, the Jewish population of Europe was about 9.5 million. By 1945, two out of three Jews had been killed.[5] From 1919 to 1922, Truman had been co-partners in a haberdashery with a Jewish man named Eddie Jacobson. The business failed, but the friendship survived. Although Truman had written in a diary in 1947 that he found the Jews "to be very selfish,"[6] he wrote that his former business partner Eddie Jacobson was "as fine a man as ever walked."[7]

After the brutality of the Holocaust, President Truman was moved by the need to help the Jews. When talk began of the establishment of a Jewish homeland in what was then called Palestine, Eddie Jacobson lobbied his old friend in the White House on a number of occasions. There's no question that the power of relationship had a significant part in helping with the reestablishment of the nation of Israel. With the exception of Clark Clifford, one of Truman's advisors, everyone else counseled President Truman against supporting Israel's nationhood. At times Truman was conflicted about what to do (after all, the number of naysayers was overwhelming), and we must wonder if he would have given in to their way of thinking had it not been for his relationship with Eddie Jacobson.

WHERE IN THE WORD?

THE BIBLE'S ROLE

Regarding the potential Jewish state, not only was President Truman moved by the pressing circumstances of the Jewish people, but he was also moved by the Bible. He believed the Jews held historical right to the land based on Deuteronomy 1:8, which says, "See, I have set the land before you. Go in and take possession of the land that the LORD swore to your fathers, to Abraham, to Isaac, and to Jacob."[1]

The following abbreviated timeline is from President Truman's library.

As early as 1939, then-Senator Truman is cited in the Congressional Record, criticizing the British White Paper in Palestine and its stringent restrictions on Jews acquiring land.

In 1945, President Truman wrote to British Prime Minister Attlee, urging him to allow a reasonable number of Jews to immigrate to Palestine.

October 4, 1946, on the eve of Yom Kippur, President Truman issued a statement indicating the United States' support for the creation of a "viable Jewish state."

November 29, 1947, United Nations Resolution 181 was passed by the United Nations General Assembly, calling for the partition of Palestine into Arab and Jewish states.

March 18, 1948, Eddie Jacobson persuades President Truman to meet with Dr. Chaim Weizmann (the chemist who had helped the

Allies to victory in WWI), President of the Jewish Agency for Palestine and the World Zionist Organization.[2]

Wednesday, May 12, 1948, 50 hours before the rebirth of Israel, President Harry Truman met with his advisers inside the oval office. Officials from the State Department were there, along with Secretary of State General George Marshall and some of President Truman's closest advisers, including Clark Clifford. According to Clifford's book, *Counsel to the President,* each of the president's advisers counseled that he postpone any decision on the recognition of this new country. When it came Clifford's time to speak, he gave reasons to recognize the new state and General Marshall erupted in heated anger, telling President Truman that if he followed Clifford's advice that he would vote against him in the upcoming election. Officials from the State Department backed General Marshall wholeheartedly and the meeting came to an abrupt end. Clifford left the meeting feeling defeated and President Truman knew he could not afford an enemy in General Marshall. Months earlier, Truman's Secretary of Defense, James Forrestal said to Clifford, "You fellows over at the White House are just not facing up to the realities in the Middle East. There are 30 million Arabs on one side and about 600,000 Jews on the other. It is clear that in any contest, the Arabs are going to overwhelm the Jews. Why don't you face up to the realities? Just look at the numbers!"[3]

May 14, 1948, David Ben-Gurion, Israel's first prime minister, read a declaration of independence that proclaimed the rebirth of the Jewish state of Israel. The United States officially recognized Israel's nationhood with the following statement from the White House: "This government has been informed that a Jewish state has been proclaimed in Palestine, and recognition has been requested by the provisional government thereof. The United States recognizes the provisional government as the de facto authority of the state of Israel."[4]

And in one day a nation was formed, exactly as prophesied in Isaiah 66:

> Before she was in labor
>   she gave birth;

before her pain came upon her
she delivered a son.
Who has heard such a thing?
Who has seen such things?
Shall a land be born in one day?
Shall a nation be brought forth in one moment?
For as soon as Zion was in labor
she brought forth her children (verses 7-8).

WAR BREAKS OUT

The very next day, May 15, 1948, five Arab states (Iraq, Egypt, Transjordan, Syria, and Lebanon) attacked Israel. Miraculously, the fledgling nation survived. Interestingly, no one was fighting over this land until it was given back to the Jewish people. Remember, nothing was growing there. It was a wasteland.

The War of Independence in 1948 was responsible for creating 700,000 Palestinian Arab refugees (many of these settled in the Gaza Strip; most of the current inhabitants of the Gaza Strip today are refugees of the 1948 war and their descendants). In contrast, David Brog notes that the war in Afghanistan has produced more than 2.5 million refugees, the Iraq war has produced more than 1.5 million, and by early 2016, the Syrian Civil War had produced well over 4 million refugees—a number that is certainly much higher at the time of this writing in 2020.[5]

It must be noted that the Palestinians have been offered a state of their own in most of the West Bank and Gaza (since 2006, the 140-mile Gaza Strip has been governed by the terrorist group Hamas, and it "has become a site for protests, bombings, land assaults and other acts of violence")[6] and in larger territories on six separate occasions. The first offer was made in 1937 and the most recent was in 2020.[7] The Palestinians turned down every single offer. After the Geneva peace talks in 1973, Israeli diplomat Abba Eban said, "The Arabs never miss an opportunity to miss an opportunity."[8] Why would they turn down these offers for a land of their own? The only plausible answer appears to be it's because they want all the land, and not just some of it. This lines up with the widespread Arab sentiment that Israel should be wiped off the map completely.

The Encyclopedia of the Stateless Nations examines the claims of 350 stateless nations, and those 350 are only a fraction of the world's supposedly 6,000 stateless nations. The author chronicled only the stateless nations that are actively seeking their independence. According to the United Nations, "Only 3% of the world's 6,000 national groups have achieved statehood." Some of these stateless nations are relatively new, such as the Palestinians, whose national identities were developed after World War I, World War II, or even later. Other stateless nations are ancient ones, such as the Kurds, who have had their own separate identities for centuries. Some stateless nations are small and unheard of, like the 790,000 Jejuvians of Korea, and the 1.3 million Majeerteens of Somalia. Other stateless nations are larger yet still obscure, like the 23 million Ibos of Nigeria. Other stateless nations have higher profiles, like the 6.5 million Tibetans in China and the 70 million Tamils of south India and northern Sri Lanka.[9]

As we can see, the Palestinians aren't the only stateless nation, but why is this one particular stateless nation the subject of so much of the world's attention? Because the Bible says that in the last days "all nations" will come against Israel (Zechariah 12:9; 14:2-3; see also Joel 3). Jerusalem will be a "cup of trembling" and a "burdensome stone" that "all the people of earth [will] be gathered together against" (Zechariah 12:2-3 KJV). Despite the existence of 6,000 stateless nations, the plight of the Palestinians will remain at the forefront of the world news, and Israel will continue to be blamed as the bad guy.

Let's take a moment to look at the "burdensome stone" mentioned in Zechariah 12:3. There are very few cities in the world that are in the news as much as Jerusalem; from a political and religious standpoint, it is the most contested city on the face of the earth. For previous generations, this passage wouldn't have made any sense. The idea of Jerusalem being a hotbed of activity and fought over was absurd. It was never in the news. Before 1948, pictures of Jerusalem revealed a mostly desolate, dusty, depressing place. But ever since the Jews fought for the city in 1967 and won, it has been in the news. When President Trump declared it the capital of Israel on May 14, 2018, the news ricocheted around the world, and many claimed this change would start a terrible war in the Middle East. Jerusalem is indeed a burdensome stone to the nations.

NEVER IN HISTORY

Back to the Palestinians. Are we concerned for them? Of course—just as we are concerned for the welfare and protection of every person who is part of a stateless group. All of these people are made in the image of God.

Do we agree with everything the government of Israel does? No, just as we don't agree with everything our own government does. Much of the world sees Israel as "occupied territory," as if Israel is occupying Palestinian land, but as we've learned from history, Israel's name was changed to Palestine, and Palestine was never a recognized country. It remained a desolate territory for nearly 2,000 years because God told us that's what would happen. On May 14, 1948, in what many Bible scholars call the greatest miracle of the twentieth century, Israel became a country recognized by the United Nations. This fulfilled prophecy that didn't make sense to previous generations, but we're the generation that sees it being fulfilled.

A rebirth like Israel's has never happened before in the history of the world. There are no ancient people groups that have lost their country, were uprooted and scattered for 1,900 years, and then were brought back into that same land and proclaimed a country again. Since 1948, against all odds and human reasoning, the nation of Israel has survived wars and constant attacks by the enemies who surround them and openly swear to annihilate them—enemies with a land mass of more than five million square miles. Israel's land mass is not quite 9,000 square miles. How does this tiny nation survive in such a rough neighborhood?

In Amos 9:15, God said, "I will plant them on their land, and *they shall never again be uprooted out of the land* that I have given them." This is the reason the Arab world was unsuccessful in the attempts to eliminate the Jewish state of Israel during the 1948 War of Independence, the Suez Canal War in 1956, the Six-Day War in 1967, and the Yom Kippur War in 1973. Nations will continue to be unsuccessful because the people "shall never again be uprooted."

Israel is the only nation in the history of the world to be driven from its land and brought back to life in one day—just as God said He would do.

WHERE IN THE WORD?

THE FIG TREE

George Washington wrote these words to a Hebrew congregation in Newport, Rhode Island, in 1790: "May the Children of the Stock of Abraham, who dwell in this land, continue to merit and enjoy the good will of the other Inhabitants; while every one shall sit in safety under his own vine and fig tree, and there shall be none to make him afraid."[1] While it's obvious that President Washington was writing that these Jewish citizens could live in safety without fear in our land (there isn't space to address the current wave of anti-Semitism in our country today), what's interesting is that he referred to the biblical symbols of the vine and fig tree when he addressed this Jewish audience.

THE LESSON OF THE FIG TREE

In the Bible, Israel is symbolically referred to as the vine, an olive tree, and a fig tree or figs (Hosea 9:10; 10:1; 14:5-6; Joel 1:6-7, 11-12; Isaiah 5:1-7; Jeremiah 2:21; 8:12-13; 11:16-17; 24:5; 29:16-17; Romans 11:17, 24). As we've learned, following Jerusalem's destruction in AD 70, there was only a remnant of Jews remaining—the fig tree was barren. But there would come a day when that would change. When the disciples asked Jesus for the signs of His coming and of the end of the age, He said in part, "Now learn this lesson from the fig tree: As soon as its twigs get tender and its leaves come out, you know that summer is near" (Matthew 24:32).

Earlier, in Matthew 21, when Jesus and the disciples were on their way to Jerusalem, they walked by a fig tree that had leaves but no fruit. Jesus was hungry, and because the tree lacked fruit, He cursed it, and it withered. After they enter Jerusalem they went to the temple, where the chief priests and Pharisees questioned His authority. During that encounter, Jesus said to them, "I tell you, the kingdom of God will be taken away from you and given to a people producing its fruits" (verse 43).

Because the Jews had rejected Jesus as their Messiah, He warned that the kingdom would be taken from them and given to people who would bear fruit. Remember, He cursed the fig tree because it wasn't bearing fruit. The withered fig tree symbolized not only the eventual barrenness of Israel, but also Israel's fruitless spiritual condition (Jeremiah 8:13; Micah 7:1; Mark 11:12-14).

In Matthew 21:43, who was Jesus talking about when He said, "The kingdom of God will be…given to a people producing its fruits"? In Ephesians 2 and Romans 11, we find reference to Gentiles (non-Jews) who are grafted into the vine. That's what has happened for nearly 2,000 years—the Gentiles have been spreading the light of Jesus and salvation.

God originally asked the Jews to take the gospel message to the far reaches of the earth, but they rejected Jesus. In *The Time of Jacob's Trouble*, I mentioned Isaiah 49:6, which says concerning the Jews, "I will also make you a light for the Gentiles, that my salvation may reach to the ends of the earth" (NIV). The Jews were supposed to take the message of salvation around the world, but the Gentiles took on that ministry when they were grafted into the vine after the Jews rejected Jesus.

In Revelation 7 and 14, during the tribulation, we see that the Jews *will* fulfill this ministry and take the gospel of Jesus around the world through the 144,000 Jewish evangelists (Elliott and Zerah in the novel). Scripture clearly states these men come from the 12 tribes of Israel, not the church. The church and the 12 tribes are always separate and distinct in the Bible, even in the New Testament. These 144,000 Jewish men will be sealed and protected, and just as God said in Isaiah 49:6, the Jews will be a light to the Gentiles and the message of salvation will spread through all the earth.

WHEN YOU SEE ALL THESE THINGS

With that as a backdrop, let's look at Matthew 24:32 again, where Jesus said to the disciples, "From the fig tree learn its lesson: as soon as its branch becomes tender and puts out its leaves, you know that summer is near. So also, when you see all these things, you know that he is near, at the very gates."

In Matthew 21, we read that Jesus cursed the fig tree and it withered, but here in Matthew 24 He said that as soon as the branches of the fig tree (that is, Israel) become tender and put out leaves, summer is near. The fig tree, or Israel, was dry and withered for nearly 1,900 years, but it put forth leaves on May 14, 1948. Jesus told His disciples that the blossoming of the fig tree was *the sign* they were to look for in connection with His coming. This would begin the countdown clock to His return. We know this because He said, "So also, when you see all these things..." He told His disciples that *in addition* to the blossoming of the fig tree, they were to look for all the things He mentioned in Matthew 24:4-28:

- deception
- false prophets and saviors
- wars and rumors of wars
- nation against nation (nation here refers to people groups, ethnic groups)
- kingdom against kingdom
- famines and earthquakes in various places (not consolidated to one region of the world)
- persecution
- people who profess to be Christians but aren't will fall away from the faith and betray and hate one another

- an increase in lawlessness, and love will grow cold
- the gospel will spread throughout the world
- the abomination of desolation will be set up inside the temple

With the exception of the abomination of desolation (the Antichrist seating himself as God) inside the temple (there isn't a temple right now in Israel), all "these things" described in Matthew 24 are converging and happening in our day. Many will argue that "these things" have been around for ages, and that's true, but Israel is the key. Israel did not exist again until 1948.

The signs are happening so quickly that it's hard to keep up with them all. As Jesus said, "when you see all these things," you know that "he is near, at the very gates." We know from the frequency and intensity of these signs that things are looking up to Christ's soon return. Jesus then said, "Truly, I say to you, this generation will not pass away until all these things take place. Heaven and earth will pass away, but my words will not pass away" (Matthew 24:34-35).

Like leaves on the fig tree—as Israel puts forth leaves and blossoms—so will all these signs grow, converging at once. As time passes, like "birth pains" (Matthew 24:8), these signs will become even more frequent and more intense. And the generation that sees all these things—the rebirth of Israel, as well as all the other signs mentioned above—will not pass away until all these things have happened. This is yet another prophecy that would have been confusing to those of previous generations because Israel wasn't a nation yet. We are the generation seeing all "these things."

The big question is this: How long is a generation? I don't know. Scripturally speaking, one generation could die out or live longer than another, but Psalm 90 says this about the length of our days:

> The years of our life are seventy,
> or even by reason of strength eighty;
> yet their span is but toil and trouble;
> they are soon gone, and we fly away (verse 10).

Psalm 90 is a prayer of Moses, and he lived to be 120. Yet he wrote that the years of our life are 70, or by reason of strength, 80. At the time of Moses, life expectancy was going down. His forefathers Adam, Noah, and Abraham lived to be 930, 950, and 175 respectively. According to the Central Intelligence Agency's *World Factbook*, the average life expectancy in the United States is 80.0 years and in Israel it's 82.5 years.[2] Moses wrote Psalm 90 more than 3,000 years ago and his words are true of this generation—our average lifespan is between 70 to 80 years.

We are the generation that's living this average lifespan, and we're the generation that's seeing the convergence of end-time signs that generations before us did not see. While we cannot know the day or hour of Christ's return, as I mentioned earlier, Jesus said we would be able to recognize the season on the basis of the parable of the fig tree. And the signs of the season tell us that these are exciting times. As Jesus said in Luke 21:28, "When these things begin to take place, straighten up and raise your head, because your redemption is drawing near."

Things are looking up!

WHERE IN THE WORD?

WHAT'S NEXT?

I'm so honored you took the time to read *The Day of Ezekiel's Hope.* My prayer is that this book has encouraged your faith, answered some nagging questions, or piqued your desire to know more about Christ so you can walk in a personal relationship with Him. If you don't know Him, you can, and upon receiving Him as your Savior and Lord, He will guide and lead you for the rest of your life.

The Bible says,

> If you declare with your mouth, "Jesus is Lord," and believe in your heart that God raised him from the dead, you will be saved. For it is with your heart that you believe and are justified, and it is with your mouth that you profess your faith and are saved. As Scripture says, "Anyone who believes in him will never be put to shame." For there is no difference between Jew and Gentile—the same Lord is Lord of all and richly blesses all who call on him, for, "Everyone who calls on the name of the Lord will be saved" (Romans 10:9-13).

St. Augustine said that God gives where He finds empty hands. Would you open your hands today and surrender to Him the sin that has separated you from Him so that He can fill your hands with His good gifts, including the gift of salvation? Would you ask Him to guide and lead your life? God knows our hearts and whether we're truly repentant, confessing and turning from our sin; He knows when we are honestly seeking Him. If you want to know Him, tell Him that. Tell Him that you believe that He raised Jesus from the dead and proclaim with your mouth that Jesus is Lord, and you will be saved. And once you've become a child of God, you'll want to ask for His help every day as you read His Word and walk with Him.

We'll explore more of the end times in the third and last book, *Daniel's Final Week*. Until then, may God bless you and keep you and make His face shine on you, being gracious to you. May the Lord turn His face toward you and give you peace—in Jesus's name.

A PREVIEW FROM BOOK 3

Daniel's Final Week

Chapter 1

The heavens shudder and galaxies, long held fast by gravity, retreat as if cowering in fright. Stars shake loose from their orbits and tumble to earth as Satan screeches before heaven's throne. With access permitted by the Most High, the ancient serpent has flown through the air relinquished by the first Adam thousands of years earlier and stands before God, condemning those sealed by the Lamb's blood.

"No! No! No!" the great dragon shouts as the heavens tremble, grabbing his sword as myriad angels sweep over the deceiver of the whole world to fight his demonic legion, who millennia ago fell from their heavenly place with the father of lies. Beelzebub's wings spread and his face twists in rage as he charges the throne. "I won't let you!"

Michael the archangel tosses the prince of demons aside, and when the lawless one regains his footing, his wings rise high over his head like a black menacing storm as he flies toward Michael.

"I cast you to the ground forever!"

The Most High's voice thunders throughout the heavens as the god of this age crumples before Almighty God, begging for his life. "I am the prince of the air!" Satan pleads. "The earth belongs to me!"

The Almighty will hear no more. Heaven is barred to the accuser forever, and Michael lifts up the murderer and tempter and hurls him to earth as the armies of heaven wage tremendous war against the adversary's vicious legion, throwing them from the heavenlies.

A mighty angel turns to the angelic throng and souls throughout heaven. "Rejoice, O heavens and you who dwell in them!" Together, God's armies watch Lucifer fall as a magnificent star from heaven for good. "But woe to you, O earth and sea, for the devil has come down to you in great wrath, because he knows that his time is short!"

The dragon falls to the bottomless pit, where many of his angels have been locked away for centuries on end. An angel of the Almighty illuminates the penetrating dark, holding a key and looking at the destroyer raving in vengeance. Satan takes the key and unlocks the pit as his hellish army, grateful to their master, shriek on their release, filling the air with a heinous and incomprehensible evil.

Satan wings his way in fury to Jerusalem, where the wounded or dead are being recovered from the massive earthquake that toppled a tenth of the city, killing 7,000 people. To his horror, the two hated witnesses who were murdered have risen from the dead and into the skies in front of the watching world. The lawless one knows that if he is to rule the entire planet there has to be one final bloodbath—Israel must be annihilated and the Jews destroyed so his enemy cannot return and reign from here.

The ruler of this world hovers above the city, listening as the swine cry out in fear and watching as the body of Victor Quade is pulled from the rubble, his head bloody from a monstrous wound. Hearts are broken as the news spreads throughout the globe that their hero, the very one who saved them from the devastating plagues sent by the two witnesses, appears to be dead. The evil one waits as more cameras and phones are focused on the horror of Victor's wound and seemingly lifeless body before making his move.

Two thousand years ago, he entered Judas, and to his delight, Judas betrayed the devil's great enemy. Satan roared in triumph as his enemy died on a cross outside Jerusalem, but the enemy rose in devastating victory and today he lives, and his people who reek of Satan's own end live as well. But now, for all eternity, they will die, and he will live forever.

With the blackest of rage he swoops down through the air and slithers into the body of Victor Quade. Victor's eyes flash open, and his mouth turns up in a smile.

NOTES

WHERE IN THE WORD? THRASHING TIME

1. Carolyn Arends, "Headless Snakes and Other Matters," *Carolyn Arends*, October 15, 2014, https://carolynarends.com/headless-snakes-and-other-matters/.
2. Paul McGuire and Troy Ansderson, *The Babylon Code* (New York: Faithwords, 2015), 8.
3. David Jeremiah, "5 Signs of Christ's Return," *DavidJeremiah.blog*, https://davidjeremiah.blog/5-signs-you-may-see-christ/.

WHERE IN THE WORD? THE COALITION AGAINST ISRAEL

1. "Immigration to Israel on way to passing last year's numbers," *Jewish Telegraphic Agency*, December 16, 2019, https://www.jta.org/quick-reads/immigration-to-israel-on-way-to-passing-last-years-numbers.
2. Kyle Rempfer, "Russia's probably not leaving Syria antime soon. Here's why," *MilitaryTimes*, July 27, 2018, https://www.militarytimes.com/flashpoints/2018/07/27/russias-probably-not-leaving-syria-anytime-soon-heres-why/; "Turkey promises 'safe zones' in Kurdish-held parts of Syria," *MilitaryTimes*, September 24, 2018), https://www.militarytimes.com/flashpoints/2018/09/24/turkey-promises-safe-zones-in-kurdish-held-parts-of-syria/; "Israel has 'freedom to act' against Iran inside Syria: Netanyahu," *Arabia Day*, https://arabiaday.com/israel-has-freedom-to-act-against-iran-inside-syria-netanyahu/.
3. "The US, China, Russia and Iran All Agree with Pakistan's Position in Afghanistan," *Eurasia Future*, https://eurasiafuture.com/2018/04/04/presidents-of-russia-iran-and-turkey-meet-in-ankara-erdogan-thanks-russia-and-iran-for-support-in-operation-olive-branch/; "The Latest: Iran, Russia, Turkey presidents meet in summit," *Fox News*, September 7, 2018, https://www.foxnews.com/world/the-latest-iran-russia-turkey-presidents-meet-in-summit.
4. "Joint statement by presidents of Iran, Russia, and Turkey at end of Sochi summit," *Mehr News Agency*, February 15, 2019, https://en.mehrnews.com/news/142523/Joint-statement-by-presidents-of-Iran-Russia-and-Turkey-at-end.
5. Joyce Chepkemoi, "The Richest and Poorest Economies in the Middle East," *WorldAtlas*, August 1, 2017, https://www.worldatlas.com/articles/the-richest-and-poorest-economies-in-the-middle-east.html.
6. "21 Israelis ranked in Forbes 2019 Billionaires list," *Globes*, March 5, 2019, https://en.globes.co.il/en/article-21-israelis-ranked-in-forbes-2019-billionaires-list-1001276833.
7. "Israel has 131,000 millionaires, and its wealth is growing," *Times of Israel*, https://www.timesofisrael.com/israel-has-131000-millionaires-and-wealth-is-growing-quickly-report-finds/.
8. Jordan Yerman, "A Startup Nation: Why Israel Has Become the New Silicon Valley," *Apex*, May 22, 2019, https://apex.aero/2019/05/22/startup-nation-israel-become-silicon-valley.
9. Paul Alster, "Potentially game-changing oil reserves discovered in Israel," *Fox News*, updated December 8, 2015, https://www.foxnews.com/world/potentially-game-changing-oil-reserves-discovered-in-israel.

10. Ariel Cohen, "Israel's Leviathan Energy Prize: Where Will the Gas Go?," *Forbes*, February 19, 2019, https://www.forbes.com/sites/arielcohen/2019/02/19/israels-leviathan-energy-prize-where-will-the-gas-go/#748e40738194.

11. "Karish and Tanin Field Development, Mediterranean Sea," *Offshore Technology*, https://www.offshore-technology.com/projects/karish-tanin-field-development-mediterranean-sea/.

12. "Israel inks mega gas pipeline deal with Greece, Cyprus," *Times of Israel*, January 2, 2020, https://www.timesofisrael.com/israel-inks-mega-gas-pipeline-deal-with-greece-cyprus/.

13. "Greece, Cyprus, Israel Sign EastMed Gas Pipeline Deal to Ease Reliance on Russia," *RadioFreeEuropeRadioLiberty*, January 3, 2020, https://www.rferl.org/a/greece-cyprus-israel-eastmed-gas-pipeline-russia-ukraine/30358166.html.

14. Eytan Halon, "Israel exports soared by almost 70% over past decade," *The Jerusalem Post*, December 30, 2019, https://www.jpost.com/Israel-News/Israeli-exports-soared-by-almost-70-percent-over-past-decade-612535.

15. Daniel Workman, "World's Top Export Countries," *World's Top Exports*, September 5, 2020, http://www.worldstopexports.com/worlds-top-export-countries/.

16. Nazila Fathi, "Wipe Israel 'off the map' Iranian says," *The New York Times*, October 27, 2005, https://www.nytimes.com/2005/10/27/world/africa/wipe-israel-off-the-map-iranian-says.html.

WHERE IN THE WORD? IS ISRAEL DWELLING SECURELY?

1. Eytan Halon, "Israel welcomes record-breaking 4.55 million tourists in 2019," *The Jerusalem Post*, December 29, 2019, https://www.jpost.com/Israel-News/Israel-welcomes-record-breaking-45-million-tourists-in-2019-612456.

2. Lidar Grave-Lazi, "Majority of Israelis feel safe walking alone at night, survey finds," *The Jerusalem Post*, June 27, 2016, https://www.jpost.com/Israel-News/CBS-Most-Israelis-feel-safe-walking-alone-at-night-457911.

3. Yaakov Katz, "Why Israel has the most technologically advanced military on earth," *New York Post*, January 29, 2017, https://nypost.com/2017/01/29/why-israel-has-the-most-technologically-advanced-military-on-earth/.

4. "Abraham Accords: Declaration of Peace, Cooperation, and Constructive Diplomatic and Friendly Relations," *whitehouse.gov*, September 15, 2020, https://www.whitehouse.gov/briefings-statements/abraham-accords-declaration-peace-cooperation-constructive-diplomatic-friendly-relations/.

5. "Remarks by President Trump and Prime Minister Netanyahu of the State of Isreal Before Bilateral Meeting," *whitehouse.gov*, September 15, 2020, https://www.whitehouse.gov/briefings-statements/remarks-president-trump-prime-minister-netanyahu-state-israel-bilateral-meeting-091520/.

6. Mark Hitchcock, *The End* (Carol Stream, IL: Tyndale House, 2012), 294-295.

7. Ron Rhodes, *End Times Super Trends* (Eugene, OR: Harvest House Publishers, 2017), 166.

8. Quoted and adapted from Ron Rhodes, *End Times Super Trends*, 166-167.

9. Isabella Ginor, "How Six Day war almost led to Armageddon," *The Guardian*, June 9, 2000, https://www.theguardian.com/world/2000/jun/10/israel1.

10. "The Yom Kippur War brings United States and USSR to brink of conflict," *History.com*, https://www.history.com/this-day-in-history/the-yom-kippur-war-brings-united-states-and-ussr-to-brink-of-conflict.

11. Lionel Beehner, "Russia-Iran Arms Trade," November 1, 2006, https://www.cfr.org/backgrounder/russia-iran-arms-trade.

12. Matthew Levitt, "Hezbollah Finances: Funding the Party of God," *The Washington Institute*, February

2005, https://www.washingtoninstitute.org/policy-analysis/view/hezbollah-finances-funding-the-party-of-god.

13. Adam Bensaid, "Russia is selling more weapons to Saudi Arabia and the UAE," *TRTWorld*, February 22, 2019, https://www.trtworld.com/middle-east/russia-is-selling-more-weapons-to-saudi-arabia-and-the-uae-24431.
14. "A Marriage Made in Hell," *60 Minutes*, S.51, E26, April 21, 2019.
15. Hal Brands, "Putin Conquered the Middle East. The U.S. Can Get It Back," *Bloomberg*, October 22, 2019, https://www.bloomberg.com/opinion/artcles/2019-10-22/putin-conquered-the-middle-east-the-u-s-can-get-it-back.
16. Patrick Buchanan, "Is Putin the New King of the Middle East?," *RealClearPolitics*, October 18, 2019, https://www.realclearpolitics.com/articles/2019/10/18/is_putin_the_new_king_of_the_middle_east_141530.html.
17. Jonathan Spyer, "Putin Is the New King of Syria," *The Wall Street Journal*, October 16, 2019, https://www.wsj.com/articles/putin-is-the-new-king-of-syria-11571264222.
18. Oliver Carroll, "Putin arrives in Saudi Arabia as Middle East kingmaker: 'Something Is Afoot,'" *Independent*, October 14, 2019, https://www.independent.co.uk/news/world/europe/putin-saudi-arabia-visit-king-salman-riyadh-middle-east-trump-a9155771.html.
19. Nathan Hodge and Mary Ilyushina, "Russian voters overwhelmingly back a ploy by President Vladimir Putin to rule until 2036," *CNN*, July 2, 2020, https://www.cnn.com/2020/07/01/europe/russia-referendum-putin-power-2036-intl/index.html.

WHERE IN THE WORD? THE TWO WITNESSES

1. David Jeremiah, *Agents of the Apocalypse* (Carol Stream, IL: Tyndale House, 2014), 95-96.

WHERE IN THE WORD? WHY IS ISRAEL A SIGNIFICANT PART OF THIS BOOK?

1. J.D. Farag, "Hope for the Battle Weary," *Olive Tree Ministries,* September 2020, https://olivetreeviews.org/radio-archives/.
2. Rabbi Binyamin Elon, *God's Covenant with Israel* (Green Forest, AR: Balfour Books, 2005), 12.
3. "Covenant," *Easton's Bible Dictionary* as cited on *BibleGateway*, https://www.biblegateway.com/resources/dictionaries/dict_meaning.php?source=1&wid=T0000916.
4. Dr. Senta German, "Ziggurat of Ur," *Khan Academy*, https://www.khanacademy.org/humanities/ancient-art-civilizations/ancient-near-east1/sumerian/a/ziggurat-of-ur.
5. Gerald R. McDermott, *Israel Matters* (Grand Rapids, MI: Brazos Press, 2017), 46.
6. "Arab Countries 2020," *World Population Review*, https://worldpopulationreview.com/countries/arab-countries/.
7. Alexandra Twin, "World's Top 10 Oil Exporters," *Investopedia*, October 23, 2019, https://www.investopedia.com/articles/company-insights/082316/worlds-top-10-oil-exporters.asp.
8. Daniel Workman, "Petroleum Gas Exports by Country," *World's Top Exports*, September 2, 2020, http://www.worldstopexports.com/petroleum-gas-exports-country/.

WHERE IN THE WORD? WHY THE JEWS?

1. David Jeremiah, *What in the World Is Going On?* (Nashville, TN: Thomas Nelson, 2008), 7-8.
2. "World Population," *countrymeters*, https://countrymeters.info/en/World.
3. "Muslim Majority Countries 2020," *World Population Review*, https://worldpopulationreview.com/countries/muslim-majority-countries/.

4. "2018 World Jewish Population," *Berman Jewish Databank*, https://www.jewishdatabank.org/databank/search-results/study/1060.
5. Steven L. Pease, *The Golden Age of Jewish Achievement* (Sonoma, CA: Deucalion, 2009), 16.
6. "Jewish Nobel Prize Winners," *jinfo.org*, http://www.jinfo.org/Nobel_Prizes.html.
7. Pease, *The Golden Age of Jewish Achievement*, 17.
8. Pease, *The Golden Age of Jewish Achievement*, 16.
9. Ellie Bothwell, "Top 10 universities for producing Nobel prizewinners 2017," *Times Higher Education*, October 13, 2017, https://www.timeshighereducation.com/news/top-10-universities-producing-nobel-prizewinners-2017#survey-answer.
10. Pease, *The Golden Age of Jewish Achievement*, 17.
11. Pease, *The Golden Age of Jewish Achievement*, 16.

WHERE IN THE WORD? THE PROMISED LAND

1. Gerald R. McDermott, *Israel Matters* (Grand Rapids, MI: Brazos Press, 2017), 49.
2. Joel Benin and Lisa Hajjar, "Palestine, Israel and the Arab-Israeli Conflict—a Primer," *Middle East Watch*, December 2019, https://www.middleeastwatch.net/Palestine-Israel-and-the-Arab.
3. Robert Jeffress, *Perfect Ending* (Nashville, TN: Worthy Publishing, 2014), 41-42 (emphasis added).
4. Chris Katulka, "The Reason Why," *Israel My Glory*, January-February 2020, 27.
5. Elwood McQuaid, *It Is No Dream* (Bellmawr, NJ: Friends of Israel Gospel Ministry, 1978), 18.
6. Josephus, *The Jewish War*, ed. Gaalya Cornfield (Grand Rapids, MI: Zondervan, 1982); Victor Duruy, *History of Rome*, vol. V (London: Kegan, Paul, Trench & Co., 1883).
7. "The Destruction of Jerusalem in 70 AD," *Bible History*, https://www.bible-history.com/jerusalem/firstcenturyjerusalem_destruction_of_jerusalem_in_70_a_d_.html.

WHERE IN THE WORD? THE FINAL HUMILIATION

1. Elwood McQuaid, *It Is No Dream* (Bellmawr, NJ: Friends of Israel Gospel Ministry, 1978), 38.
2. Emily Jones, "'No, Jesus Was Not a Palestinian': Why Jews, Christians Are Blasting Ilhan Omar Again," *CBN News*, April 25, 2019, http://www1.cbn.com/cbnnews/politics/2019/april/no-jesus-was-not-a-palestinian-jews-christians-blast-ilhan-omar-for-claiming-jesus-wasnt-jewish.
3. David Brog, *Reclaiming Israel's History* (Washington, DC: Regnery, 2017), 18.
4. Brog, *Reclaiming Israel's History*, 24.
5. Jonathan Bernis, *A Lasting Peace* (Lake Mary, FL: Charisma House, 2019), 31.
6. Brog, *Reclaiming Israel's History*, 32.
7. Brog, *Reclaiming Israel's History*, 35.
8. Brog, *Reclaiming Israel's History*, 37.
9. Brog, *Reclaiming Israel's History*, 43.
10. Brog, *Reclaiming Israel's History*, 49.

WHERE IN THE WORD? WHY GOD BROUGHT THE JEWS BACK

1. Mark Twain, *The Innocents Abroad*, Project Gutenberg, May 25, 2018, https://www.gutenberg.org/files/3176/3176-h/3176-h.htm#ch46.
2. Twain, *The Innocents Abroad*, https://www.gutenberg.org/files/3176/3176-h/3176-h.htm#ch52.
3. Twain, *The Innocents Abroad*, https://www.gutenberg.org/files/3176/3176-h/3176-h.htm#ch56.
4. Walter Clay Lowdermilk, *Palestine: Land of Promise* (New York: Harper & Bros., 1944), 5, 74-76.

WHERE IN THE WORD? GET READY

1. "Balfour Declaration: Text of the Declaration (November 2, 1917)," *Jewish Virtual Library*, https://www.jewishvirtuallibrary.org/text-of-the-balfour-declaration.
2. Rafael Medoff, "What FDR said about Jews in private," *Los Angeles Times*, April 7, 2013, https://www.latimes.com/opinion/la-xpm-2013-apr-07-la-oe-medoff-roosevelt-holocaust-20130407-story.html.
3. Joshua Botts, "Chapter 7: 'Out of the Frying Pan into the Fire,' 1945-1957," *Office of the Historian*, https://history.state.gov/historicaldocuments/frus-history/chapter-7, footnote 34.
4. Daniel A. Gross, "The U.S. Government Turned Away Thousands of Jewish Refugees, Fearing That They Were Nazi Spies," *Smithsonian Magazine,* November 18, 2015, https://www.smithsonianmag.com/history/us-government-turned-away-thousands-jewish-refugees-fearing-they-were-nazi-spies-180957324/.
5. "Jewish Population of Europe in 1945," *United States Holocaust Memorial Museum*, https://encyclopedia.ushmm.org/content/en/article/remaining-jewish-population-of-europe-in-1945.
6. Rupert Cornwell, "Truman diary reveals anti-Semitism and offer to step down," *Independent*, July 12, 2003, https://www.independent.co.uk/news/world/americas/truman-diary-reveals-anti-semitism-and-offer-to-step-down-95825.html.
7. "Jacobson, Edward Papers," *Harry S. Truman Library & Museum*, https://www.trumanlibrary.org/hstpaper/jacobson.htm.

WHERE IN THE WORD? THE BIBLE'S ROLE

1. Clark Clifford, *Counsel to the President* (New York: Random House, 1991), 7-8.
2. "Jacobson, Edward Papers," *Harry S. Truman Library & Museum*, https://www.trumanlibrary.org/hstpaper/jacobson.htm.
3. Clark Clifford, *Counsel to the President*, 3.
4. "Jacobson, Edward Papers," *Harry S. Truman Library & Museum*, https://www.trumanlibrary.org/israel/palestin.htm.
5. David Brog, *Reclaiming Israel's History* (Washington, DC: Regnery, 2017), xvi.
6. Julie Marks, "Gaza: The History That Fuels the Conflict," *History*, August 29, 2018, https://www.history.com/news/gaza-conflict-history-israel-palestine.
7. Shannon Pettypiece, "Trump Mideast peace plan expands Israeli territory, offers path to Palestinian statehood," *NBC News*, January 28, 2020, https://www.nbcnews.com/politics/white-house/trump-middle-east-peace-plan-expands-israeli-territory-offers-path-n1124606.
8. "Abba Eban," *New World Encyclopedia*, https://www.newworldencyclopedia.org/entry/Abba_Eban.
9. David Brog, *Reclaiming Israel's History* (Washington, DC: Regnery, 2017), xi-xii.

WHERE IN THE WORD? THE FIG TREE

1. "From George Washington to the Hebrew Congregation in Newport, Rhode Island, 18 August 1790," *Founders Online*, https://founders.archives.gov/documents/Washington/05-06-02-0135.
2. "The World Factbook," *Central Intelligence Agency*, https://www.cia.gov/library/publications/the-world-factbook/rankorder/2102rank.html.

ALSO FROM DONNA VANLIERE

A typical day at work turns into a nightmare for Emma Grady when her favorite patient and several colleagues vanish in front of her. Fear turns to chaos as Emma begins the frantic race from Brooklyn to Queens, anxious to discover if her boyfriend is safe. Subways are closed, graves are open, and countless people have inexplicably disappeared. Mayhem erupts as terror grips the residents of New York City.

What could make so many vanish in a moment? And not just in New York, but all over the globe? Emma wonders if this is the predicted end of the world and begins a desperate search for answers.

This page-turning story will take you on a riveting journey from New York City to Israel, and in the final chapters, Donna turns to the pages of the Bible, where you'll discover that God has made known to us "the end from the beginning," and that things aren't spiraling downward but are actually looking up.

Does Bible prophecy often leave you confused and frightened? You're not alone. There are some strange and mystifying Bible passages that have bewildered generations of Christ-followers. Many aspects of Bible prophecy could never be understood by our parents and grandparents simply because the signs of the end times had not yet become apparent.

But did you know that the meanings of many of these same Bible verses are being revealed before our very eyes? It is our generation that is seeing end-time prophecies being fulfilled.

Join Donna VanLiere and listen to her free podcast *Things Are Looking Up*, in which she shares significant and specific prophecies that only our generation has been able to understand, and discusses the very real connection between Bible prophecy and our world today.

www.DonnaVanLiere.com/LookingUp

To learn more about Harvest House books and to read sample chapters, visit our website:

www.harvesthousepublishers.com